SUNDAY SUPPER

K.SINKO

For my grandmothers, who taught me that the best kind of love is served on a plate...

...and who begged me to spice things up.

Hey reader!

I want to be conscientious toward your feelings regarding particular topics brought up in *Sunday Supper*. This book dives into themes of conception issues and miscarriage, as well as health-related difficulties regarding intimacy.

Given that these are prominent in the story, this book does have intimate scenes on the page. If you prefer a closed-door modification, feel free to skip chapters 18 and 25.

Love you all, xx.

Prologue

Bella was thirteen when Nonna taught her how to make her meatballs.

It was the recipe her grandmother was most famous for, the meatballs that had New Yorkers waiting in hour-long queues, crowding the front of her shop on Mulberry Street day in and day out. Russo's Deli was the beating heart of Little Italy, and her meatballs were the crown jewel. Only Nonna and her mother knew the secret recipe.

And she was about to join their ranks.

Nonna tied on her pink apron and directed her to unwrap packages of beef, pork, and veal, adding them to a bowl of crusty Italian bread soaking in milk. Eggs, freshly grated Pecorino Romano, herbs, and a whirlwind of other ingredients that Bella couldn't keep straight were also added to the bowl.

She may not have remembered all of them as Nonna listed them off, but she knew she would someday. After all, she and her family gathered for supper every Sunday night and meatballs were always on the menu. She had many more Sundays to practice.

"How come Grandpa never joins us for Sunday supper?" Bella asked as she rolled meatballs at her nonna's small kitchen table, standing in the center of her tiny one-bedroom apartment directly above the deli. Almost like the table was the center of everything in her apartment, and nothing else mattered. "I know you're divorced, but maybe someday?"

"Your *nonno* is far too busy on Sundays with his friends," Nonna swiftly replied, shutting down the idea. "Are you still meeting him for your pizza dates?"

Bella scowled. "We never go anywhere else. I wish he would let me join him in Queens."

Nonna bristled. "Queens? Why would you want to go to stuffy, boring Queens when we live in the most exciting borough in the most exciting city on earth?"

She smiled at her grandmother's bursting love for Manhattan. "I know. It would just be cool to see."

Nonna kissed the top of her head. "Do not fret, *piccola*. He may someday." She turned to wash her hands in the sink. "Now, let's get these meatballs in the sauce before your mother gets here and starts bossing us around."

Chapter One

Never in her twenty-seven years of life did Bella Russo expect a plot twist quite like this.

Bella stood in her kitchen, an open bottle of Chianti dangling from her fingertips, as she glared at her laptop screen on the kitchen table. She took a swig from the bottle, eyes not leaving the screen, unable to fully comprehend what she was looking at.

This can't be real.

A cold shiver ran down her spine, reminding her that *yes*, this was, in fact, real.

Her phone buzzed on the table next to her computer. She swiped to answer and tapped on the speakerphone.

"Bells? What's wrong? I saw you called me, like, seven million times."

She took another swig of red wine. Yes, she did dial Percy over and over as the panic sunk in. When she didn't answer after her ninth attempt, she uncorked the bottle that was now halfway gone.

"*Bella,* are you even there? I'm five seconds from calling myself an Uber—"

"I'm here," she interrupted, her voice sounding calm despite the big, fat ball of panic currently lodged in her throat. "I got my last test results back."

"And?"

Bella didn't respond. She scanned the computer screen, her mind trying to decipher how it could even be possible, her heart still in denial.

"*Shit,*" Percy whispered. Bella listened to murmuring and shuffling on the other line before her best friend continued. "Are you home? I'm coming to you."

"It's not my health, P," she reassured her. "Still no news on that end."

Bella found it infuriating. After pricking her fingers for blood, pulling out strands of her hair, and spitting into test tubes, all fourteen DNA tests she'd taken in the past month had come back inconclusive. There was nothing wrong with her. Nothing to blame for the current nightmare she was living in.

Percy whooshed out a breath of relief. "You had me scared for a minute, Bells. This is a good thing, right?"

"I still don't have answers," she replied, her voice monotone and bitter.

"I know," Percy replied softly. "We'll keep trying, okay?"

Bella brought the bottle back to her lips.

"If it's not your health, then want to let me know why you're calling me in the middle of the night?"

She set the wine and her phone on her two-person kitchen table and slumped down into a chair. "This test was a bit different than the others. It takes a look at my ancestry to see if these same issues run in my family tree."

"Okay..." Percy started, sounding confused at *why* this particular detail mattered right now.

"Everything seemed fine until I realized that my grandfather's name wasn't only attached with my mother's," Bella explained.

"But I thought your mom was an only child?"

"She is. Or, at least that's what I've been told."

"What are you saying?"

She placed her face in her hands. "That my grandfather had another son and an entire secret family that I never knew about."

TWENTY MINUTES LATER, Percy knocked on Bella's door.

She swung the door open and frowned. "You didn't need to come over, it's really late."

Percy ignored her and charged inside, kicking off her shoes and dodging the wonky coatrack. "There's no way I was going to fall asleep after you dropped that kind of news on me," she said, plopping two cotton tote bags onto the coffee table. Bella noticed a box from Zabar's sticking out the top of one, most likely stuffed with the black-and-white cookies Percy's girlfriend Yazmin always spoiled her with.

Bella sighed. This wasn't the first time her best friend had come to her rescue late at night. In the past year since moving into her Lower East Side apartment, Percy had shown up when a crying Bella couldn't get off the floor of her empty living room, wondering if she'd truly hit rock bottom. She'd been there for the initial round of discouraging doctors' appointments—and the many since. Most recently was when Bella found out Lon was engaged, less than a year after he walked out of her life. As always, Percy was there, bags of takeout and baked goods from Zabar's and wine and pajamas in tow, ready to tackle the damage. And if Bella was being honest with herself, she was tired of feeling like damaged goods.

Her friend pointed to the sleeping laptop. "Let me see it."

She did what she was told and tapped the trackpad. The screen blinked back to life, the test results still open and waiting for her. Taunting her.

Percy squinted her eyes and peered down to read. After a few painstaking moments, she spoke. "Maybe it's a mistake?"

"Maybe," Bella mumbled. "But...what if it's not?"

Percy let out a low whistle and straightened, then pointed to the bottle on the table. "Save any for me?"

She passed it to her, waiting as Percy took a long pull. She wiped at her mouth with the sleeve of her Amagansett crewneck. "How old is your mom again?"

"Sixty-two," Bella replied. "This says my—my uncle—is forty-nine."

"Which means she was...ugh, I suck at math, how old was she?"

"Thirteen," she replied. She'd already mapped it out before Percy arrived. "Meaning my grandfather had another kid a year after divorcing Nonna."

"And your grandfather moved to Queens after they got divorced, right? Lived there until he passed?"

Bella nodded, then felt that familiar pang in her heart. Even two years after the funeral she still missed her grandfather deeply, missed their monthly pizza dates at Lombardi's—*they're named after me*, he always joked—and the sweet postcards he mailed her from locations all around the city. She had them in a shoebox at the top of her closet, postcards from places like Arthur Avenue and Katz Delicatessen and a random bodega outside Astoria Park.

Yet he never told her the truth. None of her family did.

Percy placed the bottle down and pulled strands of her short blond bob into a bun at the top of her head, tiny sections flopping down to rest at the nape of her neck. She sat in front of the computer and opened up a new tab.

"What are you doing?" Bella said, the words rushing out of her.

"Doing what I do best," her friend replied. "Stalking someone on the internet."

It certainly was what Percy did best. Ever since Bella's relationship status went from happily married to depressingly single, Percy had taken it upon herself to coach her in the world of online dating. She instructed Bella to swipe right—*or was it left?*—on every suitable bachelor that came across her phone screen. When it ended up becoming a match, it was only a matter of seconds before Percy plunged into the depths of Google and LinkedIn. The number of men on dating apps who already had girlfriends and wives was horrifying.

Bella snorted. "This isn't some Hinge guy, P. This is apparently my *uncle* and he could be anywhere—"

"Already found him," she interrupted, then sighed. "I'm a little disappointed at how easy that was."

Bella leaned in next to her friend, reading what was on the screen. Percy's search was simple and to the point.

Matteo Lombardi, New York City

His name was basic enough that there should have been dozens of other Italian-American dudes come up in the search. Yet the news articles and online profiles and Google snippets that popped up featured the same man: Matteo

Lombardi, restaurateur of three New American eateries located in Brooklyn.

"That might not be him," Bella countered. "His name is really common, it's like the Italian version of John Smith."

"Forty-nine, born in Queens, in the restaurant business, lived in the city his whole life?" Percy countered. She clicked on the images tab and pictures appeared of Matteo Lombardi. Behind the bar at one of his restaurants, shaking hands with important-looking men at parties, laughing with a cocktail in hand and a petite redheaded woman on his arm.

Percy clicked on that image and pointed to Matteo's face. Specifically his nose. "Still think that's not him?"

Bella sucked in a breath. His pointed nose, his bushy dark espresso locks identical to the wavy hair trailing down her own back, the way the skin around his eyes crinkled with his lopsided smile.

Matteo Lombardi was a spitting image of her grandfather.

"I need sugar," Bella blurted. She snatched the Zabar's box from Percy's bag and peeled it open, breaking a black-and-white in half. She bit into it then dropped the other half into Percy's outstretched hand, her friend's face still locked on the screen as she scrolled through what looked to be Matteo's website.

Bella shoveled another chunk into her mouth, crumbs dropping to the floor. "It's still not enough evidence," she said around a mouthful of cookie. "Sure, he looks like my grandfather's *twin*, but I need proof."

"Then let's go meet him."

She fumbled, dropping her half of the cookie to the floor. "*Meet* him? No way, that's such a bad idea."

Percy rolled her eyes. "Chill out. We'll go undercover

and visit one of his restaurants, see what we can find out about him. And as luck would have it"—she clicked one of the restaurant locations listed on his website, then pointed to it with a smile—"I'm currently on the list to get into this one."

Bella ignored the tragic cookie disaster on the kitchen floor and felt her curiosity nudge her a step closer.

Tri

A New American restaurant with elevated dishes inspired by the cuisine of the tri-state area

Seasonal menu offerings from executive chef Wyatt Henderson and restaurateur Matteo Lombardi

"My editor assigned me this place, but I've been dragging my feet because it's all the way in Red Hook, which is *such* a slog," Percy continued. "But now that there's a little incentive on the line..."

Bella's face heated.

"What do you say, Bells?" her friend asked, clicking back to the photos of Matteo Lombardi. "Want to do a little recon tomorrow night?"

She stared at the screen, her eyes scanning that similar nose and crinkled half smile, the sight of it making her stomach flip-flop with longing and grief and something new: betrayal.

"Yes," she answered. "I'm in."

BELLA SAT on the sleek minimalist couch in the lobby of her office building as she waited for Percy the next evening, dazed. She watched the maple tree across the street sway with the gentle breeze, the deep orange leaves glowing like burning candlelight under the golden hour sun, and yet, Bella felt nothing. Fall was always her favorite season in the city, and nowhere else in the world ever came close. She'd road tripped across New England to see the changing colors, hiked the Catskills and Adirondacks during weekend escapes upstate, flown to Paris and Milan and Amsterdam and countless other cities over the years for her job as a social media consultant, yet *nothing* compared to home. Nothing ever came close to the magic of Manhattan between the months of September and December.

Except this year. This year, not even the turning leaves in Central Park or the Feast of San Gennaro in Little Italy had the power to drag Bella from her stupor. The city was bright with color and life, but in her heart, everything felt dull.

Percy burst through the revolving doors at the lobby's front entrance. The two of them looked far more polished than the girls who stuffed their faces with cookies fifteen hours earlier. Percy dressed the part as the trendy millennial food writer she was: an oversized tan blazer on her shoulders, her Ramones graphic T-shirt tucked into black leather trousers, her sleek blond bob parted at the center, and a stack of gold necklaces dangling at her throat.

Bella was a New Yorker down to her core and her wardrobe reflected that, with at least 95 percent of the clothes in her closet donning the color black. Tonight she chose her power outfit in hopes that it would infuse her with the confidence she needed—her long-sleeved silk wrap dress paired with suede pumps and her favorite black trench coat.

Bella stood up and Percy wrapped an arm around her. "You still up for this?"

It had been impossible to focus through her strategy meetings and client calls today, her stomach in knots thinking about her grandfather and Matteo and if maybe she should approach her family first before making a surprise visit to the restaurant. She may not know him, but what if he knew about *her*? Her mind volleyed back and forth between the pros and cons, wondering what would happen if he recognized her. But her curiosity won every mental tennis match, and when six o'clock finally struck, she'd grabbed her coat and headed for the elevator.

"I am," Bella confirmed. "Although, please tell me *Taster* is paying for a bottle of wine tonight."

Percy smirked. "I hear the sommelier at this place is impressive, so yes, we will absolutely be using the magazine's card to support our drinking habit. And for a car." She tapped her phone to pull up the Uber app. "There's no way I'm taking two subways and a *bus* to get to Red Hook. Or worse—a boat."

"The ferry is kind of nice," Bella protested. "Especially when the sun is setting."

Percy rolled her eyes. "City kid."

"Snobby Hamptons kid."

She flicked her off, then typed in the address of the restaurant.

"Hey, Bella."

Bella's heart squeezed at the sound of *that* voice behind her. She spun around to face Katie, who was nervously twirling a strand of her strawberry blond hair, the princess-cut diamond ring on her finger glistening against the sun that peeked through the lobby's floor-to-ceiling windows.

She gave her a tight smile and a nod. "Great job today in the strategy meeting with Dreamscape. I think they're going to enjoy what you have."

Katie's face flushed. "Thanks, I hope so, too."

Bella gave her another nod.

Katie shifted on her feet. "Hi, Percy."

Percy flicked her off as well, her eyes not leaving her phone screen as she watched for their Uber that was currently four minutes away.

Katie's flush dipped into a deeper, shameful red.

"See you on Monday, Katie," Bella said, keeping her tone warm yet dismissive enough to indicate she was finished with this conversation.

"Yeah, Monday. Have a great weekend."

She watched Katie shuffle out of the building, then beeline it down Fifth Avenue.

"I don't get how you're still nice to her after everything," Percy huffed.

"We still work together, P. What am I supposed to do?"

"Fire her. You don't just work together. She's your employee."

"She was also my friend. *Our* friend," Bella added. "And soon to be your sister-in-law."

"Have I told you how much I hate my brother? Because I do. *A lot.* With a burning passion."

"You may have mentioned it."

Percy linked an arm through hers. "He's an idiot. And for whatever it's worth, you'll always be my favorite sister-in-law and she will never come close."

"That's probably because you've known me for ten years," Bella joked.

"Even *if* Lon had been the one to bring you home and I never knew you, your personality would be far superior to someone who makes the bartender list off every type of vodka when the bottles are clearly on display."

She couldn't help the coughing fit of laughter that escaped her throat. Percy chuckled with her, then tugged on her arm. "Come on, the Uber's here."

BELLA FOLLOWED Percy into the restaurant, the sun now dipping low along the harbor, the rich red colors reminding her of Nonna's famous marinara. She eyed the Statue of Liberty, watching the ferries float by as her friend gave her pen name—Percy Chase—to the hostess.

The hostess made a small yelping noise when she realized who she was speaking with. Bella smirked, thinking how it never really got old watching restaurant workers across New York fawn over her best friend. She knew Percy had something special even back during her early days reviewing restaurants and bars on Instagram, so it was no surprise when Percy was poached by *Taster* to write a column for their online magazine. Her eager three hundred thousand followers ate up her words, and if Percy wrote a rave review, the restaurant was bound to have a month of absolute chaos from the response.

Bella watched as the hostess beamed her brightest smile, gracefully tucking two menus into her arm and motioning for them to follow her. The space was cozy, the walls painted a warm gray and accentuated with three large-printed photographs with landscapes from each of the three "tri" states. Brass pendant light fixtures hung above the bar and votive candles were sprinkled across cherrywood tables, each set simply with white plates and folded, blue-striped napkins. At first glance, the setup at Tri seemed simplistic, yet Bella could tell that every detail had been chosen with intention.

They sat down at a table near the window, giving Percy an unobstructed view of the semi-open kitchen toward the back of the restaurant. Bella used the excuse of hanging her purse over the back of her chair to scope out the line cooks plating dishes and the waiters floating them over to tables.

The sommelier came up to their table, his demeanor poised and welcoming, like talking and drinking about wine was the most natural thing in the world. "Hello, ladies, how are you this evening?"

"Splendid," Percy answered. "And thirsty."

He grinned. "Good thing I can help you with that. All of our wines come from vineyards across the tri-state area, to really tie in with the roots of our menu. Have you had a chance to peruse it yet? Any particular foods you're thinking about ordering?"

"We'll probably order a bunch of different things, so I'll trust your judgment here," her friend answered.

The man eyed Bella, as if her opinion also mattered. She gave him a shy smile. "Red, preferably."

"I have an excellent Cabernet Franc from the Finger Lakes that I think will blend nicely with a variety of menu items," he answered. "Let me give you both a taste. I'm Jayce, if you need anything."

Percy grinned. "Thanks, Jayce. You're already our best friend."

Jayce chuckled as he stepped away.

Percy dropped the menu down on the table and

scanned the people moving around the restaurant. "I don't see him, do you?"

"Haven't had a chance to really look yet," Bella whispered. She picked up her menu, realizing her hands were trembling. She took a deep breath and focused on the selection of small and large plates, each dish featuring produce that the current season had to offer. Crispy tempura eggplant with basil aioli and house-made Italian red pepper flake chili crisp. Whole salted grilled mackerel with a ground cherry sauce and leek parsnip puree. Smoked salt-cured wagyu beef cubes with a cast-iron-charred mozzarella pancake, fennel shallot crispy mushroom salad, and adobo finishing oil.

But the last small plate on the menu gave her pause, because it had nothing seasonal about it. It stuck out like a sore thumb, and when Bella read it over, she barked a laugh.

Percy's eyes went wide. "What the hell is wrong with you?"

Bella continued laughing, hard enough her eyes began to water.

"Don't get me wrong, love that you're having the time of your life right now," Percy said. "But people are *staring*. Want to tell me what's so funny?"

She dabbed underneath her eyes with her napkin, hoping her mascara wasn't running as she pointed to the listed dish. "Did you see this?"

Percy slumped over to Bella so they could read what she pointed at. "Oh, right, that."

"A *deconstructed meatball*?"

Two wineglasses were placed in front of them. Bella bit her bottom lip to contain her giggling as Jayce swiftly uncorked their bottle and poured a taste for Percy. Her friend swirled her glass and sniffed its contents like they hadn't been chugging wine straight from the bottle the night before, then took a sip and nodded. With filled glasses, the two of them huddled close as Jayce walked away.

"It's apparently his most celebrated menu item, or at least according to social media," Percy explained.

"Who, Matteo?"

"No, *the chef*."

"He's famous for a deconstructed meatball." Bella guffawed but quickly sobered when she realized Percy was serious. "That is the dumbest thing I've ever heard. What is it, like, meat, bread, cheese, and tomato on a toothpick? I mean come *on*, who in their right mind would spend"—she leaned forward to study the menu again—"twenty-nine dollars on that?"

"A lot of customers, actually," drawled a measured voice from above them.

Percy and Bella jumped apart and stared up at the man standing at their table. He wore a white short-sleeved chef's coat and held a plate of something in his hands. They remained silent as he eased it onto the table between them, turning it slightly so they could get a good view of what it was.

Sure enough, it was a deconstructed meatball, all of the elements stacked together on two thick toothpicks, a swirl of a creamy sauce coating the edges of the plate.

Bella's eyes went wide as Percy smothered a cough in the crook of her elbow, then held out a hand. "Chef Henderson, it's a pleasure to meet you."

Chapter Two

The chef didn't look in Percy's direction. Instead, his eyes narrowed at Bella. Heat climbed up the back of her neck at his penetrating gaze, and for a moment, she thought she should probably apologize to him. This was his restaurant, and she'd brazenly made fun of his menu. But then the tiniest smirk curled at the corner of his lips, like this was some kind of game he was about to win. She returned a smug smile and delicately pinched her wineglass, then leaned back in the cushioned leather chair.

He angled himself ever so slightly toward Percy and took her hand, shaking it once. "Pleasure to meet you, Ms. Chase. Thanks for joining us tonight at Tri."

"It's an honor to be here." Percy nodded. She removed her hand and motioned toward Bella. "Please ignore my friend. She's a snob when it comes to meatballs."

Chef Henderson cocked a brow, his gaze back on Bella's face. "Is that so?"

Bella wasn't sure what made her do it, especially given that she was technically here representing *Taster*. But his toying smirk made her stomach burn with something that she hadn't felt in a long time. Under his taunting gaze, she felt like everything around her was a little more vibrant. She wanted to squeeze on to that feeling for as long as she could, so she lifted her chin. "Yes. This dish is a disgrace to meatballs everywhere."

Percy wheezed out an exasperated laugh, then covered her face with her hands. She'd give her shit about this later, but right now, Bella didn't care.

The chef's expression remained the same, but she knew she'd hit her mark as she watched his green eyes flash with surprise. He pushed his wavy auburn hair from his face, then interlaced his hands behind his back as he leaned forward. "Let me guess. The only meatballs that live up to *your* standards are your grandmother's. She's probably out in Jersey and has some kind of sauce she attempts to make from scratch, which she unironically calls red gravy because it makes her feel more Italian. She asks you to call her nonna, because that makes her feel Italian, too."

Bella felt her face flush.

"That sauce probably has some kind of secret ingredient. Anchovies, perhaps? I'm assuming her meatballs have one as well, something like veal or sausage, which is, again, the furthest thing from a secret ingredient despite how much she insists it's a secret. And, let's be honest, those meatballs are probably far too dry. But you wouldn't know any difference because they're your *nonna's* meatballs, and you think they are the best in the whole world."

She opened her mouth to snap back at him, to let him know who's nonna he was *actually* messing with, when Percy kicked her under the table. Bella flinched, remembering why she was here, remembering who could be in this room. She couldn't reveal herself to this chef no matter how much she wanted to wipe that pretentious smirk off his face with a truth that would likely have him melting to the floor. He had no idea he was speaking to the granddaughter of *the* Nonna Russo, the woman whose meatballs were so renowned, they'd been served to the president and many celebrities around the world. The same woman who'd tended to a line that snaked out the door of her delicatessen in Little Italy every day for decades. Her recipe *was* top secret, and no one outside of the Russo family would ever get their hands on it. Even when chefs begged for her recipe, when numerous proposals came her way to franchise and millions of dollars were offered to sell her products in stores, she always gave those hotshots the same answer: her recipes and her secrets were for her family's eyes only.

And Bella knew them all.

But she needed to tread carefully. She had no idea how much this chef knew about Matteo or his—and *her*—family. And if this chef knew about Matteo's connection to the Russo family, well, things could get messy real quick.

So she simply cocked her head and gave him a sweet smile. "Seems you got me all figured out, Chef Henderson."

The challenge in his eyes dimmed a fraction, but he stood up straight, flicking his gaze once to Percy, then back to her. "Enjoy the rest of your meal, ladies."

Bella exhaled when he turned to leave them and snatched the napkin off her plate, squeezing it tight and letting the fabric soak up the sweat on her palms.

"By the way..."

Her eyes shot up to find the chef was back at their table, his lips still curled up. "You can call me Wyatt," he finished.

He turned and made his way to the back, then disappeared into the kitchen.

Bella faced her friend, bracing for a verbal beatdown. "Sorry, P, I couldn't help myself. That was—"

"So fucking *hot*?"

Her eyes widened. "Excuse me?"

Percy laughed and opened up her own napkin with a flick of her hands, then placed it on her lap. "That chef is so sexy I would let him sprawl me out on this table and make me un-gay."

Bella had to pinch her lips together to avoid a wine spit take. When she swallowed, she cocked a brow at Percy. "May I remind you that *you have a girlfriend*?"

"Who I think would happily watch, given how hot he is," she quipped, reaching for one of the abominable meatball creations in front of them. "I know he's a little short for your taste, but please do the universe a favor and bone that man. Then call me after and give me every single detail."

"*Percy.*"

Her friend chuckled, then slathered her meatball stick with sauce and slid all of the ingredients off the toothpick and into her mouth. She glared as she watched Percy turn her head toward the ceiling as she chewed, deep in thought. She nodded, then made some kind of note on her phone.

"Please don't tell me you're going to write good things about this monstrosity," Bella said.

"Only if you promise me you'll bang the chef."

"I will not—" Bella huffed out a sigh. She knew better than to expect Percy to let this go, and she needed to nip it in the bud *now* before it became more of a thing. She leaned closer so no one around them could pick up her words. "I will not bang the chef, especially if he's rubbing shoulders with Matteo. We came here to get *answers*, remember?"

Percy groaned. "Fine. But don't get mad at me if I write

about how this man's dish might just top Nonna Russo's as the best meatballs in the city."

"You *wouldn't*."

"You're right, I wouldn't," she teased. "But you really should try it, Bells. The man clearly knows what he's doing."

Bella scrunched her nose at the plate. Each ingredient on the toothpick matched what the menu described: thin slices of sous vide veal, pork, and beef, green ricotta encased in a caramelized pearl onion shell, with an Italian herb bearnaise drizzle and dehydrated onion flakes. She conceded, slathering the stick with the rest of the sauce on the plate, and took a large enough bite so all of the ingredients landed on her tongue. She removed them from the toothpick, then chewed.

And dammit, those stacked ingredients *worked*. The richness of the sliced meats, the sharpness of the cheese, the tanginess of the onion. Everything about each ingredient was cooked to perfection. As if the ingredients were never stacked apart and "deconstructed" but were indeed blended together into the most exquisite meatball.

"He's watching you," Percy whispered.

Bella covered her mouth as she kept chewing, then chanced a glance at the kitchen. Wyatt watched from behind the kitchen counter, his arms crossed over his chest. He lifted his brows at her, his green eyes daring her with a question. *Good, right?*

She rolled her eyes and sipped her wine.

"Okay, here's a thought," Percy said. "Befriend the chef and see what he knows about Matteo."

"Again, bad idea."

"Why? Bella, come on, *live a little*."

"*No.* I don't think it's a good idea. Especially when

there's so much I don't know about Matteo or my grandfather or even my *family*. I mean, do my parents know? Does Nonna?" She rubbed at her temples. "This is a nightmare. How could they keep this from me?"

Bella felt a squeeze on her knee. "We're not sure if they know, Bells. We take this one day at a time. You're seeing them on Sunday, right?"

She nodded and sucked in a deep breath, then lifted the stem of her wineglass and leaned back in her seat. She never missed a Sunday supper at Nonna's. It was the only day her grandmother closed the deli, the day she designated to making a special batch of her meatballs and sauce, surrounded by her family. Even during her college years at NYU, her trips to the Hamptons with Percy and the rest of the Hamilton family, her traveling escapades for work, her years lost to Lon, she made sure to be at that chestnut table on Sunday evenings. If she were to cancel now, her family would *know* something was wrong.

Percy ordered three other dishes, then launched into a story about a disaster restaurant she'd had to review earlier that week. Bella scanned the restaurant every so often, keeping an eye out for Matteo, but her presumed uncle was nowhere to be found. When Percy got to the part about a baked macaroni and cheese that'd exploded all over Yazmin's dress, she casually dropped, "It's a good thing it didn't burn her left hand, because I plan on proposing soon."

Bella gasped. "You-you're proposing?"

"Yes. I'm so sorry." Percy grimaced. "I'm a horrible friend. I've been nervous to tell you."

Her mouth flew open. "P, why would you ever be sorry about this? This is beautiful news."

"Because you had a disaster year. And I don't want to stomp all over it with my happiness."

She felt a twinge in her chest over the phrase *disaster year*. "Stomp on it, *please*. Bring some joy into my life."

Percy flashed a hesitant smile. "I also hate that my brother proposed to Katie before I had a chance to propose to Yaz. I know it's not a contest, but *still*. He knew I was planning on doing it soon and he could have waited. Especially after everything..." She trailed off, tipping her head back with a sigh.

Bella twisted her hands in her lap, unsure of how to respond. Learning that Lon proposed to the woman he cheated on her with had been a shock to her system, like a bucket of ice-cold water dumped on her head. But things had fizzled out with them to the point where their relationship was practically nonexistent, and she knew it was all her fault. Knew that she was the reason he decided to seek companionship elsewhere, to leave and be with someone who had what it took to make him happy. Who wasn't such a disaster. Who wasn't damaged goods.

Divorced. The word tasted sour on her tongue when she spoke it, even thirteen months after signing the papers. It hadn't felt real to her four months ago, either, when Katie posted that sparkling ring on Instagram and officially staked her claim on Bella's ex-husband. The image of her hand on Lon's bare chest and the sandy beaches of Aruba in the background still burned in her brain.

He deserves someone who is happy and whole and healthy, she'd told herself as she curled into the fetal position on her couch that night, letting the crushing feeling of longing in her chest take over. Even though she longed for something she was never meant to have.

Thankfully the server's covert slip of their bill filled the silence, letting Bella off the hook. Percy reached for the receipt and scanned it, then frowned. "They comped the bill."

"Uh oh," Bella joked, spooning the lemon lavender panna cotta with cherry compote in front of her. She hated to admit it, but everything about their meal was delightful, from the baharat short rib ragu with charred okra and turmeric pappardelle to the smoked oyster pâté with preserved lemon, wild garlic, and sourdough crackers. Even the dessert was divine. Bella didn't glance at the kitchen again as they ate, afraid she would lock eyes with those devious green irises and catch the tilt of that arrogant mouth.

It was always a journalistic no-no for a restaurant to pay for a meal. Paying for the meal meant they were hoping to buy themselves free press, which inevitably resulted in a biased review. *Taster* was adamantly against freebies of any kind for that reason, which was why Percy had to flag down the server and request that they be charged for the meal.

"My apologies, Ms. Chase, but this comped meal wasn't meant for you," the server explained.

Percy's smile turned giddy as she lifted the receipt. "Excuse me?"

Bella didn't notice the server walk away. Instead, her eyes were drawn to a scribbled message on the back of the receipt. Percy caught on and flipped the paper so they could both read it. Bella leaned over to get a closer look.

If you really think your meatballs are better than mine...

Then the message was followed by a ten-digit phone number.

"Oh my *god*," Percy breathed.

Bella sat up straight and finally allowed herself to glance toward the kitchen. To her surprise, Wyatt wasn't anywhere to be found.

"Bells...you—"

"Absolutely not."

She grabbed her coat and shoved her arm in a sleeve.

"Come *on*, you have to. The hot chef got ten times hotter by dropping his number like that."

Bella stood up and fastened the buckle at her waist.

"Hey, crazy lady," Percy said, grabbing her hand. "Stop for a moment and think about this."

She paused and glared down at her. "What's there to think about? The uppity, pompous chef wants further reason to taunt me from the gold dais he sits on, with his posh organic menu and his pile of deconstructed meatballs."

"*Or*, this could be a way to learn more about Matteo," Percy countered with a hard squeeze of her hand. "If they work closely, then there's a chance he knows a little bit about Matteo's family, right?"

She let out an irritated sigh. "Maybe I should drop this whole Matteo thing, you know? My grandfather kept it a secret for a reason."

"Is that *really* what you want?"

Bella slammed her eyes shut. In truth, she wanted a lot of things. But wanting never got her anywhere. Wanting got her into this mess in the first place.

She felt Percy slip the receipt in the pocket of her coat. "Just think about it, okay?"

She exhaled. "Fine. I'll think about it."

Chapter Three

She dreamt of her grandfather that night. They sat at a booth across from each other inside Lombardi's, greasy slices of pepperoni pizza on white plates, shakers full of Parmesan and red pepper flakes beside them.

Dream Bella watched as her grandfather used the shakers with both hands, in the same way he always did that made her laugh as a kid. But she wasn't laughing this time. She glared at him. She was so, *so* angry at him.

Her grandfather frowned. "What is it, kid? Are you sad because of the baby?"

"No," she whispered. "I'm not sad because of the baby."

"It's okay if you still are, my darling," he replied, his nickname for her drawing up that deep feeling of longing in her chest again. But then she remembered, and she wanted desperately to know the truth.

"Why didn't you tell me, Nonno?" she whispered. "Why did you keep it a secret all of these years?"

He placed the shakers down on the table and snatched a couple of napkins. "I'm not sure what you are talking about."

"Your other family? Your *son*? Does Nonna know? Does my mom?"

She stared into his caramel-colored eyes, the wrinkles etched across his face somehow seeming even more prominent than a few moments ago, like he'd aged years during a single conversation. He continued to stare, but he said nothing.

She stood up to scream at him, but her voice was mute. In her hazy periphery, the entire world continued on around her, unaware of her tantrum, like she didn't exist. Her grandfather continued to stare ahead at the table, then picked up his slice and took a bite.

She screamed and screamed and screamed, but nothing came out.

A car horn flared outside, making Bella bolt upright in her bed, her forehead slicked with sweat, her back drenched as well. She flung the covers to the side and shifted to sit on the edge of her mattress, looking out into the dreary morning. Sulfur and the musty scent from leaves on the sidewalk carried up to her bedroom window, the rustle of wind making the glass rattle. It seemed fitting to Bella that she would wake up to a storm. It felt like everything in her life was pouring down on her all at once.

BELLA RELAXED into her couch the following Saturday, cold cup of coffee in one hand and the receipt in the other. The waxy paper was now soft after crinkling it into a ball and unfurling it dozens of times throughout the week, her mind back in a tennis match of *should I, shouldn't I*. She stared at the ten-digit number written in black ink, her mind whirling back and forth between wanting to know the truth and wanting to avoid the chef and his egotistical attitude. But then she thought about how he made her *feel*, how that smirk and those animated brows stirred a burning heat in her chest that made her want to scream. She hadn't felt that kind of passion in a very, very long time, and she wanted to say *fuck it* and keep burning.

She placed down her mug and grabbed her phone, then opened up a new text box. She typed in the number, then after a deep sigh, wrote a message.

BELLA

I don't think my meatballs are better. I know they are.

She hit send, then placed her phone screen-down on her belly. It was drizzling outside again after a week of constant rain, the soft droplets making a pitter patter sound against the A/C unit she had yet to remove from the window in her kitchen. She wondered whether it would be so bad if she left it all year. She didn't have the energy to try to wrangle it out of its spot and somehow not drop it down the three stories below.

Her phone buzzed. She flipped it back up and sucked in a breath. He was *calling* her.

"Shit," she mumbled. She swiped it open, answering with a timid, "Hello?"

"Tell me," Wyatt started on the other line. He sounded like he was outside, walking in the rain. "How exactly are these meatballs better than mine?"

Her cheeks flushed. "It's simple," she retorted. "I can actually make a meatball. You clearly don't even know how to put the ingredients together."

She was satisfied by the raspy laugh that came down the line.

"You didn't seem to mind it the other night," he replied, his voice husky and low. She enjoyed the sound of it far too much.

"Okay sure, I'll be cordial and say that those ingredients did taste good. But, chef, you do understand what a meatball is supposed to *look* like, right?"

"I must have forgotten. It's been ten years since I graduated culinary school."

"Casually dropping that into conversation, are we?"

His gravelly chuckle sounded through the phone again. "Did it work?"

She wiggled her toes. "Nope. Completely unfazed over here."

"I'll try harder then," he replied. She heard the sound of a door swing open, the wind from the storm snuffing out. "How about this? Maybe you should remind me what a meatball is."

"You mean *cook* for you?"

"If you think you have the best meatball recipe, then yes, cooking for me would be inevitable. Unless you would like to share the recipe with me, then I can let you down easily without having to buy all of those *secret* ingredients."

She bristled. "Fat chance."

"Then it looks like I'll be coming over for dinner."

Bella coughed, surprised at how forward he was being with her. She glanced around her apartment, imagining having Wyatt in her tiny space, attempting to cook Nonna's meatballs on a stove that could barely fit her cast-iron skillet and her eight-quart stainless steel pot.

He must have caught on to her hesitation, because he continued. "What are you doing tomorrow?"

"I am nowhere near prepared to cook for you tomorrow," she volleyed. "Plus, I have a standing dinner with my family every Sunday night."

"No, not tomorrow night. I have to be at the restaurant," he said. "I mean in the morning. How do you feel about bagels?"

She pursed her lips. "I grew up in Manhattan. How do you think I feel about bagels?"

Bella waited for Wyatt's response, listening to the faint sound of chopping and sizzling pans. She heard him murmur a suggestion to someone, something about adding more stock, then some footsteps and the soft click of a door.

"I think that means you have strong opinions," he finally replied. "Have you been to South Slope Bagels?"

"Yes, but I never go. The line is horrendous."

She could almost hear his grin when he responded. "Good. Meet me there at ten."

"Did you hear what I said about the lines? There's no way they'll have any bagels left by ten."

"I'm not worried about it," he said, his voice assured. "All right, I have to hang up, we're about to sit down for a family meal. But before I do, mind telling me the name of the woman with the best meatball recipe known to mankind?"

Bella sat up straight. *Will he know my name?* If she told him she was Isabella Russo, he could easily pick up that she might be related to Nonna Russo. Or worse, realize the connection she had with Matteo, who was *his boss.* But what if she gave him a different name? She'd never legally changed it, never made a trip to social security during her three years of marriage. Though that wasn't a detail Wyatt needed to know. Plus, it wasn't like this would actually *go* anywhere. She was simply hanging out with him to get more information about Matteo.

So, she bit her cheek and gave him a name.

"Isabella Hamilton," she said. "My friends call me Bella."

"Bella," he whispered, his voice warm with something that almost sounded like satisfaction. "See you tomorrow?"

"Sure, tomorrow."

She ended the call, settling back down on the couch with a groan, and buried her face in her hands.

HER PHONE RANG AGAIN three hours later. Bella paused the show playing on her laptop and placed her box of vegetable lo mein down on the coffee table. She squinted at her phone skeptically, wondering if *he* was calling her again, and tensed. Her mom's contact brightened the screen, a picture they'd taken at the Reservoir in Central Park staring back at her.

She had yet to speak to her mom—or the rest of her family—since finding out about Matteo. Not that she did during a normal week; they saved their catching up for Sundays. Still, it wasn't enough to stop the simmering guilt in her stomach of knowing such a secret.

Bella cracked her knuckles, swiping at her screen and pressing the phone to her ear. "Hi, Mom."

"Sweetie, can you do me a favor?"

"Of course, what's up?"

"Russo's was extra slammed today and I didn't get the chance to run over to Bianca's to grab a loaf for tomorrow night. Your father has this brunch with the faculty in the morning that he wants me at, so I can't go then either—"

"I can get a loaf of bread, Mom, it's fine," Bella interrupted. "But does it have to be from Bianca? I'm...sort of busy in the morning as well."

"Sort of busy?" her mother teased. "With what?"

Shit. "Um, I'm going to get bagels with a friend."

"Percy?"

She slammed her eyes shut. "No. Someone I met this week."

There was a long pause. Bella knew her mother well; she knew she was likely calculating her response, wanting to wring as much information out of this situation as possible. There hadn't been any romantic *anything* in Bella's life since the divorce, and despite Percy's push for her to try dating apps or her mother's covert comments about "getting out there again," she had yet to meet anyone who felt remotely interesting enough to take that step.

"Oh yeah?" her mother said, the tone of her voice casual. Bella smirked, picturing her mother on the other line, probably grinning from ear to ear, potentially doing a little dance in the stockroom at the deli where she always took her calls.

She sighed, resigned to it. "Yes, I met *him* when I was out with Percy. He asked me to get bagels in the morning."

She heard a distant squeal, and despite Bella's vague description of where she and Percy actually *were* or how she and Wyatt actually met, she smiled at her mother's failed attempt at keeping calm and collected about her love life finally coming alive after its lengthy sabbatical.

"Mom..."

"I know, I know, it's *bagels*, not a *date*," her mother emphasized. "Although, your father and I had our first date over gelato, which pretty much sounds like the same thing. But—"

"*Mom*, just bagels," Bella interrupted her again. "Don't make it weird."

"I won't make it weird," she insisted. But Bella could hear the breathlessness in her mother's voice. She was definitely dancing. "You know me, sweetie. I'm just worried about you. I want you to be happy."

"I know," she whispered.

"You deserve that, after everything you've been through."

Bella curled herself into a ball, tucking her knees inside her large crewneck. "But, Mom, what if it's all pointless? What if I find someone new and it all happens again? What if I can't—"

What if I can't have a baby?

She was unable to finish her thought, emotion clogging her throat, her eyes burning with tears. She swiped them away, frustrated that even a year later, this conversation had her feeling like a charred piece of firewood, abandoned to the flame.

Getting pregnant had been unexpected. It was the summer after they graduated from NYU. Percy had been bringing Bella to her family's house on Long Island, out in Amagansett, every summer since they'd roomed together freshman year. Bella expected her weeks in Amagansett to be spent bike riding downtown and at the beach, drinking cold cocktails, and scarfing down lobster rolls. What she didn't expect was the Hamiltons' private chef at the house, their multimillion-dollar "beach house" with bedrooms the size of Nonna's entire apartment, and an older brother who irrevocably stole her heart.

Lon spent his summers in Amagansett between his

years at Boston University, and Bella couldn't help being drawn straight to him. Their stolen glances and flirty inter-actions quickly transformed into hidden kisses and late-night rendezvous. She could still hear the squeal that came out of Percy when Bella admitted to falling for her brother, and for two years of her life, Lon was her world. He moved to the city after he graduated to work at an investment bank down on Wall Street, and as soon as she graduated, she moved into his apartment on Sullivan Street. It was small but with lots of natural light and thankfully a dishwasher, and more importantly, they were happy. Two months later, when her cycle was six days late, she took a test, and those two pink lines changed everything.

Freshly graduated and twenty-three years old, only two months into her job as an assistant at a top social media agency in the city, nervous didn't scratch the surface of how Bella felt at the time. But Lon was calm—happy, even. And a month later, he got down on one knee with a diamond that made Bella's head roll at how stupidly huge it was. Preg-nancy hormones took over and she cried and jumped into his arms, thinking it was the journey of a lifetime with a man she was deeply in love with.

The wedding was quick; a small thing with family on the beach in Amagansett. Nonna made meatballs, despite the private chef's resistance, and everything felt perfect. Bella wore an ivory dress that hugged her slightly rounded belly, and she pinned white azaleas to her hair. Lon looked at her like she was the only thing that mattered in the world, and at the time, she believed it. It was that look of pure love and adoration that kept her going through the months of grief that followed.

When she'd gone in for her 16-week appointment, the ultrasound technician's shoulders slumped and she'd informed Bella there was no heartbeat. The nurse kept saying "I'm sorry" and "it was likely a chemical imbalance," but Bella couldn't hear a thing. Her mind went blank at the lack of sound coming from the monitor beside her, from the baby in her belly that she dreamed about for weeks. The baby that would make her and Lon a family of three.

Reeling with grief, Bella went home that night and slept, not leaving bed until the following Monday when she was expected at work. After so many weeks of imagining what life could be like with a little one in her arms, the surgery that followed and the subsequent heartache was unbearable. She knew miscarriages were common—knew the statistics, that one in four women experienced them. But even the stats couldn't change how she felt, how grief stuck to her chest like hardened gum on a Manhattan sidewalk, impossible to remove.

With babies fresh on their minds, they decided to try again. Her doctor said that her fertility would be heightened after her pregnancy, so they decided to go for it. Getting pregnant again wasn't hard, and while they grieved their first baby, they were exhilarated about having another life to love. Only to lose this one again eight weeks later. They gave it one more try, and nine weeks later, found themselves in the same spot.

Bella let herself drown. She stopped caring about what she looked like. She stopped caring about her marriage to Lon. The only thing she *could* control was her job, so she doubled down in her work and got herself a promotion and a corner office that overlooked the Manhattan skyline. But during those endless happy hours where she drank to try and forget, she hadn't realized everything she was losing in the process. Including her husband, who'd fallen in love with someone else.

The phone's crackling silence slowly pulled her back to the now, and she heard her mother say, "Sweetie, no matter what, you are deserving of love," with that same tone she'd always given Bella as a kid. The one that made her feel comforted and loved and cared for during her years growing up in an impossible city like theirs. "We will pray to Saint Gerard for a little one to join us, but if not? You *will* have a full life. You'll find a man to enjoy it with no matter what, Isabella."

Bella's body tensed. She knew in a city like New York, where dating apps gave men plenty of options to choose from, that she would never truly live up to what they wanted. She'd always have that whisper of self-doubt taunting her about her worth, about how most men would rather a sure thing than risk the possibility of failure.

"I know," she whispered into the phone, not fully believing it but desperate to break free from the painful memories.

"So, who is he? What's he like?" Mom asked, dropping her casual demeanor and allowing her eagerness to take the reins.

Bella sat up on the couch and tried her best to focus on the task at hand: find out what her mother knew. She wondered if mentioning Tri would spark any kind of reaction and decided to just go for it.

"He's actually the executive chef of this restaurant in Brooklyn," she responded, keeping her tone even despite the nerves that sparked in her veins. "It's called Tri, have you heard of it?"

"Tri? What kind of restaurant name is that?" her mother scoffed.

"It's supposed to be named after the tri-state area with a

menu inspired by it, or whatever. Percy was assigned to cover it."

"Is it farm-to-table?"

She doesn't know about this restaurant, Bella surmised. Unless her mother had suddenly become an expert at play-acting naivete... She shook her head and grinned, recalling the stockroom song and dance not ten minutes ago. Which meant she genuinely didn't seem to know a thing.

"New American," she replied. "Although, honestly, I don't know if there's a difference between the two."

"Well maybe you ask him, then report back," her mother teased. "And take note of his bagel order. You can tell a lot about a man from his bagel order."

"Oh yeah? What does dad's poppyseed with plain cream cheese say about him?"

"That he doesn't order anything with garlic or onion because his breath would smell bad in front of a lady," her mother quipped.

"So you're saying I should order a garlic bagel with scallion cream cheese tomorrow?"

"*Bella.*"

She chuckled at her mother's exasperation. "Kidding, Mom. You of all people know I've been ordering the same thing since I was a kid."

"Pumpernickel, veggie cream cheese," she droned off. "I swear it was the only way I could get you to eat any kind of vegetables when you were five."

"I'll take vegetables in cheese form any day."

There was some shouting on the other end, followed by clanging of pots and jars. "And I think that's my cue," Mom said. "You sure you can grab bread for tomorrow?"

"It's bread, it's not rocket science," she replied. "And it's time I start contributing to supper again, yes?"

Her mother sighed. "Yes. I never want you to feel burdened though."

Bella felt her chest squeeze with so much love for her mom, her dad, and her nonna. When everything was crumbling around her, she relied on the three of them to be a steady rock. To always show her love in the form of hugs and kind words and bowls of meatballs.

Chapter Four

THE MORNING WAS GEARING up to be one of those picture-perfect fall days. The kind that reminded New Yorkers why they dealt with the rats and the stench and the never-ending sounds of construction and honking horns. The sky was a baby blue, the yellows, reds, and oranges of the maple trees glistened under the sun, and the air was crisp enough for Bella to bundle up in her favorite black cable-knit sweater and leather jacket. She shifted from foot to foot at South Slope Bagels, thankful that she decided to wear her sneakers instead of her leather boots, especially if she was going to be standing in this line for eternity. Everyone in Park Slope dressed far more casually than the Sunday brunch crowds in Manhattan, so her sneakers and her knit beanie fit right in.

The line inched forward ever so slightly. Bella checked her phone for the tenth time in the last five minutes, waiting for the clock to strike ten so she could give the chef crap for being late. But she didn't get her chance when someone stepped beside her.

"Why are you in the line?" he asked.

Bella looked up at Wyatt, eyeing his version of Park Slope casual: corduroy jacket, loose blue jeans, Boston clogs on his feet, his wavy auburn hair tucked inside a flat-brim hat.

She frowned at him. "Because if I didn't get here early, there wouldn't have been any bagels left."

Wyatt's green eyes twinkled with amusement. "You got here early?"

"*Yes*, at nine."

He rolled his eyes, and then to her shock, he took her hand and pulled her out of the line.

"Oh my god," she cried. "What are you doing? I wasted a whole hour of my life for that spot!"

Wyatt turned around, tugging her along, holding her hand with both of his at his back. She followed him as he slipped around the people waiting at the door and stepped inside.

"You can't *walk up to the counter*," Bella seethed. "These people have—*oh*."

Her angry rant died in her throat as Wyatt guided her behind the counter and deeper into the bagel shop. He opened a swinging metal door with his foot, keeping his hands clasped around hers.

"Asshole!"

Bella froze, realizing what was happening.

Wyatt grinned, releasing her hand and giving the bearded man in black overalls—the one who called him an asshole—a tight hug with one arm. He didn't seem to mind having to lift up on his toes to reach his friend, who easily towered over six feet compared to Wyatt's smaller build. Bella put him at a few inches taller than herself, probably around five-foot-seven or so. But that didn't stop him from exuding that quiet confidence, like he was at ease with who he was and where he stood in the world.

The two men exchanged words, but Bella didn't comprehend any of it, her gaze darting back and forth between the commotion of the kitchen staff shaping and boiling and baking bagels around her.

"Who's this?" asked the bagel man.

Wyatt smiled and cocked his head. "This is Bella."

She scowled. "Of course you know the guy who runs the place. I should have known."

He smirked. "This is Benji. We went to culinary school together."

"And this is Asshole," Benji joked, slapping Wyatt on the back. "A pretentious one, might I add."

Bella crossed her arms. "I've picked up on that."

Benji belted out a booming laugh, then turned to Wyatt. "I like her."

"Seems to be a theme," he said, his eyes on a sheet of golden sesame bagels a line cook was pulling out of an oven.

Her stomach dipped at his comment.

"What would you like, Bella?" Benji asked. "Any woman who can stand five minutes with Wyatt deserves a bagel on the house. It's the least I can do for all the pain you're about to endure."

Wyatt gave him the finger.

"I usually order a pumpernickel with veggie, but..." She trailed off, watching one of the line cooks fold up a bacon, egg, and cheese combo. She didn't mean for the small moan to fall from her lips at the sight of it, but it did.

"Sounds like it's a BEC morning," Benji teased.

"Make that two," Wyatt said.

You can tell a lot about a man from his bagel order. Bella considered her mother's words, realizing that Wyatt was ordering the same thing as her. What did this tell her about him?

"And add the ketchup to both," he added.

She scrunched her nose in response. "Ketchup?"

Wyatt moved closer to her, close enough for their arms to brush. Her hand twitched, still tingling from the memory of his hands on hers. "Trust me, it'll be worth it."

Benji took it upon himself to make their sandwiches, despite having a kitchen full of cooks around him to handle it. After sliding folded cheesy eggs on the bottom halves of fresh-from-the-oven pumpernickel bagels and topping them with three thick-cut slices of bacon, he reached into the fridge and grabbed a clear container of a thick maroon spread.

"That's ketchup?" Bella asked, watching in amazement as Benji slathered a spoonful of the stuff on the empty top slices, then pressed the sandwiches together. He sliced the bagels in half and slid them in their direction.

Wyatt nodded his head, watching as Bella lifted half of her bagel and took a bite. Her eyes fluttered shut at the buttery, cheesy, greasy glory of it all, the robust flavor from the ketchup adding that perfect hint of tang with each bite. Another moan escaped her lips as she chewed.

She opened her eyes and noticed Wyatt and Benji watching her, both with wide grins on their faces.

"That never gets old," Benji said wistfully.

"It sure doesn't," Wyatt agreed.

She swallowed. "What doesn't?"

"Watching someone light up as they enjoy your food," Benji explained.

Bella's eyes slid to Wyatt, realizing she recognized the smile on his face. It was the same one from Friday night, when he watched her eat his abominable deconstructed meatball.

She shook her head and stuck out her tongue at him, then felt her face flush as she listened to his raspy chuckle in person. Her chest ignited with that burning feeling again, the one that made her feel excited and hopeful and *alive.* But this time, it wasn't anger that burned in her ribs. It was something else entirely, and she was nowhere close to being ready to admit to herself what that could mean.

After finishing their sandwiches and trying a new cinnamon pumpkin bagel Benji was testing for October, Bella followed Wyatt around the crowd of customers and out of the shop. He walked a few paces away toward a tree that hung low along the sidewalk, then turned to face her. He didn't move to reach for her hand again or brush her arm, but he remained close, and Bella could taste the static energy on her tongue from his proximity.

"So," he finally said after a beat of silence, his mouth pulled into that smirk. "There's a farmers' market I like just a few blocks down. Want to join me?"

She cocked her head. "Do they sell bread?"

Wyatt's eyes widened with amusement. "If they didn't, would you say no?"

She shrugged. "I need to grab bread for dinner with my family tonight."

"Yes, they have bread. Some of the best," he tacked on. "But I'm still waiting on an answer."

"Someone's bossy," she joked. "Is this how you are in the kitchen, chef?"

"I try to aim for authoritative yet kind."

"Like forcing a girl to eat her bacon, egg, and cheese with ketchup."

"Again, didn't see you complaining."

She chuckled, then noticed the way his eyes dipped to her lips when she laughed. She hid them from his sight, pressing them together in a thin line.

He looked back up and met her gaze. "Please join me."

"We have now resorted to *begging*."

"Is it so bad that I want to get to know you?"

Yes, she thought to herself. Being around Wyatt made her feel electric—and nervous. She had no idea how much she should reveal. But hanging out with him also meant getting answers, and after her conversation with her mom the night before, she had a feeling answers were not something she would be getting from her parents. Learning the truth was up to her, and despite her better judgment, her curiosity took over.

"Depends on what you want to know," she finally replied.

He stepped aside and held out an arm, motioning for her to walk with him down the street. She followed, tucking her hands in the pockets of her leather jacket.

"How about we start with how you know Percy," he said.

Bella frowned. "If this is your attempt to get a good review..."

"It's not, don't worry. Just genuinely curious."

She huffed, playfully turning her head from him in distaste.

"You're really making me work for it, aren't you?"

"Is it working?" she teased back, recalling his sentiment from their phone conversation the night before.

"Tremendously."

Feeling satisfied, she relented. "Percy and I met at NYU. We went from assigned dormmates to best friends pretty quickly. I was there for the inception of her Instagram account, which was mostly reviews of cheap hole-in-the-walls and grungy dive bars because that's all we could afford."

"You find some of the best food in those places."

She grinned. "I swear I discovered the best tacos in the city at this tiny joint in the Village, but it closed during the pandemic. RIP, Uncle Julio's."

"Gone too soon," he bantered.

The grin on her face at this point was comical, like it was painted on for good. "Anyway, we got an apartment and were roommates, up until she met her girlfriend Yaz, and I..."

Bella trailed off, the grin now slipping from her cheeks.

They stopped at an intersection and waited as cars drove by. Wyatt remained quiet and patient, clearly giving her the space to decide if she wanted to continue.

"...and I moved in with my ex."

"Ex-fiancé or ex-husband?"

The little white stick figure signaling to cross blinked at them from the other side of the street, but Bella didn't move. Her eyes fixed on Wyatt's. "How..."

Fingertips brushed her left hand, grazing her ring finger. "You have an indent here. I'm assuming from a ring."

"Y-you noticed that from holding my hand once?" she breathed, her stomach fluttering obnoxiously from his touch.

"I noticed that at the restaurant, when you picked up your wineglass."

Her eyes widened. "That is fifty shades of creepy."

He shrugged, dropping his hand away from hers. "Or observant."

"'Observant' is the kind of word a creeper would use. Or a serial killer."

His face flushed. "I'm sorry, you're right. But I can't help but notice you."

She furrowed her brow. "Why? What's so special about me?"

He shrugged again, the screen counting down for them to cross, but he didn't move. "You were honest to my face about my food."

"So you like people dissing you."

"You are—" He chuckled and closed his eyes, shaking his head.

"Noticeable?"

"Yeah," he agreed. "Noticeable."

The countdown had reached three. Bella snatched his hand and pulled him across the street. When they reached the other end, she looked down at their joined hands, realizing what she'd done, feeling too warm beneath her beanie and jacket all of a sudden.

He squeezed her hand once, then dropped it and laced his hands behind his back. He kept his eyes ahead as they continued down the sidewalk. "Being an executive chef is kind of weird. People treat you differently; they compliment or praise you to your face but are a lot more honest behind your back. Unless it's bad management...they're never afraid to tell you what they think."

Matteo, she thought. "Are you dealing with bad management?"

"Not now, no. I was at my former restaurant. The owner I work with now is the best in the industry."

Her heart swelled knowing that someone in her family

—albeit family that she'd yet to *meet*—would be considered as "the best in the industry" by a chef like Wyatt. She resisted the urge to press him for more, deciding instead to keep her cool and be subtle with her digging.

"What was your former restaurant?" she asked.

Creases lined his forehead as he scowled. "Hyacinth."

"You were a chef at *Hyacinth*?" It was one of those critically acclaimed restaurants in New York, the kind that had three Michelin stars and a two-month waitlist to get in. Lon tried to get them on the list years ago, but when things started falling apart, he stopped checking the reservations page.

He sighed. "For three years."

"Were you there when they got the Michelin stars?"

His frown deepened. "No. That happened after my time."

"I'm assuming bad management?"

He gave her a curt nod. She could tell that whatever it was, he wasn't ready to divulge. She allowed for the silence to linger between them, the sound of rustling leaves in the wind and distant raucous laughter from children at a playground filling the space comfortably.

The farmers' market was bustling with couples trailing dogs on leashes, families with strollers, and kids on scooters. Wyatt walked her through the different tents, and at this point, she wasn't shocked that every vendor knew him. One called him over to try a slice of their multi-colored heirloom tomatoes. Another wanted him to scan their selection of oyster mushrooms, which pleased him enough that he bought a pound to experiment with for a dish he was developing for his winter menu. Then there was the pickle guy and the vegan cookie lady. Bella scanned the crowd and the tents, feeling overwhelmed, not paying attention as a woman hugging a large pumpkin bumped into her. She lost her balance and tipped back.

Wyatt snatched her waist and caught her, his hands firm as he steadied her upright.

Her face flushed. "Th-thanks."

He smirked, his hand still lightly on her back as he pointed to a tent across from them, wire shelves tightly lined with fresh loaves wrapped in plastic.

"Bread," he said, dropping his hand.

"Bread." She coughed, her cheeks still hot. "Do they take card?"

Wyatt reached into his wallet and slipped her a twenty. "Here. I need to chat with Sunrise Farms. They have a shipment coming to me in a few weeks."

She stood there, bewildered, hand clutching the twenty-dollar bill, as he made his move a couple tents down. The man selling pasture-raised pork—she assumed from Sunrise Farms—looked flustered that Wyatt was there. But whatever Wyatt was saying softened the farmer's demeanor and the two of them shifted into easy conversation.

Bella stepped up to the tent labeled Grainy Goods and tracked down a loaf of ciabatta. When she approached the register with her loaf, the woman behind the counter asked if she wanted to pay with cash or card.

"Oh! My friend thought you didn't take card," she said.

"Or I wanted to pay for you," Wyatt said, back to standing beside her. He opened a cotton tote bag and held it out to her, giving her the option to slip her bread in the bag.

She frowned. "I can carry my own bread. And pay for it."

"Benji wouldn't let me pay for bagels, so *please* let me buy your bread."

"Well, in that case," she teased, slapping the twenty

down on the counter and smiling at the baker. "Keep the change."

The woman's eyebrows shot up. Her eyes darted back and forth between her and Wyatt. "What?"

An amused smile teased at his mouth as he turned toward the counter. "You heard the woman. It's all yours, Angie."

Angie couldn't seem to comprehend, so moments later, she and Wyatt found themselves walking away with another loaf of ciabatta and three cranberry scones in a paper bag. They grabbed coffees from a local roaster three tents down, the smell coaxing Bella into buying a whole pound of beans, then made their way to Prospect Park. They rested on a bench underneath an oak tree with pale green leaves that'd already started to turn, shimmering with streaks of gold.

"So, what do you think?" Wyatt started. "I'm not so bad. You can have me over for dinner."

Bella scrunched her face and turned toward him, tucking a leg underneath her. She held up her paper cup. "That's still up for debate. You could have slipped poison into this coffee, you serial killer."

"Poison at the hand of a chef is way too obvious. I would think of something more creative."

Her mouth fell open.

Wyatt grinned. "Come on, cook me dinner. I promise I won't make any remarks about those top-secret ingredients."

"They are top secret," she jested. "Plus, you won't actually see me make them. It's kind of an all-day process."

She watched as he cocked a brow, looking intrigued. "All day, huh?"

Her face flushed. "I already said too much. My nonna is very secretive about her recipe."

"So you *do* call her nonna."

"Benji was right. You *are* an asshole."

Wyatt grinned again, and *god*, she liked that grin. She liked his pearly white teeth, the freckles dotted across his nose, and the way his wavy auburn hair stuck out the back of his flat-brim. It was intoxicating—*he* was intoxicating. And she felt royally screwed.

"Do you need me to sign a legal document promising that I won't repeat or use this secret amazing recipe?" he asked.

"Yes." She reached for the wallet in her crossbody purse, then pulled out that worn paper receipt. She held it out to him with a pen. "I need it in writing."

Wyatt reached for the items slowly, his eyes on hers. "You kept it."

She rolled her eyes. "Duh? I did text you, remember?"

"But then you kept it after that," he said. "I must have been noticeable, too."

Bella flushed as he unfolded the receipt, flattening it out on his thigh. She watched as he scribbled something down, then signed his name and handed them back to her, his fingers brushing against her own.

She cleared her throat and squinted dramatically, making a show of reading what he wrote. "I, Wyatt Henderson, hereby promise not to repeat or reuse any of the secrets revealed regarding Bella's meatballs on Tuesday, September 30." She cocked her head. "This Tuesday?"

"The restaurant is closed on Tuesdays. Are you free?"

She hummed. "I'll need to call my lawyer first and make sure that this legally binding contract is aboveboard."

"And how long will that take?"

"I don't know. I'll fax it over to him after this and get back to you."

Wyatt chuckled, and Bella found herself admiring him again. For a long beat, they stared at one another, the late morning passing them by around the park, the warm sun on her skin feeling something akin to anticipation.

Wyatt curled a finger around the hem of her leather jacket at her wrist, then gave it a small tug. "And if he approves of this agreement? What then?"

Bella kept her eyes on his hand, the way his finger lightly traced the fabric of her coat. *Yep*, she thought. *So, so screwed.*

"Then I guess I'll see you on Tuesday," she whispered.

Chapter Five

It's NOT like meeting and flirting with a handsome man like Wyatt was a bad thing; Bella knew that. It was all the other factors that had her mind in a tailspin. There was the fact that he worked for Matteo, who was her grandfather's secret son, although she still wasn't 100 percent sure if Wyatt's boss was the Matteo she was looking for. Then there was the fact that he didn't know her real name, or that her nonna was arguably the most famous Italian granny in the city. And then there was the soul-crushing reality that even if it all worked out, even if he found out the truth and he still found her *noticeable*, she still might not be able to give him the future he wanted, and that could be a deal-breaker.

She shivered at the thought as she stepped off the subway at Canal Street, the cotton tote bag holding her ciabatta bread and leftover scones swinging at her shoulder. It was only *one* date, or whatever that was between her and Wyatt today. She was getting ahead of herself.

She sucked in a breath of the sharp evening air as she

turned onto Mulberry Street, heading for Russo's Deli. Nonna refused to move out of the apartment that stood above her shop, even though she knew her grandmother could likely afford something bigger, and without so many stairs. But her stubborn nonna stayed put, arguing that the deli and the apartment were her family legacy, purchased by her mother and father when they immigrated from Sicily in 1912.

Mulberry Street was electric as hordes of tourists made their slow descent down the center of the road, eyes wide at the twinkling *Welcome to Little Italy* sign that hung proudly at the entrance. Someone was singing New York ballads outside of the Cannoli King again, attempting to lure tourists in with espresso and crispy cannoli stuffed with various sweet ricotta cremes. Gelato cart attendants scooped flavors onto tiny cones, sticking small plastic green spoons and vanilla wafers at the top before handing them off to greedy hands. She smiled at the chaos of it all, allowing herself to blend into the crowd of tourists still lingering in the city after the Feast of San Gennaro the week before, when the street was covered with vendors selling greasy grilled sausages and sandwiches, fresh squeezed lemonade, and zeppoles heavily dusted with powdered sugar.

She finally made it to the front of Russo's Deli, which, unlike the rest of the street, was completely dark. Sundays were sacred to her nonna for two reasons: Sunday mass at St. Teresa's, and supper with her family. Even if tourists flooded Mulberry Street during that second half of the weekend, even if she could milk their wallets with containers of meatballs and sauce, Muffuletta heroes, and boxes of rainbow cookies, she never budged. She was the most stubborn person Bella knew. But also the most fiercely loving.

Bella took a deep breath as she looked at the dark deli, attempting to give herself a pep talk for tonight. After their conversation last night, she assumed her mother was completely oblivious of Matteo and her grandfather's secret. But she wouldn't be surprised if Nonna was aware, because how could her ex-husband have an entire family and she *not* know about it? Bella tried imagining what her life could look like in that situation—Lon starting a life with Katie, having kids, and Bella living her life completely oblivious to it. It was unfathomable.

She *could* go in there and simply demand answers, but in her heart, she knew that wasn't the way to handle this. If Nonna truly knew about Grandpa's other family, then she kept it a secret from her mother for a reason. This—this *thing* had lots of layers. And if she wanted answers tonight, she needed to get crafty. She needed to act like her normal self and broach topics casually, hoping they'd steer her in the right direction. Maybe give her a little more insight into the situation before figuring out how to eventually admit the truth.

She unlocked the door next to the shop with her key, then followed the scent of marinara and basil as she made her way up the stairs to Nonna's.

"*Piccola!*"

Bella grinned as she stepped through the front door, propped open with a wooden chair. Nonna remained at the stove stirring her sauce in the stockpot in front of her, but her brown eyes twinkled with delight at her granddaughter.

"*Ciao, Nonna,*" she replied. She dropped her bag on the table and wrapped her arms around her grandmother's shoulders. "Everything smells amazing, as usual."

"Only the best for my sweet." She scooped simmering marinara with the wooden spoon in her hand, blew on it, then lifted it to Bella. "Taste. What do you think?"

Bella tried it, her brows lifting. "Ooo, spicy this week."

"Yes, too much?"

She shook her head. "I like it. Red pepper flakes?"

Nonna beamed with pride. "Of course."

Bella washed her hands. "You know, one of these weeks you're going to put an ingredient in that sauce that I won't be able to recognize."

"Impossible. I taught you that palette. If you get something wrong, then I have failed you," she teased with a flick of her spoon.

Bella chuckled as she reached for the bread she brought, then began slicing it in half, prepping it with butter and minced garlic. "Is the oven on?"

"Of course, it's all ready for you," Nonna replied, eyes fixed on the ciabatta. "That is a nice loaf you have there."

She flushed. "I picked it up at the farmers' market today in Park Slope."

"And I hear you were not alone?"

Bella rolled her eyes. "Mom told you, I'm guessing."

"You know your mother, never can keep a secret that one," she teased.

She must really not know then, Bella pondered. *Because then I probably would have known.*

"So tell me about him," Nonna pried.

Before Bella could think up the proper response, one that would *maybe* steer the conversation to Wyatt's restaurant and Matteo, her mother and father came bustling through the open doorway, their cheeks flushed.

"Sorry we're late, *Mamma,*" Mom exhaled, dropping her purse with a *thud.* She wore her espresso-brown hair in a loose bun low at the nape of her neck, the top of her head peppered with streaks of gray.

Dad reached for her coat and peeled it off her shoulders, then gave her a kiss on the cheek. "It was my fault. The faculty brunch turned into an all-day thing."

Bella's father was an adjunct professor of Italian Studies at Columbia University. It was how her parents had met. Curious to learn more about the culture that ran deep in her family's history, Mom took a class on Italian Literature and Culture her senior year, and it was Dad's first year teaching it. When she placed her final exam down on Dad's desk, she looked at his eyes through those round tortoise glasses and asked him out for gelato. "And that was that," Mom always said.

The four of them fell into their usual Sunday supper rituals, moving around each other effortlessly. Bella slipped the toasted garlic bread out of the oven and sliced it up, placing the pieces into a lined breadbasket. Mom whisked together the vinaigrette and tossed the leafy green salad as Dad set the table and Nonna added final touches to her sauce before motioning for them to fill their bowls. They gathered around the table in their usual spots—Bella sitting in between her parents, Nonna sitting across from her—and over steaming bowls of meatballs, her grandmother said her prayer of blessing. *Bless us, O Lord, and these Thy gifts, which we are about to receive from Thy bounty, through Christ, our Lord. Amen.* Then, after silently signing the cross to their bodies, they dug in.

"I was asking Bella about her man," Nonna declared.

Mom perked up. "Oh yeah? How'd that go?"

Bella sopped up some of the sauce in her bowl with a slice of garlic bread, keeping her eyes on the food and *not* on her mother's eager face. "He's not my man."

"Is he nice? Did he kiss you?"

She coughed, then took a long sip of wine.

"Angela..." Dad warned.

"What? Innocent questions!" Mom exclaimed.

Bella placed her wineglass down and sliced a meatball in half with her fork, the smell of salty pork and oregano filling her with joy. "No kiss. We're just friends, remember?"

"Mmmm." Nonna nodded, like she was pretending to better understand the situation. But Bella wasn't blind; she could see the way her grandmother's eyes sparkled. Even if she was better at channeling it, she was clearly just as hopeful as Mom.

Bella set down her fork and looked at her grandmother, deciding that this was likely the best transition to getting to the *real* conversation she wanted to have. She gave Nonna a smile. "Did Mom tell you that he's a chef?"

Nonna lifted her brow. "He is, is he?"

"Yes, he's the executive chef at this really nice restaurant out in Red Hook."

"What's the restaurant called?" she inquired. "I do keep up with these kinds of things. I might have heard of it."

"It's called Tri."

Bella watched her grandmother's face *very* closely after she said it, on the lookout for any hint or sign of recognition. Her face remained blank, those eyes still bright, that smile still wide. But if she wasn't mistaken, Bella noticed a small twitch at the top left corner of her grandmother's lip. It could have meant nothing; a tiny nerve spasm, perhaps. But a twinge in Bella's core told her there was something more to that smile. Something else hiding behind those sparkling brown eyes.

"I've never heard of that one, actually," Nonna replied. "What type of food is it?"

Bella went on to explain Wyatt's intricate menu, then the deconstructed meatballs, which had Nonna hooting with laughter as she recounted her first conversation with the chef.

"He thinks his meatballs are better than mine, if you even call those things meatballs," Bella quipped. She looked down at her plate and shrugged. "I'll be, um, cooking for him this week. You know, to prove him wrong."

"Cooking *my* meatballs?" she inquired.

"Don't worry, I already made him swear a blood oath that he will not repeat anything he sees or hears. And he will never see the recipe."

Looking pleased at that, she leaned back in her chair. "Good. We've come too far to have some fancy chef steal my recipe."

"You know, *Mamma*, it wouldn't be so bad to let yourself share it with the rest of the world...maybe that new management offer to sell them in Costco?"

"Pssssh, never." Her grandmother waved off Mom's comment.

"It would be nice for you not to be on your feet all the time down there."

"Well, thankfully I have you helping me," she replied, patting the top of her mother's hand on the table.

Bella watched her mother slump into her chair. It was the same conversation, brought up in a different way. Her mother was always looking for ways to monetize the business so they wouldn't have to be the ones running the show all the time.

But Nonna never complained, never once considered

franchising or selling products in stores or offering her recipes in cookbooks. She thrived behind the counter at Russo's and was committed to holding on tight to her family's secret recipes with those tiny, wrinkled, well-worked hands.

Chapter Six

"SHE REALLY PRETENDED TO KNOW NOTHING?" Percy asked.

Bella pierced a strip of chicken and spinach in the salad bowl at her desk, then sighed, regretting not buying the sandwich she'd been coveting. The sad nineteen-dollar salad in front of her was really not doing it for her. "I'm still not totally sure if she knows, P."

"Come *on*. Can you imagine not knowing if Lon remarried and had kids?"

"Trust me, I have," she grumbled.

There was a beat of awkward silence between them. Bella took another bite of chicken, chewing slowly as she fidgeted with the headphones in her ears, then tapped the phone screen beside her to make sure Percy was still on the call. She was.

"Sorry," Percy finally mumbled. "I keep bringing him up. I'm ruining the best-friend code."

"He's your brother, Percy. Do you really think I expect you not to talk about him?"

"I guess not," she grumbled. "On the bright side, the fact

that he *is* my brother made it so much easier to beat him up."

"You're using past tense like you have, in fact, beat him up."

Another beat of silence.

"*Percy!*"

"Okay, I didn't *beat him up*, per se. Just, you know, a swift kick in the balls when he got back from Aruba. I told him he didn't deserve to have children."

Bella dropped her fork. "Please tell me you didn't."

"I would like to, for your sake. But...sorry, babe, it's true."

She groaned. "Your mother must have loved that."

"Luckily I'm past the point of being grounded. But she did tell me and Yaz to get out of the house for the day."

"And Yaz?"

"Said she's never been prouder of me."

"I've always liked her," Bella muttered.

"I would happily do it all again, too. You mean everything to me, Bells. The meatball to my spaghetti."

At that moment, her phone buzzed on the table. She scanned the text, realizing it was from Wyatt.

"I literally made a reference to *meatballs* and you didn't even acknowledge it," Percy quipped.

"Wyatt just texted me."

"The chef?" Percy squeaked. "You're on a first-name basis with *the chef?*"

"You told me to get information from him, remember?"

"Whoa, whoa, whoa. If you don't tell me what's going on *right now*, I'm going to lose my damn mind."

Bella relayed her weekend to Percy, from his phone call to the bagels and their walk around the farmers' market. She even mentioned his keen awareness of the indent on her finger, how he picked up that she used to wear a ring.

"I might have done something kind of dumb, though," Bella continued.

"Okay...?"

She sighed. "I, um, told him that my last name was Hamilton."

A beat of silence. "*Why* would you do that?"

She groaned. "When he invited me to hang out, I wasn't sure how much he knew about Matteo's connection to my family."

"And does he?"

"I don't think so."

"So you'll tell him?"

Bella was silent for a moment. She *should* tell him, but her stomach soured at the thought. Did she need to? Did it even matter if he knew the truth?

Except it wasn't. Her mind drifted to the way Wyatt looked at her with those dark green eyes, the way his lip curled into a smirk when she messed with him, the way his raspy laughter made her feel warm down to her toes.

Yet, besides the small touches on her back or the brief moments holding her hand, he didn't make any other move. He seemed to enjoy the static energy between them, keeping her close without actually touching her. His small tug of her jacket as they sat on that park bench had left her feeling heated all over.

"What does his text say?" Percy inquired.

Bella swiped open her screen. Instead of a text, Wyatt sent a link from *New York Magazine* with a headline that made her eyes roll: *The Best Meatballs in New York.*

"Seems like *New York Mag* published a roundup on meatballs," she replied, clicking on the link.

"Bastards," Percy grumbled. "I pitched that same thing to my editor."

She scrolled through the article, the writer counting down the top ten restaurants with the best meatballs in the city. When she reached number two, she groaned. "Wyatt's meatballs are number two."

"Of course they are, but what's number *one*?"

Bella scrolled down, then sighed with relief. "Russo's."

She smiled at the image of the Meatball Duo on her screen; two meatballs served in an oval container, drowning in Nonna's marinara, topped with chopped basil and shaved Pecorino Romano cheese.

"She'll always be the queen," Percy said.

Another buzz from her phone had Bella closing the link and reading the text that came in.

WYATT

Still think your meatballs are better than mine?

Bella smirked, then typed back.

BELLA

I guess you'll have to find out.

"If you're texting the hot chef, I want a play-by-play," Percy demanded.

"I'm...well...I might be having him over tomorrow night."

"You're having him OVER?"

Another text buzzed through.

WYATT

The lawyers OK'd our contract?

She smirked.

"BELLS!"

"*Yes*. I'm going to make him meatballs."

"Nonna's meatballs? Is he even worthy?"

Bella remembered the smile on his lips when she bit into that bagel, when she enjoyed food in front of him. She wondered what his reaction would be to her meatballs. Would they surprise him? Would he hate them? Would he make fun of her? Or...would he be so enamored by her meatballs that he would maybe kiss her?

She shook the thought away. Kissing Wyatt was off-limits.

"It's all a game, to prove him wrong," Bella replied, stabbing into her salad. "And I'm hoping to pick his brain about Matteo."

"You minx, I love it," Percy said. "You better call me the second he leaves. I want every juicy detail."

She smiled. "P, don't you have an *engagement* to plan?"

As soon as she asked it, a knock sounded at her door. Bella looked up and noticed Katie standing outside of her office, a tablet in her hand.

"Oh, I've had it planned for months, literally not worried about it," Percy replied. "Which, by the way, are you available on October 25th?"

Bella watched as Katie took a seat across from her desk. Her gaze instinctively locked to the flickering diamond on her colleague's finger, like a moth drawn to a flame.

"Too distracted by your hot chef to answer me?"

Bella shook her head and looked away, swiveling in her chair so Katie couldn't look at her directly. "*No*, I was checking my schedule. I'm free. Let me know if you need me to do anything, okay?"

"Just come to the after party and look like your usual sexy self. Feel free to bring your new boy toy."

She rolled her eyes. "I gotta go, I have a meeting."

"Tell hot chef I said hi!"

Bella hung up and turned back around. "Katie, hi, sorry about that."

"Guessing that was Percy?"

She blushed. "Yes."

"Was she talking about the engagement party?"

She nodded, then tapped on the mouse of her computer and typed in the password.

"We'll be there," she said. "We're so excited for her."

We. Bella swallowed down the dry ache in her throat at Katie's use of that word. It still felt strange to her that her *employee* was engaged to the man she thought she would spend the rest of her life with. Bella had never been someone's boss before, so she'd figured it was rather harmless to invite Katie out one night for drinks. She *liked* Katie. Ever since she interviewed her for the content creator position, she knew Katie was perfect for the job. Better yet, Katie was perfect as a new friend. Happy hour drinks after work transitioned to weekend brunches and girls' nights in. Percy started tagging along, and Katie became the third person in their duo, the three of them constantly sending memes in their group text and getting together weekly for rom-coms and takeout at Katie's studio apartment in Williamsburg.

Looking back, Bella must have had an inkling that becoming close with her employee in this way could complicate things, but when one miscarriage turned into three, she'd stopped caring. Because it was Katie who was always there for her after a long workday, pulling her to the bar and ordering her a drink. It was Katie who made herself available to Bella to talk things out, or simply joke and laugh and drink until Bella was sufficiently numb and ready to go home. It was Katie who always greeted Lon warmly when he joined them for the night, made him feel part of the group, getting him to laugh in ways that Bella couldn't seem to do anymore.

She should have seen it coming, should have seen it through their lingering glances and small smiles. But she was too distracted by her grief to notice. Too distracted to try to save her marriage. When Lon finally told her that he was in love with Katie and he was leaving, Bella felt like she deserved it. She hadn't given him what he wanted, what he *deserved*. It wasn't her right to hold on to him any longer.

Bella coughed, turning her face toward her screen. "The feeling is mutual."

This engagement party would be the first time she'd have to see her ex-husband face-to-face since the day he walked out. Could she do it? Walk into that party and look at them and not feel like a bullet singed through her chest? Or worse, once Percy was engaged, would she be able to handle everything that came with her wedding? Could she survive another round of wedding planning and festivities with her former in-laws without things getting awkward? She was bound to be in the wedding, but would Lon be a part of it, too? How much would she have to interact with him?

Her mind drifted to Wyatt and she let herself imagine him there by her side. She thought about his coy smile, his considerate gestures, the way his body felt next to hers. A constant presence she could rely on.

But then she shrugged it off. *Ridiculous.* It was time she faced reality. When he found out why she *really* wanted to get to know him, he'd want nothing to do with her. Because she was kind of, sort of, using him.

She took a deep breath. "How's the content plan coming for Dreamscape?"

Katie handed Bella the tablet in her hands. She scrolled through the document, impressed by Katie's thorough strategy to revitalize this luxury real estate brand's social media. Even after everything that happened between them, Bella had yet to feel any regret about hiring Katie for this job. She was undeniably one of the best in the business.

"Six videos a day on TikTok?" Bella inquired, scanning Katie's bullish plan.

"We don't need to shoot six videos, we would reuse footage we have and use it with new trending audio, post replies to comments from viewers, that sort of thing. Plus, TikTok functions like a black hole, it's unlikely someone would actually see all six based on that algorithm."

She nodded. "I understand. But I want to avoid burnout on your end."

"I won't burn out, Bella. I know how important this client is."

Bella looked up from the screen and into Katie's turquoise eyes. "Those are two contradicting thoughts."

"Yes, well, I—"

"Let's drop it to three and circle back in two months," Bella interrupted. "The client doesn't even know what good social media numbers look like, given that their platforms are dormant. Which means any numbers we give them will look good, be an improvement. So let's start there and evaluate between the two of us to see if it's worth increasing our output or shifting our focus to something else that is drawing more attention and brand awareness."

Katie nodded. "Okay. But I really don't mind—"

Bella raised her brow at Katie, making it clear this wasn't up for discussion. She watched her former friend sigh, her shoulders relaxing. Yes, this client *was* important for their agency. Their boss had made a point to highlight how Dreamscape would be the highest paying client Gotham Media Agency worked with in their mere eight years of existence. Yet Bella had a sneaking suspicion that the content plan had to do with more than simply impressing the client. She hadn't seen Katie this aggressive with a strategy since her early days working at the company.

"Dreamscape approved us for three of their spaces to shoot content. Send me a checklist with a breakdown of options so we can be as efficient as possible," she said.

"You don't have to do it, Bella, I can—"

"*Katie.*"

Katie pressed her lips into a line, her expression sheepish.

"Big client, remember? You will not rush our content days. You will need hands to produce the best work."

"You're right, I apologize," Katie replied timidly.

Bella nodded. Her phone buzzed again by her side.

WYATT

Happy to add another clause to the agreement and commit to bringing a bottle of wine, if that will help speed things along with legal.

She couldn't help the laugh that huffed out of her chest. Without thinking, she lifted her phone and fired back two texts.

BELLA

The legal department said we are a go.

And I prefer red.

She placed her phone down and looked up at Katie

sitting across from her. Her eyes were wide, a small smile curled at the corner of her lips.

Bella coughed. "Anything else? Are you good with the workload for your other clients?"

Katie nodded, that playful smile still on her face. "Nope, things are all good."

She looked back at her computer screen, clicking into her email, hoping to look busy and unfazed by Katie's knowing expression. "Send me your content checklist by Thursday end of day."

Katie agreed, then stepped out of her office with a backward glance that Bella studiously ignored.

Chapter Seven

Bella stirred the simmering pot of marinara when the buzzer sounded by her door. The sound startled her, the wooden spoon in her hand spraying sauce across the front of her shirt.

"Of course," she grumbled. She tossed the spoon in the sink and slid over to the intercom, pressing the talk button. "Who is it?"

"Your legally binding contract," said a raspy voice.

She smirked, then pressed the buzzer to open the door below. In a haste, she tossed her shirt into her overflowing hamper and grabbed a clean T-shirt from her dresser, a white one with *Russo's* written in that familiar red script across the chest.

"Shit." She shoved the shirt back in the drawer and closed it, panicking as she scanned her apartment, clocking the small details around her place that told the story of who she was. A picture of her and Nonna making meatballs in her apartment. Dish towels hanging on her stove with the Russo's logo.

A knock sounded out the door.

Shit, shit, shit. She ran the items to her room, shoving them inside her box of postcards above the closet, and reached for her favorite navy silk tank top. She tucked it messily into the front of her dark-washed jeans, then flipped her hair and ruffled her waves as she made her way to the entrance of her apartment and opened the door.

Wyatt dipped his head and smiled, wearing an all-black ensemble of jeans, a loose sweater, and a flat-brim hat, his curly hair spilling out. He held a bottle of red wine in one hand and a bouquet of white lilies in the other.

Bella crossed her arms. "Flowers? I don't remember that being part of the contract."

"I can't not bring something if I'm asking a woman to cook for me on our first date," he admitted, stepping into her apartment.

His body was close to hers in the cramped entryway as she closed the door behind him. Shadows enveloped them, but the warm light coming from the kitchen was enough to make out the twinkle in his eye.

She swallowed as he handed her the flowers. "This is our first date?"

He shrugged. "We'll see how the meatballs are."

Bella clicked her tongue and stepped away from him, making her way back to the kitchen. She went back to stirring her pot of sauce as she listened to Wyatt slip off his shoes and approach her. Too nervous to look him in the eye, she snatched her ceramic pitcher and filled it with water, then began trimming the flowers.

Wyatt remained silent as he scanned her apartment, the tiny open kitchen next to her couch and coffee table, a gold-trimmed bar cart by the window. He shrugged off his coat as he eyed the doorway leading into her bedroom, which was only big enough for her queen-sized bed and her vanity dresser.

He stepped right up to her, his arm brushing hers, and broke the silence. "Nice place."

Her stomach lurched at his proximity, the heat radiating from his chest close by. "There's nothing much to it, I know."

"I think it's quaint."

"Which is the polite way of saying *tiny*."

His laugh was low and husky, and it did absolutely nothing for her ability to stand up straight. She felt his fingers brush against hers ever-so-gently, which certainly wasn't helping either.

"Wine opener?"

"On the bar cart. Wineglasses are hanging below it."

Bella placed the trimmed lilies into the pitcher, then watched as Wyatt swiftly opened a familiar-looking bottle in his hands.

"Jayce said you enjoyed this the other night," Wyatt explained, like he was reading her thoughts. Sure enough, he opened a bottle of the same Cabernet Franc she enjoyed with Percy at his restaurant. Dinner at Tri, finding out about Matteo...that already felt like a month ago, not a mere six days.

"Talking to your somm about me?" she teased, trying to keep things light to avoid the mental spiral she was about to go down.

Wyatt smirked as he poured the wine, then stepped right up to Bella again and handed her a glass. They clinked in silence, eyes lingering on one another as they took sips.

He placed his glass down, then peered into the pot. "Is this it?"

"No, this is the poison."

He nodded. "Does that make you the serial killer?"

"Wouldn't you like to know." Bella smirked.

She relished the way he chuckled at her again, loving the sound that rumbled out of him. She wondered if hearing it would ever get old. She wanted to hear it again. Then again.

"Did you make the sauce from scratch?"

She pointed to the empty jars in her sink that needed to be rinsed. "My nonna and I make a special batch of her sauce every August. She'll buy forty pounds of tomatoes and make all this sauce to can so I have jars throughout the year."

"You have a whole stash?"

Bella nodded and opened the slim pantry next to her kitchen. Her shelves were covered in jars, except for one that held all of her other pantry items.

Wyatt whistled. "That's impressive."

"Thanks, chef. Hopefully it lives up to the hype. Otherwise this would be the most awkward not-first date."

"Well, I hope they live up to the hype, because I would very much like for this to be our first date."

Bella felt her face heat at his admission, at how near he stood to her. Wyatt reached an arm around her and for the briefest moment, she wondered if he was going to curl it around her waist and close the space between them. But he only reached for his wineglass, raising it to take a long sip, teasing eyes on her the entire time. Like he could also tell what she was thinking.

She brushed it off and turned to her pot of meatballs, giving it a stir.

"Need help with anything?" he asked, glancing inside her stainless-steel pot again.

Her heart pattered hard in her ribcage. "Um—" She

scanned her kitchen, trying to reorient herself and not think too much about the heat coming off his chest. "There's, um, a bowl of greens on the table. I was going to whisk a dressing but haven't gotten that far yet."

"I can do that," he said, and as if he lived there, he reached into her cabinets and started retrieving items: bowl, whisk, oil, vinegar, seasonings.

"Kind of defeats the purpose of cooking for you, don't you think?" she teased as she stirred.

"How about you whisk the dressing when you come to my place for dinner, and we'll call it even."

Bella lifted a brow. "Confident the first date will go that well?"

"Aren't you?"

Bella sucked in a breath, the knots in her stomach tightening. It was getting harder and harder to convince herself that she was only hanging out with Wyatt Henderson as a means to gain information about Matteo. Wyatt's banter, his eyes on her, the way that he made her feel even if his touches were featherlight or barely existent at all—they were opening up something in her chest that had been locked away for a long time.

She gave the sauce a taste as she listened to Wyatt toss the salad with his dressing, wondering if she should fess up.

But what if he doesn't want to stick around after he finds out? The thought of tearing whatever this was apart before it even started felt like the antidote to whatever spell she was under when Wyatt was around.

She felt a tug on her tank top. She turned to find him close beside her again, his fingers playing with the silk material.

"Where'd you go?" he asked softly. Had she just been staring at her backsplash this whole time?

"Sorry." She stepped out of his reach and grabbed two shallow pasta bowls in her cabinet, all the while trying to remember his question. "I'm a bit—um—nervous."

"Did I make you uncomfortable?"

Her eyes widened. "No, no. You're great. I just—"

I just lied to you about who I am.

"I just haven't been on a date since my divorce," she rushed out.

Wyatt didn't betray any emotion as he nodded and took in this information. "Tonight is a big deal."

"Yeah," she breathed out. "A big deal."

"Then we'll take things slow, okay?"

He reached out and tugged on her tank top again. Bella smiled, realizing that he had yet to really touch her. Like he'd been waiting for her permission. Like he'd already known she would need to take things slow.

She relaxed. "Yeah. Slow sounds good."

Bella pulled the Italian loaf from her warm oven and filled up their bowls with steaming meatballs, then they made their way to her two-person table by the window. Wyatt's dressing on the salad smelled exquisite, something far more complex than her usual olive oil and balsamic vinegar. He scraped some of the salad onto side plates as Bella reached for her basket of garlic bread.

"I know it's probably a little strange to eat meatballs without pasta, but it's a tradition in my family," Bella explained. "Hope that's okay."

"More than okay. I need the full experience."

"Good." Bella propped her elbows on the table. "All right, chef. It's time."

He grinned as he twisted the fork in his hand, then slowly cut into a meatball. Bella's chest swelled with pride at the way the meatball sliced in half like warm butter while still retaining its shape, exactly like Nonna taught her. She kept her eyes locked on him as Wyatt broke off a piece and took a bite.

His eyebrows shot up in an instant, his eyes wide with what looked to be disbelief. Wyatt chewed, looking down at the meatballs and sauce in front of him.

He swallowed. "These taste like—" He broke off, shaking his head. She felt her chest tighten, wondering if she'd be so unlucky that he would identify Nonna Russo's meatballs from a single bite. *Has he had them before?*

"Never mind. These are..." Wyatt trailed off again as he took another bite.

Relief washed over her. Bella leaned back in her chair, feeling smug. "Did I render you speechless?"

"I think you have."

She smiled. They ate in silence for a few minutes, listening to the distant honking of cars outside, the cacophony of voices from people entering and exiting the rows of restaurants and bars lined up below her building. Bella couldn't seem to keep her eyes off of Wyatt in her space, the way the moonlight made his hair glisten, his comfortable posture as he crossed a foot over his knee and took a sip of wine.

His eyes met hers. She flushed and looked down at her own plate, then shoveled a large bite of meatball into her mouth.

"How long have you been divorced?" Wyatt asked, the tone of his voice gentle. "If you're comfortable talking about it, of course."

"It's okay," she reassured him. "Almost fourteen months."

"Did you marry young?"

She nodded. "I was twenty-three, he was twenty-five. We were married for three years, but then—"

Her throat squeezed around her next words, like they weren't ready to jump out. She blinked back tears, moving her gaze down to her plate.

"Is Hamilton his last name?"

He was giving her an out, a natural flow out of the sticky truth of *why* she ended up divorced. Her shoulders relaxed, even though the question he used to evade these hard truths was no easier to answer. She *did* give him the last name that was supposed to be hers by marriage, but after everything that happened, she didn't have the chance to change it. Yet deep in her heart, she knew it was much more than that. Giving up the Russo last name never seemed right to her. Even her own mother refused to give it up, and her father ended up switching *his* name after marriage. Bella half hoped Lon would suggest the same, but he'd been insistent. He wanted her last name to be Hamilton.

"I didn't get the chance to change my last name," she admitted.

At least it wasn't a lie, but Bella knew at some point, all of these truths would have to be revealed. She hoped he wouldn't run, too.

Bella took another bite of her meatball, her mind dizzying.

Knuckles grazed underneath her chin as Wyatt guided her closer to him, the smile on his face kind. He brushed the corner of her lip, and she was horrified to notice the smear of marinara sauce on his finger.

He grinned as he leaned away from her. Heat pooled in her belly as she watched him suck on his thumb and lick the sauce clean.

"That was kind of hot, chef," she whispered.

He shrugged and twisted his fork as he dug back into his plate. "You're kind of hot."

Dear god, this man. Bella's cheeks flushed as Wyatt casually continued eating, like what he'd done and said didn't completely upend her. Confident, patient, undeniably sexy. She no longer wanted to go slow with him. Not in the *slightest*.

She grumbled to herself as she returned to her own dinner, the heat in her belly slowly stirring, reminding her that it had been a long time since she did anything with a man.

Wyatt placed his fork down in his empty plate. "It seems I forgot what a meatball was after all."

Bella hummed. "Admit it. I was right."

He tilted his head, the left corner of his mouth dipping into his cheek. "You were right."

She raised a fist in the air in triumph.

Wyatt let out a low laugh. "I guess this is our first date, then."

Her eyes narrowed. "On one condition."

His face lit up at her challenge. "Hit me."

"As you can see, the dishwasher in this place is nonexistent. You might be a chef and all, but how are you at cleaning dishes?"

He flashed his pearly whites as he stood up and reached out his hands to her, pulling her up as well. They stood there for a beat, chest to chest. Even if the man was on the shorter side, she liked how he was only five inches above her, his face close to hers.

He threaded his fingers with hers, her stomach somersaulting at his touch. "Every chef starts out as a dishwasher, so lucky for you, I'm *very* good at cleaning dishes. A professional, really."

"So I don't need to tell you not to wash my cast-iron skillet with soap."

"I wouldn't dare."

"Good boy."

Wyatt chuckled again as he released his hands, collecting their dishes on the table. He placed them in the sink, then turned on the spigot. "Has anyone ever told you that you're hilarious?"

She grabbed her dish towel and leaned against the counter next to him. "My mother says that I have lots of *personality*. Is that the same thing?"

Wyatt handed her a clean plate to dry, tipping his head down to face her. "I like your personality."

"That's good. Otherwise this first date would be *really* uncomfortable."

Bella watched as Wyatt smiled to himself, cleaning her dishes with efficiency. Neither spoke as they finished the task at hand, brushing against one another and stealing heated glances until the oxygen in the small space was all but snuffed out.

Lo-fi jazz played from her sound system as Bella eased onto her two-person couch. Wyatt poured the rest of the wine into their glasses, sitting down close beside her. She felt the heat from his thigh against hers and forced a breath into her lungs.

Bella took a long sip from her glass, then as casually as she could, brought up the question she'd been dying to ask him since the moment they met. "So, chef. Tell me about the restaurant."

He leaned back against the couch. "What do you want to know?"

"Everything. What your staff is like, how you create a new menu...if you like the owner you work with."

She watched him as he took a sip from his glass, waiting with bated breath.

"The last one is easy. Yes, I like the owner. Matteo is a great boss. He gives me freedom to do whatever I want with the menu and trusts me completely."

Bella nodded, forcing herself to go slow and pace herself through this conversation. Nonchalance was key. "How'd you end up working for him?"

"He contacted me after I left Hyacinth," Wyatt admitted. "He had an idea for a restaurant to highlight the area's local cuisine. I've always liked finding ways to involve local vendors and farmers in what I'm working on, so his concept intrigued me."

"And he's kind to you?"

"Very. Much better than what I was working with before."

She really wanted to ask him more about Matteo, but an opening like *that* could not be ignored. "What were you working with before?"

Wyatt let out a long breath. He placed his glass of wine on the coffee table, then pushed his wavy hair back. His struggle was evident, and Bella felt a rush that he was sharing with *her*. "A verbally abusive manager whose only mission was to earn those damn Michelin stars."

"Is that why you left? Because they were abusive?"

He shook his head. "Unfortunately no, there's a lot of abuse in kitchens. But earning the executive chef position at Hyacinth was a career highlight for me, and I put myself in the firing line to save my staff from her wrath. I knew what I was signing up for."

"Then why did you quit?"

Wyatt's eyes dropped to his hands. She wondered if she'd pushed too far, wondered if she should return the favor and change the subject, save him from answering.

But to her surprise, he reached for her hand and entwined their fingers once again, as if hers was the comfort he desired to keep going.

"I didn't quit. She fired me because I didn't get her the ratings she wanted."

"That's—" Bella had no idea how to continue. Every word that came to mind didn't feel right. *Horrendous. Vile. Despicable.*

He drew circles on her hand with his thumb. "Embarrassing."

"Wyatt," she whispered.

The chef tipped his head back and rolled it her way, his eyes now on her. His admission made him look tired, like he'd set down a massive brick that weighed on his chest.

"It's not embarrassing, and it's certainly not your fault."

"It kind of is, though. My cooking wasn't good enough. Five months later, Hyacinth was awarded three Michelin stars. The chef she hired after me was able to give her what she wanted in less than a year."

Images of Wyatt's food at Tri popped in her head. The baharat short rib ragu. The lemon lavender panna cotta. The charred cabbage quarter with caramelized miso hollandaise and feathered pancetta curls. How could this man possibly think his cooking wasn't good enough?

Her chest burned. "Then prove her wrong."

Wyatt shook his head. "I'm done trying for a star. And thankfully, Matteo doesn't care either."

"He doesn't want awards for his restaurants?"

His brow furrowed. "How did you know he has multiple restaurants?"

Shit. Bella felt heat rise up from her neck and into her cheeks. "I, um, well...I might have looked him up?"

Wyatt remained silent, his brow still furrowed.

"After I looked you up?" she continued.

His face relaxed at that. "You googled me. How cute."

She rolled her eyes, relief flooding every crevice of her body. "Fine, I admit I was curious."

Wyatt released her hand and scooted even closer, sliding his arm around her. He tucked a strand of her hair behind her ear. "It's okay, I looked you up, too. Or tried to, anyway."

Her mouth went dry. "And what did you find?"

"Nothing. There are a lot of Isabella Hamiltons out there."

She let out a breath. *I am really playing with fire here.* "I keep a low profile online."

"Lucky you."

"Can't do that as a hot chef?"

He smirked. "You think I'm hot?"

"You called me hot. Seemed only fair."

He shook his head, looking amused.

"So...how come Matteo doesn't want to win any awards?"

"He said it has something to do with his father."

Bella felt like she was going to faint.

Thankfully, he didn't notice her body stiffen. "His father always told him that food is about taking care of others first."

Her mind flashed to their usual booth at Lombardi's, an untouched pepperoni pizza between them. She was in eighth grade and frustrated that her life seemed to revolve around her family and the deli. The girls she went to school with were leaving the city for the summer, off to their beach houses or their summer camps. But Bella was stuck in Manhattan, forced to spend her days in the stockroom at Russo's or melting outside in the concrete jungle. She voiced to her grandfather at their monthly lunch that she was angry at how stuck she was to this place, and to her surprise, her grandfather defended Nonna and her business.

When we feed people well, we love them well, her grandfather said that afternoon. *With her meatballs, your grandmother is able to love the entire world.*

She forced back tears, reminding herself who she was with. "That's really beautiful," she whispered.

Wyatt curled his hand around her neck. "*You're* really beautiful." Her heart beat faster in her chest as he stroked his thumb across her cheek. "Is this okay?"

"Yes," she whispered.

He continued to stroke his thumb up and down, tracing her jawline and down to her collarbone. The heat in her abdomen flared again, making her want in ways she hadn't in far too long.

Breathless words tumbled out of her mouth before she could think twice about them. "Kissing me would also be okay."

He let out a long sigh, a new expression flashing over his face. Something like nervousness. Or regret.

He dropped the tone of his voice to something more careful. "You're not the only one who needs to take it slow, Bella."

Chapter Eight

Bella felt like she was going to cave in on herself, sucked right out of that embarrassing moment and into a doom spiral. She was sure Wyatt caught on because moments later, after he'd slipped into his coat, he cupped her face and told her how beautiful she was again, then quietly exited her apartment.

Unable to stop her brain from replaying that moment over and over throughout the night, Bella was too anxious and exhausted to focus on anything at work the following morning. She texted Percy about meeting for lunch instead of their usual midday phone call.

When Percy entered the Mediterranean fast-casual spot, she grabbed Bella by the arms and shook her. "What's wrong? News from one of your tests?"

Bella's eyes widened. "What? No! I'm fine."

Percy exhaled and dropped her head. "Jesus, Bells. You can't scare me like that. I thought you were going to tell me you had cancer."

She enveloped her friend in a fierce hug. "No cancer

and no health scares. But I need to talk through something super weird that happened last night."

Percy sighed into her embrace. "With hot chef?"

"*Yes.*"

They ordered their hummus bowls and took seats at the back of the restaurant.

Percy popped the lid on her bowl and hummed. "Okay. Spill."

She started with her conversation with Wyatt about Matteo, about what she learned regarding her uncle.

"He's absolutely my grandfather's son," she explained. "He repeated the phrase my grandfather always said, word for word."

"Damn." Her friend leaned back in her chair. "Didn't I tell you banging the chef would get you some answers?"

"I'm *not banging the chef.*" She huffed. "In fact, I have a feeling no banging will be happening for a while. Maybe ever."

Percy frowned. "What do you mean?"

She went on to explain the rest of the night, rehashing Wyatt's comments about taking it slow despite his gentle touches and the things he said to her.

"What if he's not actually into me?" Bella asked sheepishly.

"Hot chef called you hot *and* beautiful, and you don't think he's into you?"

She shrugged.

Percy pursed her lips. "I don't buy it, babe. There's something else going on here."

"I even wore the silk tank top. My boobs look *so* good in that top."

Percy smirked. "I'm sure he noticed."

"Doubtful. He was too busy saying things like *I like*

your personality to admire my tits. They're good tits. Which he would know, if he'd given up this whole gentleman act and grabbed my boobs like a real man."

Percy coughed out a laugh.

"What?" Bella asked.

Percy pointed her fork at her. "My girl is back."

Her face flushed. "Back?"

"The chef might be a little confusing right now, but he clearly did something that I could not."

She frowned. "Which is?"

"Bring Bella's sass back from the dead."

"YOUR VITALS and numbers look good, Bella."

She blinked down at Dr. Roscoe. "Nothing came back from my bloodwork?"

The doctor shook her head. "If it did, we would have called you right away. Everything looks perfectly healthy."

She sighed. "It doesn't make sense."

Dr. Roscoe sighed along with her. "I understand this is frustrating after what you have been through. Fertility can be fickle that way. When you want to start trying again, we can focus on specific things that might help. Your diet, stress management, medications. Do you and your husband think you'll be ready anytime soon?"

Bella bristled. "Oh, um, actually...we separated."

The pinch in her chest tightened when she watched her doctor's mouth form a silent O. "Separated for good?"

"I'm afraid so. Signed the papers last year."

"I'm sorry. That must have been especially difficult. After everything."

She nodded, surprised at how she was able to keep her emotions at bay during this conversation. "Yes. But, maybe for the best. Or at least that's what I try to tell myself."

"Well, when you do decide if you want to try with someone else, I will be here, and I'll do everything I can to help you, okay?"

Tears finally sprung up in her eyes. "Yeah, okay."

She felt a comforting hand pat her knee. Dr. Roscoe had been there with her through it all; the ultrasound appointments, the surgeries, the endless pricking of blood and tests Bella insisted on taking to seek some kind of answer to why her body wouldn't carry her babies to term. She was her doctor, but in many ways she felt like a friend, determined to find solutions for a problem that didn't seem to exist.

"Bella."

"Hmm?" she responded, lifting her head to face the doctor.

"We *will* try everything we can. But as someone who has been through the trenches with you, can I give you some advice?"

"Y-yes, of course."

Another pat of her knee. "Adoption is a beautiful thing. There are many babies in the world to love, and this should never stop you from being a mother. You have options, my dear."

"I know," she whispered.

Bella exited the building twenty minutes later, out onto Wall Street. It was Friday afternoon, and the streets were buzzing with tourists, commuters, and finance bros on the hunt for early happy hour drinks. She sucked in a breath and closed her eyes, the sulfur from the asphalt below and the smells of the halal cart at the corner filling her nose. She had a feeling her annual checkup would prove to be completely useless. She wondered if it was time to let it all go, to move on and simply take the risk. With life. With someone new.

She exhaled and reached for her phone in her purse, her fingers moving over the screen.

BELLA

All clear at the doctor. I think I'm done hunting for a solution that might not exist. It feels scary and risky, but I just want to move on.

Percy immediately typed back.

PERCY

Thank fuck. Proud of you babe.

Her phone buzzed as a new text came in. She smirked when she saw who it was from.

WYATT

What are you doing next Tuesday?

She typed a message back to Wyatt.

BELLA

I understand you loved the meatballs, but no, I will not make them again.

He called her two seconds after she sent it. Smiling, she answered. "Obsessed much?"

"Phone calls are so much easier," he said matter-of-factly. "While those meatballs were...*surprising*, that's not exactly what I had in mind."

"I can see the review now. 'Isabella's meatballs weren't just good, they were *surprising*.' What every cook wants to hear."

"I'd be happy with that review."

She rolled her eyes even though he couldn't see her. "You wouldn't get that review because *you barely make meatballs.*"

"Says the woman who looked like she was having a religious experience while enjoying them."

"That's beside the point."

He laughed. "Can we get back to why I called, please?"

Bella started her walk to the subway station. "No. Let's keep fighting about meatballs."

"Could we maybe fight about meatballs on Tuesday, after this special dinner Matteo is hosting at the restaurant?"

She perked up. "Special dinner?"

"*Now* she wants to hear about it."

Matteo is hosting a dinner at the restaurant. Yes, she very much wanted to hear about it. "Are you about to offer me free food?" she asked breezily while her heart thumped.

"Is that all I'm good for? Free food?"

"Seeing as you haven't *kissed* me yet, I would say yes."

She wondered if that was too far, but to her delight, he huffed a laugh. "Matteo hosts our vendors for a special dinner once a year, and I put together an entirely new menu for it. You should come try it and meet him."

Her hands trembled as she reached for her MTA card. "Meeting your boss after only one date? Someone's confident."

"He's been grilling me about you already, so you might as well save me from my misery and come say hi."

She froze. "You told him about me?"

"He's thoroughly impressed by how nonexistent you are on the internet."

Because I technically am nonexistent on the internet.

She suddenly felt very, *very* thankful that she gave Wyatt a different name.

"I probably would have gotten away with not telling him if I didn't show up to work on Wednesday smiling like a damn fool," he continued.

"You were smiling?"

"Because of the meatballs, obviously."

"Sure, sure. *The meatballs.*"

He hummed, and *oh*, she liked the sound of it. Smooth and low, like a warm, gooey caramel sauce. She felt a sharp twist of desire in her chest. "Tuesday, huh? You're not free at all before that?"

Wyatt groaned. "Unfortunately, no. The weekends are my busiest. And Sunday morning my sous chef wanted me to sample this menu she's working on..."

"It's okay," she reassured him.

"Are you sure?" His question sounded pained. "You're not mad?"

She made a face. "Why would I be mad? You're a chef with a very different schedule than mine. It'd be like me asking if you're mad that I work nine to five."

He was silent for a beat, and Bella wondered what that beat meant. There was something going on for him here, and she was three seconds away from poking at it when he finally responded. "Yeah, okay, you're right."

Now they were both silent. Bella swiped into the station, the humid underground making her blouse stick to the back of her neck.

"You sure you're cool with coming? Is it weird that I asked you to meet Matteo?"

In any other circumstance, Bella would probably find it a bit odd. But in this situation? She was thankful that Wyatt was making it *very* easy to access her long-lost uncle, who she was now set to meet in four days.

"Yes, it's cool," she answered. "And no, it's not weird. I would love to meet him."

She sensed his pleasure from the other end of the line as a second soft hum sounded through. "Good. I'll see you then."

She rode the train back to her apartment with a smile on her face. She knew it was risky, whatever this was between the two of them. But *life* was full of risks, and she was finally ready to take them again.

Chapter Nine

Bella stepped into Tri the following Tuesday feeling the sweat already pooling underneath her armpits. The place was packed to the brim with a variety of characters: produce farmers, wine mongers, fishermen, butchers, all dressed to the nines for their big night in the city. She gazed back and forth, wondering where she should even go, when a warm hand graced her back. A tall, familiar looking man dressed in a maroon suit with a skinny floral tie appeared beside her.

"Hello again," Jayce said. He guided her around a laughing crowd and toward the bar. "We have a place for you right over here."

"Th-thanks," Bella stuttered.

"How'd you enjoy the wine the other night?" Jayce asked, holding out a tan hand to a single set spot at the corner of the bar.

She eased out of her coat and stepped up to sit. "Oh, it was just as delightful as the first time. Thanks for telling Wyatt which bottle it was."

Jayce smiled, his gaze a little menacing. "So you *did* hang out with him last week."

Bella felt the blood drain from her face. "I thought you knew?"

"Oh, I assumed when he asked which wine you drank at the restaurant that he was doing his research. But I had no idea it was so he could bring you a bottle."

"I figured he—"

"Chef telling me about a woman he's into? Honey." Jayce clucked his tongue. "That's rarer than a 1947 Cheval Blanc."

He held out his hands to take her coat. She gave it to him, watching him delicately fold it over the crook of his arm.

"Let's just say the chef *never* invites women to the restaurant," Jayce explained. "When he told our host Delilah to set a plate at the best seat in the house, it set the whole staff in a tizzy. Secretly, of course. They would never dare ask him the truth."

She glanced around, noticing the waiters, bussers, and bartenders sneaking glances in her direction, then immediately averting their eyes.

"Why is this the best seat in the house?" she murmured.

Jayce leaned over and pointed across the restaurant. Directly in Bella's line of vision was Tri's open kitchen, and standing in the middle of the chaos was Wyatt. He was wearing his white chef's coat, his wavy hair slicked back enough to remain out of his face. He was talking to one of the line cooks as he examined a finished plate of a salad, fixing the mint leaf garnish with tweezers. He placed the dish on the metal counter in front of him, and then his green eyes flashed in her direction. His smile was slight, like he was mastering himself while he worked in his kitchen, yet his expression seemed pleased.

"Red or white?" Jayce asked.

"Um..." She was flustered. By Wyatt's attention to detail for her arrival. By the staff that was not-so-subtly staring at her. By the fact that she was in the same room as her mysterious uncle and had yet to lay eyes on him. "Surprise me," she said in a rush.

"Sparkling it is."

Jayce returned moments later with a coupe glass filled to the brim with sparkling wine and placed it before her with a paper menu. "The menu is fixed tonight, but you have two options for dinner."

Bella scanned the menu, picking up on the different vendors showcased. Cold smoked oysters from Long Shore Docks served with a mignonette made with Riesling from Harrington Vineyards. Shaved beet salad from Green Harvest Fields with orange sumac dressing, chèvre cheese, pecans, and mint. The dinner options included a pumpkin risotto from Mason County Pumpkin Patch and wine-braised pork shoulder from Sunshine Farms, reminding Bella of the man Wyatt spoke with days earlier at the farmers' market.

"I can only have one?" she teased. "How do I decide?"

"Pick the one that calls to you, they are both delicious," he drawled loudly. Then he turned to face her and mouthed, *Get the risotto.*

"Pumpkin risotto sounds lovely." Bella smiled, handing him the menu.

"Great choice." Jayce grinned back as he took it from her, then pivoted on his heels and left to talk to a waiter.

Bella sipped on her wine and scanned the crowd, hoping to find Matteo somewhere in it. Everything about the evening felt cozy and familiar, the tables full of banter and food and laughter. The staccato of silverware on plates and clinking glasses harmonized with the warm jazz that played through the speakers. Her gaze fell back on the kitchen as she watched Wyatt wipe down a plate, listening to a petite woman whose short black hair streaked with cobalt blue was tucked behind a white bandana. Wyatt nodded at whatever she said and responded with a "Thank you, chef," then scanned the rest of the dishes that were placed in front of him, eyeing each one to make sure every single detail was perfect before handing them off to the waiters on the other side of the counter.

"He's the best in the biz," said a booming voice next to her.

Bella turned to find herself face-to-face with her grandfather. Or at least a much younger version of him.

Matteo Lombardi.

"Matteo Lombardi," he said. He held out his hand to her.

"Isabella," she muttered, the end of her name dying in her throat.

"I know," he said confidently. "It's great to finally meet you."

Matteo's resemblance to her grandfather was uncanny, his features sharper and saturated compared to the photos. Everything about him, from his long, pointed nose to his dark hair and the crinkles at the corners of his eyes and mouth, was like stepping back in time. Even his caramel-colored eyes were exactly the same. It was hard to deny the truth when she looked at this man. She wasn't sure she needed the confirmation to know this was her uncle. His face already told the entire tale.

Bella coughed, realizing her bout of silence likely came across as rude. "You as well. Your restaurant is absolutely stunning."

He beamed. "Thank you. I know it's taboo to pick a

favorite child, but I have to admit, I think Tri is my favorite out of all of my restaurants."

She smiled. "Your secret is safe with me."

His grin made her heart skip, and for the briefest moment, she was sitting at the booth at Lombardi's, eating pepperoni pizza.

A steel dish covered in ice with three oysters was placed in front of her, the riesling mignonette dolloped on top.

Matteo placed a large palm on her shoulder. "Enjoy your meal. We can gossip about Wyatt later."

"I like gossiping," Bella quipped.

"I think it's a requirement to be a true Italian." He winked when he said it, and then he was walking away, already chatting up the two farmers from Green Harvest that were digging into their beet salads.

She could feel the cadence of her heart loud in her ears as she watched him, her mind racing. *Does he know who I really am?* She thought about her grandmother at last Sunday's supper, how she denied knowing about this restaurant when the expression on her face told a different story. Something didn't feel right, and the fact that her precious nonna never told her any of it made her burn with frustration and hurt.

Bella lifted an oyster and after one bite, her mind was lost in a sea of delectable flavors and textures. Every single dish was exquisite, every sip of the wine Jayce handed her unique and divine. When the risotto arrived, she understood why Jayce told her to order it. The dish was served in a small roasted sugar pumpkin, with decadent sage brown butter garnished with pickled kohlrabi. The waitress that came to take her empty pumpkin gave her a lingering smile, and when Bella smiled back, she blushed and scurried off.

She took a sip of her wine when another bowl was placed in front of her. Bella turned to find the petite woman Wyatt spoke with earlier. Her eyeliner was winged with excellent precision, the tip so sharp it could probably slice you whole. Bella had a feeling it matched the personality of the woman before her well.

"Compliments of the chef," she said.

Her gaze lingered on the bowl, noticing it was a small slice of the wine-braised pork shoulder. "I thought we only got one option?" she inquired.

The woman tilted her head, as if Bella's observation was amusing to her. "Not when the chef insists on giving you special treatment."

She glanced back at the kitchen and found Wyatt watching her again. He raised a brow in challenge, clearly curious about what she thought of this dish. The portion was small enough to eat in two bites, but Bella finished it in one, relishing the savory taste of the fatty meat and the tangy red wine.

"Wow," she blurted, covering her mouth that was still full of food.

"We like the word wow. I'm Marissa, by the way."

She chewed and swallowed before speaking, like an actual polite human and not whatever animal she portrayed from her massive bite. "Bella. Sorry that he has you doing his bidding."

"I'm his sous chef, it comes with the job description." She retrieved her empty plate. "Dessert will be out in a few."

A "few" meant over twenty minutes, but Bella didn't mind. She leaned back against the wall, the wine in her hand and the food in her belly making her feel sleepy and content. She watched as various guests said their goodbyes. Matteo stood by the door, thanking each of them for making the trip and for their continued partnership, his booming laugh filling the space in the same way a lit fireplace warmed up a room. Her lingering gaze on her long-lost uncle distracted her from the white coat making its way across the restaurant and to her corner, a plate of apple tarte tatin with cardamom ice cream in hand.

"Sorry for the delay on dessert," he said as he placed the dish in front of her. "But the chef was selfish and wanted a few minutes of your time."

"How rude of him," she quipped.

Wyatt leaned against the bar, his back facing the lingering eyes and whispering mouths in the kitchen. He stood close enough for their conversation to be private, but still held an appropriate distance. They were in front of his entire staff, after all.

He watched her as she sliced into her tart, then dipped it in the ice cream and took a bite. "Never mind." She let out a part moan, part sigh. "This dessert makes up for it."

"I hear the word wow was used earlier."

She shrugged. "It doesn't mean much. I mean, wow is also used as an acronym for a gym, and going to the gym is basically like going to hell on earth. So the word could have many meanings."

Wyatt closed his eyes and dipped his head with a chuckle. When he lifted it back to her, the smile on his face made her heart swoop. "What does it mean in this context?"

She fidgeted in her seat, then relented. "It means 'wow, chef, this meal was the best I've ever had.'"

"High praise from the master of meatballs."

"The master of meatballs? I thought she was over at Russo's."

Bella felt her blood go ice cold as Matteo stepped up to them wearing a wide smile. He handed Wyatt a glass of red wine.

"I don't know," Wyatt replied, winking in her direction. "I think Russo's might be dethroned."

She smiled at him, at a loss. She knew there wouldn't be another set up quite like this, so she took a sip of her wine, squared herself toward Matteo, and asked, "Have you ever tried the meatballs at Russo's?"

"I actually haven't," Matteo replied. "My father and the owner were apparently not on the best terms."

Because they were divorced!!! "He never told you why?"

He shrugged. "Nope, and it never occurred to me to ask. If I'd known how little time we had, I might have."

Her head was spinning at his response when Matteo turned to Wyatt and asked him if he'd ever been to Russo's.

"Once, when I first moved to the city."

"Really?" Bella blurted.

He nodded. "I have to admit, they live up to the hype."

Her heart swelled with pride, then fell flat when she realized how complicated all of this was getting. How long was she going to be able to keep up with this ruse?

"Have you been there before, Bella?" Matteo asked.

"Oh yeah," she said in a rush. "I grew up in the city. Been there plenty of times."

"No kidding! City kids, up top!"

Matteo held up his hand. Bella smiled and high-fived him. She finished off her wine as Matteo and Wyatt discussed the evening. She wanted to tune in, wanted to hear every detail from Matteo to try to decipher more about his life, but her exhaustion finally seeped in. She leaned on the counter, the lids of her eyes feeling heavy.

Jayce came up to her from behind the bar and took her empty wineglass. "What did you think?"

"I think it was so good I'm entering a food coma," she replied with a yawn.

She felt a warm hand brush against hers. Matteo walked off and made his rounds with the staff, thanking them for all their hard work.

"How'd you get here?" Wyatt asked.

"Two trains, then a bus," she replied. "Red Hook isn't the easiest to get to, chef."

"Was that your plan to get home as well?"

She shrugged. "The way back will be one train instead of two, since I came from work."

"It's eleven," he stated.

"And?"

"And I really don't like the idea of you getting on the train. Or a bus."

She scrunched her nose. "Then I'll order an Uber."

He furrowed his brow, then reached for her hand under the bar, twining it with his. "How about you stay at my place tonight. I'm a five-minute walk from here."

Bella sat up straight. "That doesn't sound like taking it slow." She yawned again, her body defying any fight she had toward this absurd plan.

"I promise I'll be on my best behavior." He cocked his head. "Please? I can drive you back in the morning."

Her jaw dropped. "You're only telling me now that you have a *car*?"

He smirked. "Is it working for you?"

"Tremendously."

"Good." He squeezed her hand. "I need to finish a few things up and then we'll go."

"Okay," she whispered. Her heart did that swoopy thing again as she watched him walk back to the kitchen, his staff scurrying around him in an attempt to look busy after their obvious ogling.

Chapter Ten

BELLA RESTED her head in her palm, chastising herself for blowing her shot with Matteo. Yet as Wyatt came around to her and offered to carry her work bag, she realized any attempted conversation would have been pointless in her current state. She was *wrecked*.

She let the chef carry her bag in one hand, his tightly rolled knife bag tucked under his other arm as they made their way down a quiet cobblestone street.

The sound of soft waves felt innocent in contrast to the bright city lights of Manhattan across the river. The Statue of Liberty was also in view, a beacon among the dark lapping water and the trees of Governor's Island in between.

Wyatt slowed in front of a gray brick building with a sleek back door and pulled his keys from the jeans he'd changed into back at the restaurant.

She yawned. "What made you decide to live in Red Hook?"

"It's close to the restaurant. I also enjoy how quiet it is here."

He wasn't wrong. Compared to the rest of Brooklyn and Manhattan beyond, it felt like a whole other world. You couldn't hear the constant chorus of sirens and traffic. You could hear birds. You could even smell the briny river.

He unlocked the door and held his arm out, inviting her to step in. She did, climbing up the single flight of stairs, fully expecting to reach an apartment door. But the stairs opened up into a living room space, next to a massive kitchen with an island counter separating the two spaces. Beyond the room was a wall of glass, followed by a charming patio with plush chairs. Vines climbed up and down the protective railing, and beyond was a stunning view of the skyline.

Her mouth fell open as he placed his knife bag on the counter and took off his corduroy jacket, then came around behind her and slipped her trench coat off her shoulders.

"This entire place is yours?" she breathed, still in shock.

He nodded as he opened up a closet and hung their coats. "I bought it two years ago when I started at Tri."

She kicked off her heels. "You *bought it*? How? Does Matteo really pay you that much?"

Wyatt reached for her hands and guided her down the hall. "Let's get you ready for bed first, then I'll tell you the sob story."

She felt a pang in her chest cycling through Wyatt's confession about the verbal abuse at Hyacinth, about getting fired for not being good enough. This man had *another* sob story?

Wyatt led her into his bedroom, which was as impressive as the rest of his apartment. A king-sized bed stood at the center, covered by a soft white duvet and matching wooden nightstands. He pulled a drawer open from the dresser across the room, a modern canvas painting hanging above it. She was seriously impressed by the design of this place, then thought of the intentional, thorough man before her. Wyatt had perfected every dish that left his kitchen that night, fixating on the tiniest details, like the setting of a mint garnish on a salad. Of course his apartment would be set up with the same kind of care.

He held out a red sweatshirt, the color muted like it had been well worn, and a pair of boxer shorts. "Will this be okay to sleep in?"

She nodded, taking the pile of clothes from him, emotion building in her throat. He was being careful and intentional with her, too. It made her feel horrendous knowing that she was partially lying to this man.

"I need to shower," he continued, grabbing another set of clean clothes for himself before closing the drawer. "Feel free to change and get right in bed. You don't have to wait up."

Her eyes widened as she turned to look at his bed, the plush sheets beckoning. "But where will you sleep?"

"It's a big bed."

She swiveled back to face him, ready to protest, but he was already closing the door of his bathroom.

She sighed as she slipped out of her clothes and into Wyatt's. His sweatshirt smelled like a medley of herbs: rosemary, thyme, sage, parsley. She wondered if he grew them on his massive patio, or if the oils from the herbs he worked with slowly seeped into his clothes over time. She breathed it in as she settled under the covers, his bed the perfect balance of soft and firm, the pillows the kind you wanted to burrow in and never leave.

She was half asleep by the time Wyatt exited the bathroom. She peeked at him in his boxers, at his impressive set of abs as he pulled on a white T-shirt. He ruffled his wet hair with a towel, then hung it up in his bathroom and switched off the lights, the illuminated skyline outside the French pane window saving them from complete darkness.

He crawled into bed beside her, and true to his word, he kept a respectable distance as he settled down on his pillow. "Hi," he whispered.

She nuzzled into the duvet. "Hi back."

"Comfy?"

"Mmmm."

His white teeth gleamed as he smiled. "Good."

"Want to tell me the sob story?" she whispered.

"You seem tired, we don't have to."

She frowned. "Tell me a bedtime story, Wyatt. You promised."

"It's a depressing bedtime story."

"*Pleeease.*"

He sighed and closed his eyes. "I was able to buy this place because of my parents' inheritance."

"They're gone?" she whispered.

He nodded his head once.

"I'm so sorry, Wyatt."

"Thank you. I'm okay, I knew I would lose them early. My mom had me when she was forty-seven. My dad was fifty."

"Wow," she breathed, shooing away the intrusive thought that a woman was able to successfully carry a child at *forty-seven*, yet she'd been unable to do the same in her early twenties.

"Dad passed first when I turned thirty, and mom two years later," he continued. "They were stockbrokers and ran a company together. I'm their only child, so I received everything."

"So you bought this apartment. And the car."

He nodded. "I was fortunate to be able to afford those things, yes."

"Can I ask how old you are?" she whispered.

"Thirty-five."

Only three years since he lost his mom, she thought. *How devastated he must feel.* "Do you miss them?"

He shrugged. "Our relationship wasn't really a warm one. They were supportive of me going to culinary school instead of a traditional college, but I never felt like I connected with them in the way other kids do with their parents."

"That must have been hard."

"I became friendly with solitude," he continued. "Then I moved to New York and found people who feel like family. Like Benji and Matteo."

She squeezed her hands around the duvet. "You and Matteo are close?"

"He's kind of turned into the big brother I never had," he replied. "He doesn't have siblings either, so we bonded over that."

But he does have a sibling. Matteo had to be unaware of her own mother, who also grew up thinking she was an only child.

Wyatt reached an arm over to her and tucked a strand of hair behind her ear. "Okay, you've been to the restaurant. You met my people. You now know my sob story and my age. I think it's your turn now."

She faked a yawn. "I'm so tired, though."

"Tell me a bedtime story, Bella."

She stuck her tongue out at him, and she was rewarded with her favorite raspy laugh.

"Fine," she relented. "What do you want to know?"

"Why did you get divorced?"

She shivered. "Really jumping into it, huh?"

"Sob story for a sob story?"

"Don't you want to know other things first? Like…what I do for work? Or my favorite color?"

"Your favorite color is black," he replied confidently. "It's the only color you wear. Except for a navy tank top I can't stop thinking about."

He totally checked out my tits. "Hm. You're right. What about my job? Know that one, too?"

"Something that requires you to be in a fancy office in Manhattan, or at least I assume so based on the killer wardrobe."

She smirked. "I work for a social media marketing agency. We focus on luxury clients, like real estate firms or car companies or restaurants."

He raised a brow. "Restaurants, huh?"

"I don't mix work and pleasure," she cooed.

He grinned. "Duly noted. Do you make the content?"

"I used to, but now I have minions that do it for me."

"So you're the boss."

She shrugged. "Got a corner office and everything."

"That's so hot."

"Not as hot as having an entire kitchen staff gossiping about you and the only woman you've apparently *ever invited to your restaurant.*"

He sighed. "Was it that bad?"

"You didn't notice?"

"I have to keep away from the gossiping staff or I'll lose my head," he answered honestly.

"Well, it was hot to watch," she joked.

He booped her nose with his finger.

She sighed. "Sob story?"

Wyatt nodded.

Bella felt nowhere near ready to tell him the naked truth, about the multiple miscarriages or the pills she'd had to take so her depression wouldn't swallow her whole. But despite how *unique* this was with Wyatt—she was currently *in his bed*—they were still only getting to know one another. She didn't have to take all of those steps at once. Especially when she had plenty of other secrets she needed to reveal to him at some point.

One thing at a time. She sucked in a breath, afraid she would lose her nerve, and finally spoke. "My husband left me for someone else."

His face darkened. "Are you kidding me?"

She shook her head. "For one of my employees, actually. She was a close friend. We all hung out a lot. It was happening right under my nose."

"Does she still work for you?"

Bella nodded. Her eyes had grown used to the dark, enough for her to be able to see the red that crept up his neck. Feeling bold, she lifted a hand and stroked a finger down the column of his throat. He relaxed at her touch.

"He confessed, then left me to pack up my stuff. He owned our apartment, so I had to find a new place. We finalized the divorce a month later."

"What a jackass."

"They're also engaged," she added. Tears sprung up and trickled down her cheeks. "He proposed four months ago."

Wyatt slammed his eyes shut and took three deep breaths. She felt a hand curl around the curve of her waist. "Can I hold you?" he asked, his voice low.

She wiped at her tears with the sleeves of his sweatshirt. "Hold me?"

He nodded.

"Okay," she croaked.

Wyatt pulled her close to him, wrapping an arm tight around her waist while the other cupped the back of her head. He brushed his fingers softly through her hair, the motion soothing as Bella sniffled and let the tears fall.

"I'm so sorry," he whispered.

"I should be over it by now." It's what she always told herself. It was her fault Lon left in the first place. She gave up after everything happened, didn't try hard enough to get him to stay.

"It's okay if you're not," Wyatt responded.

He kept combing her hair with his fingers, his comforting touch lulling her to sleep. If she wasn't mistaken, she felt his lips press at the top of her head and heard a soft whisper before she entered sweet oblivion.

Sleep well, mia bella.

THE SMELL OF HOT COFFEE, sugar, and spices woke her in the morning. She blinked her eyes open to find Wyatt sitting beside her, rubbing her shoulder to slowly wake her up. He was already dressed in his jeans, sweatshirt, and jacket, his clogs on his feet.

"What time is it?" she asked.

"Six forty-five," he replied, brushing her hair out of her face. "I wasn't sure what time you needed to be up for work."

She nodded and sat up in the bed, realizing the smells she woke up to weren't a dream. A hot cup of coffee and a brown paper bag were waiting on the nightstand.

"You went and got me coffee," she said, exasperated.

She snatched the bag and opened it up. "And a cinnamon roll."

"It's a pumpkin cinnamon roll."

She gawked at him. "You're joking."

"I remembered your face when you ate that pumpkin bagel at South Slope and figured you'd like it." He shrugged, grinning. "My hunch was confirmed when I watched you annihilate the risotto last night."

She blushed and poked his rib, then sniffed the bag. "Wow. Where did you get this?"

"Bakery around the corner. I know the owner so they let me in early."

"Of course you do," she muttered.

He smirked. "I also grabbed you a toothbrush, and there are washcloths and towels in the bathroom."

She thanked him and stepped into his bathroom to brush her teeth and wash her face, eyeing him every few moments. He sat on the bed scrolling on his phone, his gaze sporadically flicking to hers too. When their eyes met, he smiled, and her heart did that big swoop again, like the first big fall down the Thunderbolt at Coney Island.

She shivered when she stepped out of the bathroom, noticing he'd folded her dress and tights and placed them in a cotton tote. "Any chance you have sweats I can borrow for the ride home?" she asked.

He nodded and reached in his dresser for a pair of black joggers and handed them to her. She slipped them on, then laughed at how absurd she looked. "Think I should go to the office like this?"

Wyatt chuckled as he stepped up to her and placed one of his flat-brim hats on her head. "There. Now you're ready for the office."

"Everyone's going to love my wardrobe upgrade."

Wyatt carried her bags as she sipped on her coffee and followed him out of the apartment. The air was chilly, the cobblestone streets of Red Hook slick from the rainstorm that rolled through in the middle of the night. Wet colorful leaves scattered the alley on the path to his car, a Lexus with black leather interiors.

She sat down in the passenger seat and nibbled on her cinnamon roll as he started up the car.

"Need me to navigate?" she asked.

"I remember how to get there," he answered, and pulled out of his spot.

"You drove the other night?"

He nodded. "Much faster than a bus and a train."

"Because you chose to live in a neighborhood of Brooklyn that is impossible to get to?"

Wyatt glanced at her as he turned onto the road. "How'd you sleep last night, Bella?"

"Like a damn rock."

"And do you now understand why I live in Red Hook?"

She scowled. "All right. You win that one."

He smiled, letting her enjoy the cinnamon sugar and pumpkin spice in peace. Bella watched him as he sipped on his coffee while he drove, the sunrise over the Brooklyn Bridge warming her skin.

Ludlow Street was still blanketed in that early morning calm when Wyatt pulled up to her apartment building. He killed the ignition and turned to face her. "When can I see you again?"

She sipped on her coffee. "My my, chef. Some would say you have grown an obsession."

"You slept in my bed, and you're sitting here in my clothes. Obsession doesn't even come close."

"It was the navy tank top, wasn't it?"

He flushed and leaned his head back on his seat. "It's a great tank top."

"And the meatballs."

"And the meatballs," he repeated.

She gave him a wicked grin. "My scheme is working."

"Tremendously."

Bella laughed. She *really* liked him. His attention to detail. His charm. The way he could take her sass and come back at her with a wit that made her laugh. She knew it was a bad idea to keep things going with him. But how could she pump the brakes when he bought her pastries and coffee and toothbrushes, or held her tight as she cried herself to sleep? It was becoming harder and harder for her to convince herself that she shouldn't dive headfirst. Shouldn't let herself crest that roller coaster and hold on.

"I think seeing me again will be up to you," she replied. "You're the one who works nights."

He lifted his hat and smoothed back a lock of hair with a sigh. "Yeah, that's the crappy thing about dating a chef. You'll never get a weekend date night."

"Are we...dating?" she asked.

Wyatt dropped his hat in his lap and reached his hand over the center console to grab hers. He brought it up toward his face, brushing a thumb over her knuckles. "Do you want to be dating?"

"Hmmmm." She squinted her eyes. "I only date guys who are willing to kiss me."

He smirked, and to her shock, he pressed his warm lips against her knuckles. Tingles spread from her hand and up her arm, slicing right into her belly.

"There," he teased.

She rolled her eyes. "That doesn't count"

"You didn't specify."

She shook her head and removed her hand from his grasp, then reached for the hat on her head. "Want this back?"

"No. I want you to wear it to the office."

"I don't think I'm ready to unveil my new wardrobe *quite* yet," she hedged, reaching for the door.

He stopped her with a hand on her leg, his palm covering her knee. "I'm sorry if I overstepped last night. You hopped out of this big relationship and I don't want to force you—"

"Wyatt," she muttered.

The expression on his face was similar to the one she saw when he told her about Hyacinth. He looked embarrassed. Small, even.

"You didn't force me to do anything," she reassured him.

"I'm not moving too fast?"

"Aren't *you* the one insisting we take things slow?" She smirked. "Plus, you haven't even kissed me."

"I did, actually."

Bella rolled her eyes. "Just because we've had a lot of deep conversations in the past couple weeks doesn't mean we're moving too fast. We're...still getting to know one another."

He nodded, his expression unreadable.

"Don't worry about me," she reassured him. "I promise if it feels like too much, I'll tell you."

"All right." But his words didn't change that expression on his face, as if his thoughts were elsewhere.

Her brow furrowed. "Is everything okay?"

Wyatt closed his eyes, then nodded once.

Chapter Eleven

WHATEVER EXPRESSION FLITTED over Wyatt's face that morning, whatever had him deep in his thoughts when she got out of the car and he drove off, was enough for him to create space. Bella had yet to hear from him since Wednesday, no texts or calls or *anything* for four days. She knew it was ridiculous to think he was no longer interested—what was four days in the grand scheme of things?—but his silence left her wary. Was he backing off? Did she say something to make him change his mind? Did he no longer find her *noticeable*?

Percy came over on Saturday morning with bagels, and Bella was grateful for the distraction. She poured coffee from her French press as her friend unloaded the goods, snatching plates from cabinets like she, too, lived in this apartment.

"So you haven't heard from him?" Percy asked as they reconvened on the couch.

Bella shook her head. She opened up her pumpernickel with veggie cream cheese and took a bite of the top half. "Not since he dropped me home."

"Maybe he's busy during the days the restaurant is open. Working in a kitchen can be grueling."

She sighed. "Not even a text?"

"Is he the texting type?"

Bella took another bite of her bagel, thinking it through. When she first texted Wyatt last weekend, he had called her. The only time they texted was to set plans for their dinner, but nothing else.

"Maybe not," she replied.

Percy dipped the cream cheese on her bagel into the everything seasoning that'd fallen off the top. Bella had watched her do this ever since they first shared bagels together their freshman year. *Why waste all the good stuff? This way I get seasoning with every bite.* Bella knew right then she would be best friends with Percy Hamilton.

Percy launches into a story about a restaurant she had to review that week, but Bella half listened, her thoughts on Wyatt and if he actually wanted to see her again. Did she do something to offend him? Push him too far with the kissing thing? Did he no longer want to date her?

Maybe it's for the best. I was sort of lying to him.

"Bells?"

She looked up at her friend, who was now frowning at her. "Y-yeah?"

"Did you hear what I said?"

"I'm sorry," she rushed out as she crinkled her empty wrapper. "I got lost there for a minute."

Percy sighed, taking the wrapper from Bella's hands and crossing to the kitchen to throw out their garbage. "I know you've been through a lot, and I will always be your girl and be here for you. But I just told you my plans for proposing to Yaz and you weren't even paying attention." She crossed her arms and looked down at the floor.

Bella's heart twisted in her chest. "Oh god, P, I—"

"Part of me feels like I had to go the extra mile to take care of you, because it was *my* brother who fucked everything up."

She jumped off the couch and went for Percy, grabbing her friend's hands. "You're right. You're about to do this massive thing in your relationship and I haven't cared enough about it."

"I understand there's so much going on right now, with Wyatt, Matteo, your family, figuring out stuff with your health. But it's hard feeling like second place after so long, you know?"

"You will never be second place," Bella replied earnestly. "You are my number one, you always have been."

Her friend audibly sighed. "Promise?"

She pulled Percy to the couch. "Promise. Now tell me your plans and don't spare me a single detail."

Bella watched as Percy smiled a genuine, joyful smile, then launched into her proposal idea. She gave her friend her rapt attention, probing about the particulars. It would be three weekends from now, on a Saturday in Central Park, under the tree where they had their first picnic date. When Percy had finally mustered the courage to ask Yazmin Kashani out, she insisted on having a date *not* at a restaurant so she wouldn't be distracted. In those days, after landing her gig as a columnist at *Taster*, she couldn't even go to a midnight diner without scrutinizing the cutlery or lighting or playlist choice.

"Do you need any help with it?" Bella asked. "Need me to hide and take pictures? Take Yaz on a girlie date to get her nails done?"

Percy waved her off. "I have all of that handled. After I propose, I know she wants our families to meet for khastegāri, and then a celebration after with all of our friends. I even convinced the restaurant to let Yaz's mom bring tahchin. It's her favorite. I want you there."

We'll be there, Katie had told her in her office last week. *We're so excited for her.*

Bella smiled and nodded, hoping she looked pleased despite the queasiness she felt. It would be her first time seeing Lon and Katie together in person *as a couple*. She rolled her shoulders, remembering that this night wasn't about her but her best friend. She would push all of those feelings aside and focus on the more important task at hand: Percy's happiness.

Her phone rang on the coffee table. Bella ignored it as she took a sip of her coffee, her eyes not leaving Percy's.

"Are you not going to answer that?" Percy said, a wicked grin climbing at the corner of her lips.

She shook her head. "Nope. I'm with my best friend. Whoever is calling is second place compared to her."

"*Bells*," she teased, reaching for the phone. "You don't want to know if it's hot chef?"

"Nope, I couldn't care less."

"So you won't mind if I just..." And before Bella could snatch her phone away to stop her, Percy answered and held it out to Bella.

She fumbled, coffee spilling onto her lap as she cradled the phone to her ear. "H-hello?"

"Hi," said her new favorite voice.

She melted at the sound of it. "Hi."

"I'm sorry I haven't called," he started. "I'm busy in the afternoons and evenings, and by the time I go to bed or wake up, you're likely already asleep or at the office and I didn't want to distract you. The timing—"

"Never worked out," Bella finished for him. "That makes sense."

Wyatt was quiet for a moment. Bella looked up at Percy sipping on her coffee, that cocky grin still on her face. Bella stuck her tongue out at her.

"Are you mad?" he asked softly.

There was that apprehension again. "No, Wyatt, I'm not mad."

"Because this is usually when—" His sentence died. He was silent for a beat, then coughed.

Bella really wanted to dive into whatever he was about to say. *Usually when...what?*

"Never mind," he said. "Are you free tomorrow?"

"I am, except for dinner with my family."

"Matteo's family has this Sunday supper tradition. It's usually a dinner thing, but once a month, he has it around brunch time so I can go before heading to the restaurant, and he told me to invite you this weekend."

Despite the loose clothing she wore, her skin grew hot and tight, her tongue tied into silence. *He hosts a Sunday supper?* Having dinner on a Sunday was common for families, especially any family that grew up Italian, where sitting down for a big meal was a heralded tradition. But the fact that he referred to it exactly as her nonna did—"Sunday supper"—had her losing her marbles. The similarities were uncanny, and now, it was pretty clear. Did her grandfather bring that tradition to his new family? Did they have meatballs and sauce like her nonna's?

"Meet Matteo...and his family," she said.

Percy's eyes widened with a sharp inhale.

"If it's too much..." he started.

Bella watched as her friend silently nodded her head. *Do it,* she goaded.

If she was going to play with fire, she might as well go all in. The opportunity to attend Matteo's Sunday supper and see how much information she could grasp was too good to deny.

Even if that meant deceiving the man she was undeniably falling for.

"It's not too much," Bella blurted. "I would love to join you."

His sigh sounded relieved. "Good. I'll pick you up at eleven?"

"In the car?" she teased.

"Yes, *the car*. He lives in Astoria."

Of course he does. Astoria was where her grandfather moved after his divorce with Nonna.

"Okay," she responded. "See you at eleven."

It was drizzling the next morning when Wyatt picked her up, but she didn't mind. No matter the weather, Bella thought New York City would always be the most beautiful place on earth. She had her moments growing up when she felt otherwise, when she felt frustrated that her life wasn't *normal* like other girls—in a big house in the suburbs, at a public high school that wasn't cutthroat like the private institutions her peers competed to get into. But anytime she left the city, even for the occasional beach trips with Lon at his family's house in the Hamptons, it was only a few hours before she missed the screeching sounds of an incoming subway and sparkling skyscrapers. She knew this was her forever home.

When she got in the car, they both blushed as they

exchanged bashful hellos. Thoughts of his warm arms twined around her, his fingers combing through her hair as they fell asleep, bombarded her. He might not have *kissed her* kissed her yet, but something about being around Wyatt this way felt far more intimate. He wasn't intoxicating because of his looks or his touch. He intoxicated her because of how attentive he was, how he made her feel seen and heard.

They made their way north up the FDR, rain pattering the windshield as Norah Jones softly played through the speakers. She was wringing her hands in her lap, her nerves on the brink of explosion. She was about to step into Matteo's home, meet his family, maybe hear about her grandfather. She had to pretend like she didn't know the man, pretend like Matteo's father wasn't also a man that she loved and missed with all of her heart.

Wyatt gently poked her thigh. She looked down at it as he flipped his palm up, inviting her to take it. She did, lacing her fingers through his as she looked at him. A smile curled at the corner of his lips.

"How was the rest of your week?" he asked.

She sighed and leaned her head back. "It was okay. We sent this big content plan to a client. I'm hoping they approve so we can tackle it soon."

She'd stepped into her office on Wednesday morning, humming from the sugary pumpkin cinnamon roll she devoured and the feel of Wyatt's lips on her hand, to find Katie's plan printed and neatly placed in a file on her desk. She read through it as she sipped on her second cup, feeling annoyed at how much she wanted to hate Katie for every-thing that had happened but simply couldn't because the girl was still spectacular at her job. The plan was not only submitted ahead of schedule, it was *flawless*. There'd been nothing left to do but ping Katie and tell her to send it to the client for approval. The fact they hadn't heard a response yet had her on edge.

"How was yours?" she pressed, desperate to change the subject.

"One of our waitresses dropped three plates on Friday night. One every now and then happens—it's a restaurant, we're used to it. But three?" He shook his head. "I had to pull her into my office."

Bella sucked in a breath. "Did you fire her?"

His eyes widened. "Fire her? Jesus, no."

"Then what happened?"

"I told her to be honest with me. Turns out her father recently passed, but she didn't tell us because she needed the money from work to afford a flight home."

"Oh my god, is she okay?"

"I hope so. She's currently sitting on a flight heading to Omaha."

Bella felt like she was going to melt in her seat. "Did you...buy the flight for her?"

He nodded. "I told her that the restaurant deserves her best, and if she isn't able to give that, then she needs to come talk to me so we can work it out."

She shook her head, looking out the window and across the East River. "You're amazing."

"I don't know about *that*..."

Bella squeezed his hand. "You are. Having a boss like you means all the difference in the world."

"Most of my employees don't get paid time off. It was the least I could do."

"Most managers wouldn't even bother," she countered.

He squeezed her hand back. "Most managers wouldn't keep an employee who betrayed them, either."

She hummed, ready to squash this conversation like a bug. "Subject change?"

He grinned. "How'd the office like your upgraded wardrobe?"

"I think the hat goes nicely with stilettos."

They crossed the Queensboro bridge and continued their way north, through the streets of Long Island City and up to Astoria. The neighborhood was much quieter compared to Manhattan, or even some of the busier parts of Brooklyn. It reminded Bella of Red Hook and the quiet cobblestone street outside of Wyatt's apartment, the slice of serenity in a noisy, rambunctious city.

He pulled off the road and parked at the curb, outside of a beige brick-walled single-family home. Carved pumpkins lined the stoop, with an intricate fall wreath hanging on the arched door.

Wyatt kept his hand firmly in hers as they made their way up the stoop. He barely knocked before the door flew open. Two little girls squealed at their feet, their dark espresso-colored hair bouncing as they jumped up and down with delight.

"Uncle Wyatt!!"

He grinned and crouched down to hug them. Bella's chest constricted as she watched their little arms fling around his shoulders, their hands covered in colorful marker streaks. The youngest of the two burrowed her face in Wyatt's neck as the other stole his hat and placed it on her head.

When she noticed Wyatt wasn't alone, she looked up at Bella with wide bright-blue eyes, mouth agape. "Uncle Wyatt, did you bring your girlfriend?"

"Yeah, he did!" cheered a booming voice down the hall.

Bella watched as Matteo made his way from the kitchen

to the foyer. He scooped up his oldest daughter into his arms, then grinned as he faced Bella. "Nicola, this is Wyatt's friend Bella. Can you say hi?"

Nicola balled the fabric of her blue floral dress, a delicate lace Peter Pan collar adorning her neck. "Hi," she said sheepishly.

She smiled. "Hi, Nicola. I like your dress."

The girl grinned back, a gap in her front teeth. "Thanks. Momma made it for me."

"Did she? That's so cool!"

"We're a big crafting family," said a sweet voice with a slight southern drawl.

Bella recognized the petite woman from the photos of Matteo online. Her red hair was longer now, tied back in a braid with a white ribbon. She wore a lace white button-down, tucked into a loose pair of jeans. She pegged her as the kind of Mom that Bella wished she could be. Making dresses for her girls, coloring with big fat markers that got all over their hands.

Matteo kissed his wife's cheek. "Bella, this is Claire."

Claire looked at her, and if she wasn't mistaken, she noticed panic flash across her face. Bella chalked it up to maternal protectiveness around a stranger and gave Claire a genuine smile, hoping it would ease her worries.

Wyatt stood close, the littlest one still clinging to his leg. "This is Haley Jo," he said. Her dress was similar to Nicola's, but in a soft peach color with yellow daffodils.

"She's in love with our Wyatt," Claire joked. She no longer looked panicked, her smile warm.

Matteo's laugh boomed in the hallway. "All right, the fried chicken is almost ready."

Wyatt handed Claire the bottle of chilled Sancerre he brought in his cotton tote. "Need any help?"

They ambled toward the kitchen. Wyatt snatched his hat back from Nicola, making her shriek with laughter. Bella brought up the rear, right behind Claire. But before she stepped into the kitchen, a cold, slim hand grabbed her wrist.

"I'm going to give Bella a tour of the house while you gentlemen debate about the proper way to fry chicken," Claire called out.

She tugged on Bella's arm, forcing her down the hall and into what seemed to be their bedroom. She closed the door lightly, then turned to face her. That sweet, warm smile transformed into a cold, dagger-like stare.

"What in the hell do you think you're doing here?" Claire snapped.

Chapter Twelve

Every muscle in her body tightened with panic as she stared back at Claire, who looked like she was going to burn her alive. Her eyes in slits, her face stern.

Fake it, fake it, fake it.

"I-I don't know what you're talking about," Bella rushed out.

"Isabella Russo, right?"

Her stomach dropped to her feet.

"I know exactly who you are, so don't play dumb with me," Claire continued. "I want to know why you're here."

Bella felt heat rise from her neck up to her cheeks. She pressed her hand to her forehead and took a deep breath. "How do you know about me?"

"My question first. You're in my *home.*"

"Okay, okay," she said, swaying slightly. "I-I took this DNA test to find out my family medical history, and it led me to this family tree where I saw that my grandfather had another son."

Claire's eyes went wide with surprise. *Interesting.*

"How do you know about me?" Bella repeated.

"When your grandfather passed and his ex-wife didn't even bother to show up for the funeral, I was curious. I did some digging of my own."

Those words felt like a hammer to Bella's gut. "Wait... there was a funeral?"

"*Of course* there was a funeral. Did your grandmother really not tell you?"

"I-I..." Any attempt to respond died in her throat as she thought it through. When Nicholas Lombardi passed two years ago, Nonna told them that he requested for there to be nothing big, for there to be a day of celebration instead of mourning. They laid flowers at his freshly dug grave, then true to his requests, Nonna hosted a small gathering at Russo's and invited all of his closest friends in Little Italy. Bella was too wrapped up in her grief to think much of it. So was her mother.

Her silence must have been confirming enough. Claire sighed and shook her head. "Unbelievable."

Fury burned through her. Bella began to pace. "So you did your digging, then what? Tracked down Nonna?"

"She's not difficult to find," she said. "I stopped by Russo's. She pulled me aside and told me why there was never any contact. Why your mom and my husband don't know about one another."

"*Why?*" Bella pleaded, her heart pounding in her chest. *This is it.* She was finally going to get her answers.

But Claire shook her head, refusing to explain. "This is not my story to tell. Now, I would like to know why you are *here.*"

"Because I'm seeing Wyatt," she explained, her voice hesitant.

Claire crossed her arms. "Mighty convenient that you're seeing *Matteo's chef.*"

"I looked Matteo up. Then I visited his restaurant, and met Wyatt."

"Does Wyatt know?"

She looked down at her wet boots and shook her head.

Claire huffed. "Do you even like him?"

Hurt flashed over Bella's face as she looked up at Claire. "Yes. I'm not faking how I feel."

"Yet you're faking who you really are?" she inquired. "Matteo told me your last name is Hamilton."

"It was supposed to be my married last name. I never changed it."

Bella watched as Claire paced the floor. The bedroom was bigger than most, Queens was known for being the borough with more space, but it was still cramped enough for Bella to feel stifled.

She cleared her throat. "So Matteo doesn't know either?"

Claire's blue irises dimmed.

Bella heaved a sigh of relief. "I'm not the only one keeping secrets."

"I'm protecting my husband. You being here is *not* helping."

The fury was building to a breaking point, and Bella was more than ready to snap. "What was I supposed to do? It seems two of the most important people in my life have lied to me, kept big secrets from me, and I'm...what? Not supposed to be curious? Not supposed to look for answers?"

"Yes," Claire rushed out. "After tonight, leave him alone. Leave Wyatt alone."

All of the fight drained from her. *Leave Wyatt alone?* "You want me to stop seeing him?"

"You've been lying to him. Do you really think that's a

good start to a relationship? I already know Wyatt deserves better."

Bella covered her mouth to muffle her cry. *Lon deserved better. Wyatt deserves better.* Maybe Claire was right. Wyatt was good and kind, and she was...well, all she had to do was look into Claire's eyes for her answer.

The woman before her squared her shoulders. "We will go in there and have lunch and be civil. Then Wyatt will take you home, and you will never come here or see either of them again. Do you understand?"

No. She couldn't understand. She couldn't make sense of *any* of this.

But she silently nodded, because what else was she supposed to do? She was the one intruding, walking into Matteo's house in an attempt to pry for answers. Now she had them, and it didn't make her feel any better. Instead, knowing more left her feeling hollow with hurt.

"It's funny," Claire said, the tone of her voice somber. "I'm surprised Matteo didn't notice."

Bella wiped at a tear that trickled down her cheek. "Notice what?"

She was surprised to see a smile on Claire's face. Her heart hurt, wondering if in another life they could have been friends. If she could have been the cool older cousin to those beautiful little ones in their floral dresses, covered in marker.

"Notice how much you look like my girls," she breathed. "They're your spitting image."

Bella shuffled behind Claire as they made their way back to the kitchen.

Wyatt leaned against the counter, beer bottle in hand as he laughed at whatever story Matteo was telling him. The sound of that laugh she'd come to crave made her want to weep.

You lied to him, she reminded herself. *He deserves better than you.*

He pulled on his beer as he found her across the kitchen. His brow furrowed at whatever expression must have been clear on her face. So she schooled her features and gave him a reassuring smile, then asked if they needed her to do anything.

"Not a thing, darling," Matteo said as he dipped a spider strainer in a pot. "Except to pour yourself a drink."

Before she could ask, Claire stepped beside her with a pleasant smile—all of that animosity erased from her features. She handed Bella a glass of white wine, then held up her own. Her brow raised in a challenge, as if they were sealing their secret agreement.

Bella looked over at Wyatt, holding a lined sheet pan as Matteo transferred thick strips of breaded fried chicken from the pot.

She turned back to Claire, then nodded as she clinked her glass.

I'll do as you say, the gesture said. *I'll leave them alone.*

But she still had a whole lunch ahead of her, and if she was forced to never see them again, she was going to squeeze every detail out of Matteo that she could.

They all made their way to the table, the girls already at their seats, digging into bowls of homemade macaroni and cheese. Bella took in the food, noting the traditional Southern dishes: fried chicken, collard greens, mac and cheese, fluffy biscuits ready to flake apart with greedy hands.

"Matteo's spoiling me tonight," Claire drawled from across the table. "These are all of my childhood faves."

Here we go. Bella grinned at Claire. "That's so sweet." She turned to Matteo as he passed plates of fried chicken to everyone. "What are your childhood favorites, Matteo?"

Claire frowned.

Matteo didn't notice as he passed Bella a plate. "My mom was a classic casserole kind of woman, but my father's Italian roots ran deep. Veal parmesan, carbonara, meatballs—"

She felt her throat close up.

"—I miss his cooking the most," he finished.

Bella couldn't remember one moment where she experienced her grandfather's cooking. Their days together were always out, exploring corners of Little Italy. She'd asked him plenty of times if she could visit him in Astoria when she was in college, but he told her it would be "way more fun" to meet up in the city. She didn't think much of it at the time. But now?

"Did you lose both of them?" Bella asked softly.

He nodded. "Within a year of each other. It was pretty unbearable. But thankfully I had family to step in and take care of me."

She watched as Matteo reached a hand around and gripped Wyatt's shoulder with a firm hand. Wyatt gave him a nod back, something unspoken and intimate settling between them.

They really are as close as brothers. Bella wiped her sweaty hands on her jeans underneath the table. This web was intricate and complicated, and she berated herself for thinking she could bulldoze right through it.

"How'd you like growing up in the city?" Matteo asked her. "You were in Manhattan your whole life?"

Bella confirmed, giving vague details about her upbringing. She explained that her father was a professor and her mother helped her grandmother during the day, evading any explanation on what her mother helped her out *with*. She cleverly turned the conversation back on him and asked about his restaurants, which carried them through the rest of the afternoon. Matteo beamed when he spoke about his work and his restaurants, how he loved creating spaces in the city that made customers feel safe and valued. A respite from the chaotic concrete jungle.

"Your father must have been proud," she said, the words slipping out of her like water.

"He was," Matteo said with wistful longing. "And I believe he still is."

She glanced at the woman sitting across the table. Claire took a sip of her wine, eyes not leaving Bella, the expression on her face saying it all. *I don't trust you.*

A familiar poke on her thigh brought her back to her senses. Bella looked down to her lap and found Wyatt's hand there, palm up. A secret offering under the table.

She cupped his hand and squeezed. Then, a beat later, she let go.

THEY REMAINED silent on the drive back to Manhattan. Bella noticed the curve of a smile on Wyatt's lips. He looked content. *Happy.* Like a man who took his new girlfriend to meet his family.

That was the word Nicola used. *Girlfriend.* Was that

what Wyatt called her? Was that what he meant by them "dating"?

Bella shimmied down into her seat cushion and closed her eyes. She knew from the start that getting involved with Wyatt would be messy. Yet now that she had her answers, stepping away from him felt utterly impossible. In less than two weeks, the chef had somehow carved into the hollows of her heart and her pain and taken a seat, like he was always meant to be there.

Wyatt pulled the car up to her apartment building and parked. She zipped off her seat belt and gave him a casual smile, trying her best to keep things light, even though she knew this was the last time she'd see him. "Thanks for inviting me."

"Thanks for coming," he said. Lines creased his forehead in worry. "Bella, what's wrong?"

"Nothing's wrong!" she said, her voice artificially cheery. "Just falling into a food coma. Probably need to take a nap before I'm off to see my family."

Before she could lose her nerve, Bella opened the car door and stepped out. She told him to have a good night at the restaurant, then closed the door with a wave and scurried up the stoop.

She heard a car door open and close behind her. Bella thrust her key into the door and made to step inside, but a hand grabbed her wrist and pulled her back out. Wyatt positioned her right in front of him, his mouth inches from hers. She noticed the faintest freckle at the top left corner of his lip as he licked them, like he wanted to taste her.

Against her better judgment, she waited. Waited for him to close the gap and take a bite. Waited to see what those feelings would turn into under a flame.

But he never budged. His throat bobbed as he examined her lips.

Maybe it was never meant to be.

"Good night, chef," she whispered, then escaped into her building.

Twenty minutes later, when she watched his name pop up on her screen with an incoming call, she ignored the call and typed out a text instead.

BELLA

I don't think either of us is ready to be dating. I'm sorry.

HE TRIED CALLING her a second time. Then again, another hour after that. By five o'clock, she knew the restaurant would be open and he wouldn't keep calling, yet she still turned off her phone as she walked to Russo's. The frigid air cut deep after the day's rainfall, her light trench coat no longer warm enough for cold autumn nights. She shivered, quickening her pace in an effort to warm up. It was the classic New Yorker trick: walk fast to get warm, or have another drink. Bella had a feeling she would need a few of those to get through dinner tonight, especially if she had to look Nonna square in the face for an entire meal and not scream profanities at her.

None of it made sense. What could have gone so wrong for her grandparents to live such separate lives? And why did they not trust their families to know?

Bella unlocked the door and trudged up the stairs. She beat her parents again, but she fully expected to, given she was thirty minutes early.

Nonna hovered over her pot, humming a tune. Bella shrugged off her coat, then went through the usual motions. She said hello, kissed Nonna's cheek, and got to work on the bread, completely avoiding any eye contact with her grandmother.

She didn't seem to notice as she continued her stir. "How was your week, *piccola mia?*"

"Fine," she muttered.

"Hmmm," she mused. "And the chef? How are things with him?"

Bella minced garlic for the bread, her stomach twisting thinking of Wyatt standing so close yet still so far. "I'm not sure if he's into me."

"*Impossibile.* Who wouldn't be into you?"

"Do you really want me to answer that question?"

Nonna's sigh said everything. She knew what the answer was, the one that walked out fourteen months ago.

Bella *really* didn't want to talk about Wyatt, let alone think about him. Instead, she wrapped the bread in aluminum and asked, "Why didn't we have a real funeral for Nonno?"

Nonna's shoulders tensed in her periphery.

She pummeled forward. "I've been thinking...a lot about him lately. Did he really have no other friends or family to celebrate him? Were his circles only in Little Italy?"

Bella listened to the guttural sigh that came from her grandmother's throat. "Your grandfather was a private man. He liked to keep parts of his life separate from others."

"Did he ever meet someone else?"

At this, she whipped her head around. Shadows cast across her brown eyes. "*Mi scusi?*"

"Was he single his whole life? Did he ever meet someone new?"

She watched in horror as her stern look wavered. Nonna's lip quivered at her question, her eyes softening into something fragile and sorrowful.

I've seen that look before. It was the same one she saw in the mirror every day.

Bella let her intuition take over as she dropped the bread and stepped around the table. She took her grandmother's hands and squeezed. "Nonna?"

"Your mother doesn't know," she whispered. "I-I didn't have the heart to tell her."

"That he cheated on you," Bella whispered back.

She watched in horror as a tear slid down her grandmother's cheek. She rarely ever saw her grandmother cry from sorrow, only ever tears of joy. Nonna Russo was notorious for being cheerful, facing her customers with a bright smile on her face—no matter how rude or entitled they may act toward her. Seeing her grandmother like this had her in a tailspin.

"What happened?" Bella asked. "Why—"

"Guess who brought cannoli tonight!"

Mom breezed into the apartment with a large white bag from Cannoli King, Dad not far behind.

Bella dropped her hands fast, but her nonna was faster. That sad expression vanished, replaced with a new one full of glee, like nothing had happened. She wondered how long her grandmother had been wearing that mask. She wondered if it was a mask that she, too, would have to wear for the rest of her life.

Chapter Thirteen

BELLA HAD IGNORED ALL of his calls for a week. Wyatt was insistent at first, until multiple calls turned into one a day before they petered off. The following weekend, she hadn't heard a thing, and she assumed he'd finally given up on her. She hated haunting him in this way, but Claire's words and the slit of her eyes hardened her resolve. *Wyatt deserves better.*

So, she swallowed the pain and did her best to push off how it felt to be held in his arms, the light brush of his fingers against hers, the gentle way he combed her hair, the heat that radiated from his chest when he stood close enough to graze her lips.

Bella attempted to have another conversation with her grandmother, making stops at Russo's throughout the week, but it was impossible to get her for an uninterrupted moment. The lines at the deli never relented, and it didn't help that her mother was constantly around. Bella had even arrived early to Sunday supper the following week, but as luck would have it, her parents were already there.

Now it was Tuesday, and despite the madness at work—they'd gotten approval on Dreamscape's content plan and had set dates the following week to access their properties—her mind kept wandering to how the chef was spending his day off.

Until his text came through that afternoon. She picked up the phone, desperately wishing she could text him about how much she *wanted* to see him, wishing she could tell him the truth...but now there was so much more on the line. Claire didn't want Matteo knowing anything, and if she told Wyatt, there was no doubt everything would soon end up in Matteo's hands. The two of them were close, and Bella knew she was no longer only playing with fire. She was overseeing a boiling pot, and if she wasn't careful, it would bubble over.

She watched as the gray bubbles danced again.

WYATT

I'm sorry. I overstepped when you said you weren't ready.

Fury fumed in her chest. *Overstepped?* He barely had the courage to kiss her.

She began crafting a text back, grasping for the right words. But an incoming call interrupted her typing.

She sighed, then answered. "Hey."

"Bella," he breathed. "I saw you were typing and—"

"Look, you didn't overstep, okay? You didn't do anything wrong. In fact, you didn't do *anything*."

A beat of silence. "I know."

"I don't get you," she started, knowing full well she was going to regret this conversation. But did it even matter if she wasn't going to see him again? "You're all worried about moving too fast for me, yet *you* were the one who made it clear that you need to take things slow."

Another beat of silence. Another "I know."

"You're right. You are really confusing, and I'm not sure if I can—"

"Please come over tonight."

Her attempts at cutting things off with him shrieked to a halt.

"Come over," he repeated. "I'll make dinner. We'll talk about this."

"Is there even anything to talk about?"

"Yes." It was one word, but it sounded like a confession. Her heart broke at the sound of it, and in a flash, she craved to be with him. Craved to hold him like he held her. To hear what was on his mind. Two trains and a bus suddenly felt too far.

"What time are you off of work?" he asked.

She settled her cheek against her desk, the cool wood soothing her flushed cheeks. "Six."

"Send me the address," he stated matter-of-factly. "I'll order you an Uber and have it bring you here."

Claire's face flashed before her eyes. *Say no, say no, say no*, she chanted to herself. But her heart had other plans, and when she agreed, she felt the little beating thing take flight and soar.

THE UBER DRIVER who picked her up was kind, but to Bella's dismay, he wouldn't shut up. She wanted to sit there in silence and think through her words, what exactly she should say to Wyatt so she could let him down easy. Going to his place for dinner was clearly a bad idea, but she wondered whether breaking things off face-to-face would make for a cleaner break.

If only the driver would stop with his useless facts about the construction of the Battery tunnel so she could *think*. Yet as they climbed their way up into Brooklyn and took the exit to Red Hook, it seemed her attempt at carefully crafting a speech was not going to happen. She would have to wing it.

Her phone dinged.

WYATT

Door is unlocked, come right in.

She sighed, the sweatshirt and joggers and hat that were still at her apartment flashing in her mind. She wished she had them on her so she could give them back. Was he the kind of guy who even cared about getting clothes back from a girl?

The driver pulled up in front of Wyatt's gray brick building with a smile and a "Thanks for the conversation." Bella shot him a wry smile and stepped out, her work tote tucked under her arm. She took a deep breath of the salty air, already dreading how much she was going to miss it. The quiet streets, the birdsong, the lapping East River, the way the sun glowed as it set along the skyline.

Bella rolled her shoulders, then opened the door. The smell of something rich and rustic permeated the space. She stood for a moment at the bottom of the steps, listening to the opening and closing of the oven, the sounds of pots moving and oil sizzling on a skillet. She kicked off her heels and tiptoed her way up the stairs.

Wyatt's back was to her, tongs in hand as he flipped the chicken thighs searing in front of him. His hair was tucked neatly inside his backward hat, his tongue poking out from his mouth in concentration.

Bella couldn't help the smile that danced across her lips. She silently dropped her bag to the floor and leaned against the wall, watching Wyatt cook. She'd seen him work at his restaurant, but he was rarely the one behind the pots and pans, rather the one standing in the center of the chaos, driving his staff forward as they handled order after order. She let herself imagine for a moment what it would be like to be with Wyatt, coming home to this sight after work, to a kitchen that smelled like heaven.

He nestled the chicken into a skillet of bubbling sauce, then slid the pan into the oven. He wiped his hands on the towel that was draped across his shoulder, then finally turned. His eyes widened at the sight of her. His lip twitched, almost like he wanted to smile. But she watched him harden his features as he leaned his hands against the counter.

"You made it," he said.

Bella nodded. "I made it."

They stared at one another, neither moving to close the distance.

She tore her gaze from his and noticed a leafy green salad in a bowl before him. Next to the bowl were jars of sauces, bottles of oils, vinegars, and various seasonings.

Bella cocked her head. "Waiting for me to make the dressing, chef?"

Wyatt finally pushed off from the counter and made his way to her. "I did say you could."

Her heart raced. He reached for her trench coat that she had tucked in her arm, then pointed to his kitchen. "Mixing bowls are in that far cabinet, and I have smaller whisks in the drawer below it."

"And the poison?" she teased, tying her hair up into a ponytail.

"Used the rest of it for the chicken."

"Excellent."

Bella washed her hands at the sink, then reached into the cabinet for a bowl. Wyatt worked around her, slicing green onions. They danced around one another but he never reached out to touch her, like they were back at square one. It stung, but her head reminded her that this was what she wanted. It would make things easier once they talked. *Eat the chicken, tell him it's over, then leave.*

She eyed the selection of ingredients in front of her and settled on making a honey dijon vinaigrette. She added a dollop of dijon and a drizzle of honey from his fancy jars, both from local Brooklyn businesses. She poured olive oil slowly as she whisked the mixture and then tossed it into the greens. By the time she was finished, Wyatt had opened a bottle of Pinot Noir and was pouring two glasses. He handed her one at the same time she slid the salad bowl in his direction.

"Taste," she demanded.

He grabbed a fork and did as he was told. He tilted his head as he chewed, then went for the basket of citrus on his counter and grabbed a lemon. He sliced it open, squeezing some of the juice on top of her salad and tossing it, then slid the bowl back to her.

"Taste," he demanded back.

Instead of reaching for a new fork, he handed her the one he had used. A flush warmed her cheeks as she grabbed it and took a bite. The light squeeze of lemon made it exponentially better.

She rolled her eyes.

He smiled, then reached for a thin maroon box that was on the counter next to his bowl of citrus. He slid it toward her. "I got you something."

Her brow furrowed, but she was too curious to fight him. She flipped open the box. Six perfect squares of chocolate were nestled inside, each with a swirling yellow design at the top.

"Isn't dessert supposed to come *after* dinner?"

He gave her that cocky smirk. "Not when you're the chef."

She rolled her eyes again, then popped a chocolate into her mouth. Sweet honeysuckle and bitter dark chocolate burst on her taste buds. Her eyes widened as she chewed, and Wyatt grinned down at her.

"Good, I take it?"

She swallowed, already grabbing for another. "Better than good. Where'd you get these?"

"One of Benji's employees is in the process of starting a made-to-order confectionary business," he explained. "He gave me this box earlier today and said, 'If this doesn't convince her to stay, then you're screwed, man.'"

She slowed her chewing, letting the taste of the sweet honeysuckle prevent her from confessing the bitter truth. *You don't have to convince me to stay. I very much would like to.* Instead, she let the silence linger as she closed the box, forcing herself not to devour a third.

Wyatt held out a hand toward his patio. She nodded and followed him as he slid open the glass door. The air was chilly, but she didn't mind, letting the frigid air recalibrate her. She searched for the right words, but as Wyatt leaned on the metal railing and glanced back at her with an inviting smile, every sentence evaporated. She joined him, restraining herself from closing the gap and letting his radiating heat warm her up from the cold. She white-knuckled the railing and turned, facing the twinkling cityscape across the East River.

Bella cleared her throat, ready to get this part over with. "You wanted to tell me something?"

She heard him sigh. "Yes."

Wyatt poked her side, right below her rib cage. She turned to face him, his hands back to where they were before, laced in front of him, his elbows casually propped up on the railing.

"I'm sorry I've been confusing, Bella," he admitted. "Truth be told, I'm not very good at this."

"This?"

He pointed between the two of them. "This. Dating. I've been told by women that I'm...difficult to date."

She considered him. "And why's that?"

"Being a chef means late nights and excruciating work-weeks. I wasn't the best at maintaining a relationship when I was at Hyacinth. My only focus was getting that damn star and I..." He heaved a sigh. "I neglected my relationships and let them fade."

"What about now? You're not at Hyacinth anymore."

"I haven't dated anyone since I started at Tri. I only recently began to feel like I've got my head above water, finally in a routine that's manageable. Starting a new restaurant also comes with its complications...and long hours."

Bella nodded, thinking this through. "So you're afraid I'll become resentful about your job?"

"It's more than that."

"Okay..."

"I've also been told that I'm not good at...certain things."

She scrunched her brows. "Certain...things?"

"*Physical* things."

Her mouth hung open, but no sound came from her lips.

He nodded.

Bella scanned the anguish on his face, the raw honesty there. "Why am I struggling to believe that?"

"I think you should," he replied softly. "I feel like I've been leading you on, right down this path where you might not like what you see."

Whatever remained of her fraying restraint snapped. She took a step and placed a hand on his cheek. Instinctively, Wyatt curled his fingers around her hip and pulled her even closer.

"I like what I see," she admitted.

"You say that now," he said quietly. "But what if you don't feel that way in a few weeks? Months?"

She chewed on that for a moment. Wyatt rested his face in her hand, his cheek warm against her cold palm.

This is the moment. It was the perfect setup, the perfect way to back out and tell him that maybe he was right. But her traitorous heart had a mind of its own as different words spilled from her lips.

"What if you don't like what *you* see?" she whispered.

"Not possible."

Bella thought about Claire and Matteo. Nonna and Russo's. Lon and her divorce. *Why* she got divorced. "You barely know me..."

"I know," he breathed. "And I think that's what scares

me the most. I'm still getting to know you, but what I do know, I already really, *really* like, and I want..."

His eyelids drooped, those green eyes staring at her lips.

"I want..." he whispered.

She hitched a breath. "Wyatt..."

He lunged and swallowed the rest of her words with his mouth.

Chapter Fourteen

WYATT TIGHTENED his grip on her waist, his other hand tangled up in her hair. She felt her knees go weak, but he kept a steady hold as his soft lips explored hers, tipping her head back so he could savor her with every roll of his lips, every stroke of his tongue. Bella gripped his sweatshirt, desperate to anchor herself when her entire body felt like it was floating on air.

Wyatt broke away with three soft kisses. "You taste sweet," he muttered.

"You fed me chocolate."

"No…" He pressed his lips to hers again, like he was deciphering the flavor. "You taste like something bright and playful."

Wyatt spun her around and walked her backward, then pinned her against the brick wall, pressing his body flush against hers.

"Strawberries," he decided.

He crashed his mouth to hers again. Bella slid her hands around his neck and combed them through his hair, letting his hat fall to the floor, his soft auburn waves like silk between her fingers. He moved a hand to her neck as he pulled away and nibbled on her bottom lip.

"Wow," she groaned.

He grinned. "And what does 'wow' mean in this context?"

Before she could respond, Wyatt ran his tongue down her jawline and neck. She tilted her head to give him access.

She swallowed. "It means…wow, I'm sorry to report that whoever told you that you were not good at this was very…"

A moan tumbled from her lips as he sucked on the soft flesh above her collarbone. His grip tightened, and she felt his chest vibrate with his own satisfied rumble.

"…very wrong," she finished, breathless.

He chuckled, tilting her head as he left a trail of kisses up the other side of her neck, nibbling on her ear.

Her eyes shuttered. "Careful, chef. You keep kissing me like that, you might have to carry me to your bedroom."

It was not the right thing to say. Wyatt froze, her earlobe still between his teeth. She could feel his body clench, then ever so subtly, he kissed his way up from the base of her throat. He ended with a long, lingering kiss on her lips, then pressed his forehead against hers as he cradled her close.

She flushed. "Too much?"

"No, that was…you are…" He sighed, and Bella wished he would say what was on his mind. Instead, he kissed her cheek. "I still want to take it slow."

She pouted. "Can taking it slow include kissing like that? Because if that's your definition, I'm in."

He laughed, a deep one from his belly. Bella grinned in response.

The timer chimed in the kitchen.

Wyatt dipped down to kiss her again with unhurried lips. He eased her off the wall and, like a dance, moved her through the open glass doors and into the amber lights of the kitchen. His lips remained on hers the entire time, teasing her with his tongue and the tips of his teeth. She liked this playful side of him.

When they reached the counter, he pulled away and slid her glass of wine over. She leaned against the cool marble as she sipped on the Pinot, watching Wyatt remove the skillet of chicken thighs in a thick, dark, bubbling sauce. He plated their meal, garnishing the chicken with the same precision she'd seen from a distance at Tri. A small crease lined his forehead as he worked, then with a satisfied hum, he lifted their plates and brought them to the table, stealing a kiss of her lips as he breezed past.

Bella took hold of their wineglasses and followed, seating herself across from him at his gorgeous acacia wood table.

He frowned.

"Aw, why so sad?" she teased.

"You're too far."

"I'm literally sitting *right here.*"

He bumped the chair next to him with his foot, then cocked his head.

Bella rolled her eyes as she stood up, then made her way to her new seat. Once the wineglasses were safely on the table, Wyatt hooked his foot around a leg of her new chair and dragged it toward him, his knee grazing hers as he took a sip of his wine. His smile curled into the dimple on his right cheek.

She giggled and shook her head. "You're a bossy little thing, aren't you?"

He lifted a single shoulder and said, "I spent an entire week away from you," like it was all the justification he needed.

"Again, someone is *obsessed*." She poked his nose.

He caught her hand before she could pull it away, then gently tugged on her arm and drew her closer to him. He cupped her face and kissed her again. She could taste the red wine on his tongue.

"Food's going to get cold," she mumbled against his mouth.

"Mmm." He brushed the pad of his thumb across her lips. "So?"

"So a hot chef made me dinner and I would like to eat it." She leaned back and grabbed her fork. "You can kiss me as much as you want when we're finished."

"Promise?"

"Yes, chef."

They ate in silence, stealing glances at one another in between bites. Wyatt's thigh pressed against hers, his confident smile making her stomach do summersaults. There was something about him that'd changed since their conversation. He was the same man, soft and attentive, but now it felt like everything was saturated. Like all of his colors came to life after he let her in on parts of him that she suspected not many people knew.

How could other women possibly think this man is not worth it? She sipped on her wine, watching as he pushed up the sleeves of his sweatshirt, his forearms flexing as he cut into his chicken. Her mind drifted, wondering what those forearms would look like when those careful chef's hands explored *her*.

Wyatt reached for her empty plate and told her to get comfortable on the couch.

She snatched it away from him. "Fat chance. You helped me clean, it's only fair."

He winked. "Oh, I wasn't planning on cleaning yet."

Bella rolled her eyes and stood up. "Work now, play later."

She listened to the rumble of his laugh as she walked to his kitchen and placed her dishes in the sink. She snatched a clean towel and dried as he washed. They only successfully finished a third of the dishes before Wyatt was curling sudsy hands around her neck and pressing urgent lips to hers.

"You promised," he whispered, leading her over to his couch. He sat down and pulled her onto his lap, his lips bruising and hungry as he kissed her fervently.

Bella let herself get lost in him, the feel of his hands on her back, how his hair slipped through her fingers.

Wyatt deserves better.

She pulled away and brought trembling fingers to her lips, staring down into his green eyes, darker now with a need to consume her.

"Everything okay?" he whispered.

She draped her arms over his shoulders and took a deep breath, tucking her chin. Bella knew she shouldn't let this continue, that there was so much more at stake here than her feelings for the man in front of her. Claire wanted to keep this secret in the dark, hidden from her husband, and she had to respect that. She thought of her nonna's tears at dinner, and her grandfather that she thought she knew so well but really didn't know at all.

But they were all *their* secrets. Her chest burned with that single truth—that she, too, was a victim to these lies. Why should she be the one to deny such happiness for the sake of keeping secrets?

Bella dipped her head and kissed Wyatt's lips once, then twice. *Screw the consequences.* She was done holding back. She wanted *him.* For as long as she could have him.

"Yes," she said. "Everything is perfect."

He squeezed his arms around her. "Do you want to stay the night again?"

She sighed. "I wish, but I have an early morning. I have to be on-site for a client."

"Want a ride home?"

She nodded her head in the spirit of taking what she wanted.

He kissed her again. "Saturday," he whispered, his lips grazing her mouth.

"Saturday?"

"We're hanging out Saturday. Before I have to be at the restaurant."

"Bossy little thing."

He smirked as he tucked a piece of her hair behind her ear. "Like you said, I'm obsessed, *mia bella*."

Bella stepped into Dante on Friday night with a smile on her face. She'd smiled so much that week, she wondered if it would remain there permanently. Wyatt called her every night around ten when she got in bed, taking a quick break at the restaurant to wish her good night. The first night he did it, the night after he kissed her, she teased him for not simply sending her a text.

"That's not exactly my style," he told her.

"What are you, an old man?"

"I'm a man who would much prefer to hear his girl's voice."

Hearing him say *his girl* had her burying her face in her pillows and smiling like a cat. His calls were brief during those breaks—one or two minutes, tops—but Bella decided she liked to end her night that way; with Wyatt's voice in her ear. *Sleep well, mia bella.*

The happy hour crowd was rowdy inside the bar. Laughter and clinking glasses chimed, small plates passed across tables, and limbs seemed loose as pop songs played through the speakers.

"Bells! Over here!"

Percy and Yaz were huddled up near the bar. Yaz sat on a bar stool wearing a stunning floor-length dress, the candlelight beside her making her light brown skin glow. Percy massaged Yaz's neck, a Negroni in her other hand as she called for Bella.

She beamed as she made her way to them, planting a kiss on Yaz's cheek before stealing Percy's drink and taking a big gulp.

"Monster," Percy quipped.

"You love me," she baited. "Yaz, I think orange is your color, babe. You look incredible."

"I don't think it has anything to do with the dress, but everything to do with the fact that Percy sent me to *a Korean spa* today."

Percy looked at Bella with raised eyebrows before snatching her drink back and finishing it off.

Bella scoffed. "No spa for me? What am I, chopped liver?"

"Eh, you're more of a bodega chopped cheese. Yaz, on the other hand, is a fine steak dinner."

"With french fries and herbed butter," Yaz added. She stood up and planted a peck on Percy's cheek. "Need to use the bathroom, I'll be right back."

The two of them watched Yaz leave until she was a far enough distance not to hear them.

Bella whipped her head toward Percy. "A Korean spa, P? She's got to know it's coming."

Percy shrugged. "I wanted to pamper her."

"Did she also get her nails done?"

"Duh? It was this all-inclusive thing. I played it off as an early birthday present. That way I don't have to worry about her nails in a week."

Bella whistled. "A week, wow. Are you nervous?"

"Very. But also...not? I don't know. I'm nervous about the day being perfect, but not at all nervous about asking her to be my wife. That part feels the most solid compared to everything else."

She sighed. "I love seeing you in love, P."

"I love seeing *you* in love, Bells."

Bella pointed at her friend in warning. "Stop that. Not in love."

"You sure about that? Because that grin you had on your face when you stepped into the bar—"

"Can I get you anything?" the bartender interrupted.

"Negroni, and a shot of cynicism," Bella answered.

"Make that two," Percy chimed in.

The bartender shook his head as he walked off.

"Want to tell me why you have that shit-eating grin on your face?" Percy asked.

"We probably have, like, thirty seconds before she comes back. Engagement details first."

Her friend grinned. "Everything is in place. The only thing is, I was hoping to get a cake or something. The bar we're going to said we could bring one in. Think you could—"

"Yes, I'll grab something. Which bar?"

"Gran Via."

Bella's face fell. Their drinks were placed in front of

them at that exact moment. She picked hers up and took a big gulp.

"I'm sorry," Percy said earnestly. "Lon's *always* there and he's friendly with the owner now. He was able to get this sick party discount for me."

Bella waved her off. "I get it."

"You're not mad?"

That I'd be back at the bar that I used to go to all the time? With my ex-husband and his new fiancée? "Nope. Not at all."

"I don't believe you..."

Bella sighed and decided to offer her friend a sliver of vulnerability. "P, we knew this was going to happen. It's going to take time before I'm completely okay with it, but this is *your moment.* We can put aside all of our drama and be happy for you."

"Have you talked to him at all?"

She took another sip of her drink. "Nothing since we signed the papers."

Percy exhaled. "You could bring hot chef, if you wanted."

"Hot chef? Bring him where?"

They jumped at Yaz's surprise reappearance. Percy shuffled to make room for Yaz, pinning Bella with a raised brow. *Answer her?*

"Oh, um, this guy I'm kind of seeing. Trying to decide if I should take him to this work thing."

Yaz's mouth fell open. "You're *seeing someone?*"

"Y-yeah, kind of."

"Kind of? How can you *kind of* see someone?"

Because he doesn't really know me. Even though he said they were dating, Bella couldn't seem to rid herself of the guilt that chewed away at her stomach.

Yaz didn't wait for a response and flicked Percy's arm. "How come you didn't tell me?"

"Because there isn't much to tell if she's *kind of* seeing someone," Percy taunted.

Bella gave her the finger.

Percy grinned, sliding an arm around Yaz's waist. "Perfect timing, though. I'm due for an update, and it's time you stopped being secretive and told Yaz as well."

Yaz glared. "Babe, *you* were the one—"

"He kissed me."

Percy's mouth fell open. Yaz simply furrowed her brow. "Just a kiss? That's it?"

Bella shifted on her stool. "Well, um, yeah. He wants to take things slow. I thought it was out of respect for me and the divorce, but turns out there's all kinds of stuff he's working through, too."

"What's he working through?" Yaz inquired.

"*That's* what you want to know?" Percy guffawed. "I want to know every dirty detail about the kiss."

Bella gave them a shy smile. "The kiss was good."

Percy cocked a brow.

"Okay, it was better than good. Great, in fact. The World Series of kissing."

"Oh my god, I knew it. Hot chef with a hot tongue."

Bella flushed. "He said I taste like strawberries."

Now Yaz was the one with her mouth open.

"I have never been more turned on by fruit. Or someone with an XY chromosome," Percy joked.

"I'm confused," Yaz interjected. "He says you taste like strawberries but doesn't take off your clothes?"

Bella shrugged. "Like I said, we're figuring things out."

"Did you tell him who you are yet?" Percy asked.

Yaz's face scrunched in confusion. "What does that mean?"

Percy hesitated, looking at Bella for confirmation.

She rubbed her neck, then nodded.

"Babe, so, there's another layer to this we need to tell you."

Percy filled her in on Bella's discovery about her grandfather, his secret family, and the uncle she'd never met. About visiting the restaurant, and how Bella started hanging out with Wyatt in an attempt to get answers.

"So he doesn't know the full truth," Yaz concluded.

Percy nodded.

"Yet you're still seeing him," Yaz added, now looking at Bella.

Bella nodded this time.

Yaz exhaled audibly. "That's really sticky, guys."

"It *is* sticky," Percy repeated, pointing a finger at Bella. "Tell him the truth."

Bella nearly slid off the pleather barstool. "I-I know. I want to. But then I met Matteo's wife, and she knew who I was. She doesn't want her husband knowing *anything,* and he's so close to Wyatt…"

"Here's what I think," Percy interrupted. "I think this feels like a lot of *other* people's problems and not your own. I think you just need to tell him."

Bella's shoulders relaxed at her best friend's insane ability to read her thoughts. Except for the whole *tell him the truth* part. "What if it's a deal-breaker?"

"Well, you can't lie forever, Bells. At some point he will learn your real last name, like when you take him to Sunday supper to meet your family."

She imagined what it would be like to bring Wyatt to Nonna's apartment. Having him join in on their traditions.

What job would the Russos assign him? He has a thing for whisking together dressings. Or maybe he would add something new to the table, something their Sunday supper was missing that they never considered before.

"I...I really want that," she breathed.

Percy set down her drink and reached for her, squeezing both of her hands. She looked at her friend, eyes misting.

"Don't you think it's time?" Percy asked.

"Time for what?"

"Time to allow yourself to be happy?"

The moisture behind her lids gathered steadily. *Allow myself to be happy?*

Her mind drifted to Tuesday night, when she finally let herself truly *want* something after her wants had disappointed her for years. Let herself enjoy Wyatt's arms and lips and the bossy way he took care of her. "Allow yourself to be happy" insinuated that she hadn't been allowing it before, and if she was being completely honest with herself, Bella knew it was true. She punished herself for her marriage failing. For her body failing her, too. Telling him the truth, *choosing happiness*, meant finally letting all of that go. Letting herself be free of her failures and moving on to the unknown.

Yaz snatched one of Bella's hands from Percy's grip and kissed her knuckles. "I think it is," she said, her voice sounding just as sweet as the personality her best friend was gone for. "You deserve all the happiness in the world."

Chapter Fifteen

Bella was reading on her couch the following morning, a cup of coffee from the corner bodega in her hand. She slept horribly again, waking up covered in sweat after nightmares of her grandfather and Nonna plagued her sleep. The image of her grandfather betraying Nonna transformed into an image of Lon, their old apartment taking shape around them as he told her the truth.

I'm in love with her, Bella.

It was six-thirty in the morning when she'd bolted upright, and after fitfully tossing in her bed, she gave up on trying to fall back asleep. She'd checked her phone and found a text from Wyatt.

WYATT

I'll pick you up in the morning at ten.

So she'd come back from the shop and draped her favorite blanket over her lap, ready to sink into a book that would drown out the memory of Lon's words. She figured it was all because of her conversation with Percy and Yaz the previous night, the anxiety that hardened in her chest at the thought of seeing Katie and Lon *together* for the first time. In front of the family she'd claimed as her own for a brief moment in time.

The sound of the buzzer flooded her with sweet relief. She flung her book on the couch and slid to the intercom, then pressed the talk button. "Who is it?"

"Special delivery," Wyatt answered.

"Oh! Well, that's weird, I didn't order anything."

"Bella, I'm about five seconds away from breaking in if you don't unlock this door and let me kiss you…"

She buzzed him in. Bella bounced back and forth near the door, then decided she probably seemed a *bit* too eager. She padded back to the couch and took a sip of her coffee, then glanced down at her sleep shorts, gray wool socks, and white Russo's T-shirt.

"Shit," she mumbled. She stripped off the shirt and started for her bedroom as a knock sounded at the door. She slipped on her NYU sweatshirt, then glanced at herself in the mirror above her bar cart and grimaced. She loosened her high ponytail and let her hair down, ruffling it with her fingers.

"Bella…" said a gruff voice on the other side of the door.

"You're so *bossy*," she chimed back, a grin plastered on her face.

She paused her ruffling, then decided to give up. Wyatt had already seen her in his sweatshirt and boxers. How was this any different?

Bella opened her door to the sight of Wyatt leaning against the frame. He was cozied up in his jacket and a beanie, loose jeans cuffed at the bottom with thick socks tucked into his usual clogs. In his hand was a picnic basket, and around his shoulder a tote bag with a blanket and a bottle of wine.

He was eyeing her, too. His gaze trailed from her lips and her hair down to her bare legs. The way he swallowed, the way he seemed physically affected by her, had heat pooling low in her belly.

"Hi, chef," she whispered.

Wyatt placed the basket and bag down on the floor, then scooped her into his arms. He rubbed his nose against hers. "Hi."

He leaned down and kissed her, his lips slow and methodical, like they had all the time in the world. His chest rumbled as he pulled away. "I missed you, *mia bella*."

She grinned into his mouth. "You saw me four days ago."

"Four days is a long time when I now know what these lips taste like." He kissed her again, gripping the back of her neck as he tilted her to him, giving him the perfect angle to devour her. She would let him, too. Let him lose complete control and do what he wanted. If only he allowed himself to do so.

She was the one to pull away this time, with three soft kisses, like he did with her. "Are you taking me on a picnic?"

"Mmm," he replied. "I was thinking Central Park. But on second thought, I wouldn't mind staying here and kissing you all day."

Bella laughed. "It is gorgeous outside..."

He groaned as she slipped out of his grasp. Wyatt waited patiently as she bundled up in her comfiest black jeans and cashmere sweater. She kept her wool socks on as she slid into her combat boots, then entered the living room. Wyatt was standing by her couch, holding up a white T-shirt that she forgot to hide.

Shit, shit, shit.

Wyatt glanced up at her with a smug expression. "Looks like someone is a fan of Russo's."

Bella crossed her arms. "Yeah? So?"

"You sure you didn't *steal* that meatball recipe?"

Her chest tightened, wondering if this was her moment. But different words rolled off her tongue. "I'm a kid who grew up in New York, remember?"

He dropped the shirt and shrugged. Her shoulders relaxed as he reached for her coat and opened it up for her. She pushed her arms through the sleeves, her heart fluttering in her chest as he untucked her hair and kissed her neck.

A shiver ran down her spine. "S-scarf," she fumbled.

Wyatt grabbed her oversized scarf, then hesitated before also grabbing the flat-brim hat hanging next to it. He stepped up to her with that cocky grin and placed his hat on her head.

"You really like me in this thing, don't you?" Bella pinched the brim and twisted it around so it was backward. "Should I wear it like you do?"

He grinned as he interlaced his fingers with hers, lifting one of her hands to kiss the inside of her wrist. "I think I would like you in anything."

She cocked a brow. "Anything, huh? How about a trash bag?"

He laughed and released his hold, picking up the basket and tote bag by the door.

She flicked off the lights and locked the door behind them, then swiveled abruptly to face him. "Oh, oh, how about *in your chef's coat?*"

Wyatt's face flushed a dark red. He blinked once, then twice.

Bella gave him a smug smirk right back. "Jackpot?"

He coughed, then nodded, unable to look her in the eye as they left the building.

The sky was a clear blue, the air chilled to the right amount of crisp, biting at her nose and her ears. Wyatt looped an arm around her shoulders and tucked his hand underneath her scarf, tracing his fingers along her collarbone. She leaned into him as they made their way down the sidewalk in the direction of the 2nd Avenue subway stop.

"No car today?" she asked, leading him into the station.

He kissed her temple. "Thought I would act like a true New Yorker."

"*Finally.* Took you long enough."

He chuckled as they swiped their cards and entered the platform. They didn't speak as they traveled north up to 81st Street, or up the platform and past the Natural History Museum. She decided she liked that about Wyatt, how he was confident enough in himself not to have to fill the silence, just simply *be* with her. Lon couldn't have been more different, always ready with something to say about work or his college friends, sometimes even political news that infuriated him. Bella never minded the constant chatter, until she was in the presence of someone who was content in the silence. She never realized how much she craved it until now.

Wyatt picked a quiet spot near Turtle Pond, across from the Belvedere Castle. Tourists peeked their heads out of the arched frames of the towers, the blueish tint of the castle's stones a contrast among the warm orange trees. She helped him lay out the blanket before they settled down. He plucked items out of the picnic basket—cheeses, meats, olives, crackers.

Bella's eyes grew wider with each item he unearthed. "Are strawberries on the menu?" she teased.

She enjoyed the way he blushed as he reached into the basket and pulled out a container of strawberries. "They're not exactly in season, but..."

Bella laughed as she crawled over to him. He tugged on her scarf and kissed her, a smile stretching her lips.

They talked briefly about their weeks as they snacked, but soon settled into silence as they watched park goers pass by; runners, moms with strollers, teenagers on skateboards, even an elderly man in a three-piece suit walking his cat with a leash.

She settled the back of her head on Wyatt's lap, letting him comb her hair with his fingers as she read her book. The breeze was soft as it swayed through the medley of red, orange, and golden-tinted trees. Distant laughter from children at the playground traveled with the wind, making her smile.

Bella looked up at Wyatt. His brow was furrowed as he stared at a pocket-sized notebook in his hand.

She placed her book face down on her belly. "What's that?"

His features softened, his eyes still on the notebook. "My shit attempt at trying to figure out the winter menu."

"Hmm. Want some help?"

He smirked. "Depends on what you got."

"Well, for starters, you should remove the deconstructed meatballs and serve *real ones*."

"Never."

She reached for his notebook. "May I?"

He nodded, handing it to her. Bella flipped it open and scanned his scribbling and his basic sketches for the presentation of each dish. There were many ingredients and dishes she knew, like arancini and olive oil cake, then others she didn't, like escarole and black garlic bavette.

"This is so impressive," she said.

"It's not, but thanks."

Bella shook her head and handed it back to him. "Why do you think it's not?"

"It's not perfect yet. I need it to be perfect."

"Why?" Her chest constricted. "Is it Matteo? Is he—"

"No, nothing to do with him." Wyatt sighed, his fingers back to combing her hair, his eyes following his movements. "Nominations for the James Beard Awards will be announced next Friday. Matteo told me last week that he submitted the restaurant for consideration."

"I thought you said he doesn't care for awards?"

"He doesn't, but..."

Realization clicked. "But you still do."

He nodded.

"And you want your winter menu to be perfect in case..."

He nodded again. "Being nominated would be an honor. *Winning* would be an honor. But the menu will transition a couple of weeks after the awards ceremony. What if guests are disappointed? What if..."

Bella cupped his cheek with her palm. "They won't be disappointed. Your food is incredible, and so are you."

He leaned into her touch. "Thank you. But...that's really hard for me to believe."

She rubbed her thumb back and forth, not sure what else to say. Thankfully she didn't have to fill the silence with her words as Wyatt dipped down to kiss her.

"You are also incredible," he whispered.

Distant, raucous laughter sounded again. Bella turned her head in the direction of the playground, watching as three kids chased each other, one of them throwing leaves while the others laughed with pure glee.

Her heart twisted violently in her chest at the sight of them. *Three. Why three?* The grief always hit her at the most unexpected times, in the most unexpected circumstances. Before she could bottle up her feelings, they bubbled over and tears began to fall.

Wyatt brushed them away with his thumb, and to her surprise, he didn't ask what was wrong or why she was crying. Instead, he asked her honestly: "Did you want kids? With him?"

She turned to face his sparkling green eyes and silently nodded. Nightmares resurfaced in her mind as she thought about Lon and her apartment, the ultrasounds with the absent heartbeats, the dark days in bed letting the world pass by. She thought about having to face him in seven days.

"D-do you ever get Saturday nights off?"

He frowned. "Why?"

"Because I...um...Percy is proposing to her girlfriend next Saturday and there's going to be this party and, well, I..."

Wyatt closed his eyes and sighed. For a moment, she thought he was going to say yes, that he would skip work and go with her. Instead, to her dismay, he shook his head. "I'm so sorry, Bella."

She swallowed, then nodded. "It's okay. You warned me. I shouldn't have asked."

Wyatt looked pained at her reaction. His eyes scanned her face, like he was trying to read what was really going on. She smiled, hoping it was reassurance enough that she could do it on her own.

Even though it was the last thing she wanted.

Chapter Sixteen

THE SOUND of her heeled boots against the cool marble reverberated across the entrance of the hushed cathedral. She grimaced but kept her pursuit, hoping it wasn't too late. She slipped in the back, eyes roving over the pews in search of Nonna. Not surprised, Bella found her in the usual spot; ten rows back on the left, closest to the red votive prayer candles. She scurried as the cantor sang a prayer to the packed congregation at St. Teresa's, something about love and forgiveness.

Bella slipped in beside her grandmother, who stared back at her with wide eyes. "What are you doing here, *piccola mia?*"

She shimmied into her warmth and dipped her head. "Joining my nonna at mass, what else?"

"When have you *ever* joined me at mass when it's not a holiday?"

"Can't today be the first?"

Nonna clucked her tongue. "I don't buy that, but I'll enjoy it nonetheless."

Bella smiled as her nonna threaded her arm through

hers. The two of them sat silently listening to the service around them, kneeling when they were told to pray, then up to the front for communion. She took her grandmother's arm again as they left St. Teresa's at the end of the service, out into another gorgeous fall day in Manhattan.

Nonna clutched the front of her jacket and nuzzled her face into it. "Walk me home and help me with the sauce?"

Bella nodded, anticipating her grandmother asking this. *Hoping*, actually. She wanted to talk to her about everything and maybe...*finally*...get some answers.

She guided Nonna back to Mulberry Street and followed her up the stairs at Russo's, into her apartment. She washed her hands and got to work on the sauce for dinner, rolling up thin slices of veal with basil and parmesan to simmer in the sauce all day. Nonna did what she did best, mixing meatballs in a large bowl with ricotta and soaked Italian bread and freshly grated Pecorino Romano. Once the sauce was assembled and the meatballs seared and tossed in the sauce, she surprised Bella by unearthing a bottle of Amaretto from her cabinets. She poured each of them a tipple over ice, then handed her a glass as they settled on her cozy couch near the window.

Little Italy was buzzing with weekend tourists, people nibbling on pastries and sipping on cappuccinos at cafés, music blasting from restaurants as hosts tried their best to lure in potential customers for a drink, maybe a plate of pasta or a *pizza napoletana*.

"Does the noise ever annoy you?" Bella inquired.

Nonna took a sip of her drink before shaking her head. "It brings me joy, seeing the community thrive. I know it's the touristy part of our neighborhood, but I wouldn't want to be anywhere else."

Bella took a sip of her drink as well—bitter at first, then

sweet. She knew there was some kind of metaphor here. Or maybe she hoped that the bitter truth of this reality they were in, the dark secrets her grandmother kept from them, would have a sweeter finish.

"Nonna?"

Her grandmother sighed. "Your mother was thirteen when your nonno came home and told me the truth."

Bella sucked in a breath but didn't dare speak. She had a multitude of questions, but she knew to give her grandmother space.

"We'd been having arguments for a couple of years by then, about the future of Russo's and our future as husband and wife." She glanced out the window, her face soft with resignation. "He wanted to move to a bigger house, somewhere in Brooklyn or Queens. I couldn't imagine leaving my home, the place my parents set roots and made this legacy after leaving their families in Italy. I love my apartment. I love my store. Your grandfather looked at those things and thought that maybe I loved them more than I loved him."

She shrugged. "Maybe I did, I don't know. All I know is that he came home and said he met someone, and she was carrying his child. But I don't think this is news to you, is it?"

Bella hesitated, then felt the fight leave her. "No," she whispered. "It isn't news."

Nonna hummed. "How did you find out, Bella?"

"I took all of these DNA tests to find...answers to my problem."

Her grandmother shook her head. "There is no problem with you, *piccola*. It is him. The two of you were never meant to be."

"Being able to carry a child to term has nothing to do with being *meant to be*. It means—"

"I know what it means, sweet one. But I believe in my heart that, while we will always mourn those babies, any man who is willing to walk out on his woman the way he did is not worthy of being in her life. You were not meant to share a family with him. He never deserved you."

"Is that how you felt about Grandpa? That he no longer deserved it?"

Nonna looked down at her glass without a response.

"I...I don't think I deserved *him*, Nonna. I could have tried harder for Lon."

"*Pffft*. I refuse to listen to that nonsense. Never say that to me, or to anyone, ever again."

Bella swallowed her words. "Yes, ma'am."

She sipped her drink. "What else do you know?"

"I know his name, Matteo Lombardi." She peeked at her grandmother, who seemed unfazed by the name. She clearly already knew it. "I also know he owns three restaurants, and that he lives in Astoria."

"And this is how you met your chef."

"Yes," she whispered.

"Is he aware of any of this?"

Bella hesitated before shaking her head. "No. He knows nothing. He doesn't even know I'm a Russo."

Her eyes widened. "*Dio mio*. And you cooked him my meatballs?"

"I wasn't sure how much he knew when I met him, so I told him Hamilton was my last name." She shrugged. "Then I was curious if the meatballs still lived up to the hype without the big Russo branding. They do, by the way. He devoured them."

"Of course he did," she quipped.

Bella tapped a finger before continuing. "Matteo's wife, Claire...she said she came to visit you? After the funeral?"

She sighed. "Claire was distraught that I missed it, couldn't understand why I wouldn't even bother to show up." She placed her drink down and twisted her hands in her lap. "What she doesn't know is that her mother-in-law visited me days before the funeral and told me my family was unwelcome at the ceremonies."

Bella's mouth fell open. "Nonno's second wife? Matteo's mother?"

"She hated me, which is reasonable. I did tell your grandfather I wanted absolutely nothing to do with his new family and to keep them far away from your mother."

"So Mom really doesn't know any of this?"

Nonna nodded.

"I made things pretty messy, didn't I?"

Her grandmother sighed.

"I'm sorry. I should have let this all go, but I...I just..."

Nonna patted her cheek with a wrinkly hand. "You are in love with the chef. I can see it."

"*Love?*" Bella choked. Why did people keep saying that she was in love? She'd known Wyatt for maybe a month. It was way too early for *that*. "No. I *like* him, sure. But not love. Especially not when he doesn't..."

She looked up at her grandmother. Those brown eyes twinkled with mischief.

"He doesn't know *things*. Like who I am and the truth about why I originally wanted to hang out with him, obviously. But also the truth about *me* and my health and—"

That hand patted her again, this time with a bit more intensity. Less of a love tap, more of a *snap out of it* smack.

"Then bring him to supper, Bella. Start letting him know the real you."

She blinked. "And Mom? Will you tell her the truth?"

Nonna's hand fell back to her lap. "I have tried to have that conversation with her so many times in the past. I don't even know where to begin now."

"At the beginning," Bella said confidently. "No more secrets."

She patted her knee, but Bella noticed the way her grandmother avoided eye contact as she did it, like she was embarrassed by what she might find there. "No more secrets for you either, my sweet."

BELLA WAS on-site with her team at one of the Dreamscape locations, a gorgeous penthouse apartment in Dumbo overlooking the Brooklyn Bridge and the East River. But even the stunning views couldn't distract her from checking her phone every five minutes. It was Friday afternoon, and the James Beard Awards had yet to post the nominations list. She refreshed the homepage, she checked her messages with Wyatt, but there still wasn't any news. If *she* was this on-edge, she couldn't even imagine how Wyatt was feeling.

Against her better judgment, she typed out a text to him.

BELLA

Did you hear anything yet?

The *whoosh* sound of the sent text was subtle compared to the pounding of her heartbeat in her ears. She stared at the screen, hoping that a gray text bubble would pop up so she could borrow his move and call him right away.

"Okay, we've got shots from every possible angle of the

upstairs bedrooms," Katie called out, stepping into the kitchen where Bella had been blissfully alone for a few minutes. "The team is coming down in the elevator so they can start shooting down here."

She frowned. "There's an elevator in this apartment?"

"A private one, yes."

Bella shook her head. "Oh, to be a New Yorker with disposable income."

"I know, right? The interns couldn't resist, they were all giddy."

She smiled, then watched as Katie smiled back, her expression almost eager.

"You, um, excited for tomorrow?" Katie asked.

No, she wanted to answer honestly. She wasn't ready to be in a small bar with her ex-husband and former in-laws, and she sure wasn't ready to do it alone. Bella had given herself mini pep talks throughout the week, reminding herself that this was Percy's big night, and it truly had nothing to do with her and her past. She needed to drop it for her best friend. She needed to not let it affect her.

Except it would, especially when a simple question like Katie's had her poised to unravel.

Bella plastered on her best grin. "Very excited. I'm so happy for them."

Her phone buzzed in her hand. Shocked by the interruption, Bella almost dropped it to the floor. She scrambled to hold it firm as she read Wyatt's name on the screen. He was calling her. She didn't bother excusing herself as she turned from Katie and answered. "Hi."

Cheering and loud, booming music came from his end of the line. Her heart hammered in her chest again at the noise. Cheering. Music. *Celebrating.*

"Hi," Wyatt said. He sounded like he was smiling. She wanted to squeal with delight.

"Sounds like a party over there," she pointed out.

"Yes, Marissa has apparently commandeered the playlist, and Jayce has popped five bottles of sparkling."

"Good news, I take it?"

Wyatt hummed, the sound of that low rumble making her knees feel weak. She gripped the marble countertop beside her.

"You should make your way down to the restaurant," he said.

Bella turned, realizing in horror that Katie was watching her. She was met with a small smirk and a head tilt, her red hair spilling over her cheek.

"I'm still at work," she replied. "We're on-site again for a client."

"Come right after?"

Bella covered her lips with her hands, doing her best to suppress her smile. "Yes, after."

She hung up and tucked her phone into the pocket of her black wrap dress, her eyes on Katie, whose gaze was curious and teasing. Bella hoped she wouldn't ask about it. Or worse, tell Lon.

Instead, Katie surprised her. "Go. I can handle the rest of this."

"Are you sure? I really should—"

"Seriously, Bella. You don't have to be here. The client already left."

She eyed the downstairs of the apartment. An associate from Dreamscape was sitting on a plush couch, scrolling through his phone, waiting for them to finish shooting content so he could lock up behind him. The rest of his crew already left. There really *wasn't* a reason for her to stick around, except to monitor her team.

She sprang into action, shoving her arms into her coat and grabbing her bag. "Call me if there's an issue, yeah?"

Katie rolled her eyes. "There won't be, but okay. Now go to...whoever just called you."

Another smirk arose as Katie raised a brow in her direction, clearly intrigued. Bella couldn't help the flush that painted her cheeks as she mumbled a goodbye and left the penthouse.

Chapter Seventeen

A PIECE of paper was taped to the front door of the restaurant, with a hurried scrawl at the center. *Closed for a private event.* Inside Tri, a massive party was underway. Bottles of wine and plates of hors d'oeuvres scattered the bar. Waiters and line cooks and bartenders filled the space, some faces she'd already come to recognize after her few visits.

She peered around them, looking for Wyatt as she squeezed her way through the people and made her way to the back. Most of the staff stood in groups, but one group sat at a table in the corner, like they were holding court. When she finally pushed her way to the table, another round of cheers erupted from their mouths.

"She's here!" Matteo cheered.

"*Bella!*" Benji added, lifting up his glass.

"Wow, that is a stunning dress," Jayce added, sizing up her work outfit. She didn't bother going home to change, she was already in Brooklyn after all.

She flushed and thanked him, her eyes finally landing

on the man sitting in the corner, clearly in the center of it all.

Wyatt greeted her with a warm, satisfied smile. He still wore his chef's coat, his hair tucked back and out of his face. He leaned his head against the wall and mouthed a *hi* in her direction.

Hi, she mouthed back.

She scanned the group, who all seemed *very* interested in their exchange. She felt her cheeks heat from the attention.

"Make room for her," Wyatt commanded.

At that, chairs skidded aside as Benji and Marissa scooted out of the booth near the wall, giving Bella room to slide in next to Wyatt. He continued to lean against the wall as his eyes dipped to her dress's neckline and back up to her mouth, but he did not move to touch her or kiss her. She gave him a slight nod, understanding the message. *We're in front of my staff, I need to act professional.*

Bella turned to Marissa as she slid back into the booth, still in her chef's coat as well. "So?"

"Two nominations," she said matter-of-factly.

She turned her gaze to the rest of the group. Matteo sat across the table, next to Jayce and a blond-haired man she presumed to be Jayce's husband, his arm slung around Jayce's shoulders, the two of them wearing matching white-gold bands on their left hands. Benji pulled up a seat at the foot of the table, wearing white overalls and a forest green button-down underneath, his hair curly and wild at the top, a rogue streak of flour behind his right ear.

Matteo grinned as he finally relayed the news she'd been anxious to hear. "Best Restaurant in the Northeast."

Hollers and *whoop whoops* sounded from the staff.

Bella watched in awe at the way Matteo's face lit up, at

how the staff celebrated. His left eye crinkled with his lopsided smile, and it made her stomach twist with longing for her grandfather.

"*And...*" Benji added impatiently.

Matteo's lopsided grin transformed into something child-like and proud. "Outstanding Chef."

More whoops and hollers and clinking glasses.

Bella whipped her head around to Wyatt. His eyes were only on hers, his smile bashful and, if she wasn't mistaken, relieved. She wanted to crawl into his lap and kiss him and tell him how incredible he was. But she kept it cool as she poked his leg under the table and whispered, "Congrats, chef. Well deserved."

His knuckles lightly brushed hers in response.

Jayce popped a bottle of Pét Nat and poured coupe glasses to the brim, handing them to Daniel—his husband, as Bella'd suspected—who then passed them out to the group.

Matteo squared his shoulders to Wyatt. "I already knew this place was worthy of awards, but it's nice to know that I'm not biased. Congratulations to you and to everyone else in this room," he said, lifting his glass as he turned to the staff.

Silent nods were shared, sips were taken, and the music somehow got even louder after Matteo's speech.

Bella took another sip of her wine, turning to Wyatt. "How do you feel?"

He pointed to his glass. "Like this wine. Effervescent. Floaty. Fully aware it will give me a massive headache in the morning."

She rolled her eyes. "Spoken like a true chef."

"No headaches, no freakouts," Marissa interjected with a point of her finger.

"We need to nail down the winter menu," Wyatt replied.

Now Matteo was the one to roll his eyes. "The man doesn't stop."

"Says the man who now has a nominated restaurant," Wyatt jested.

Matteo gave him the finger as everyone laughed.

"Can you at least promise me you won't spend your weekend off brooding over that notebook you carry in your pocket," Marissa said. "Take a break. We'll tackle it next week."

Bella's eyes widened. "Weekend off?"

Wyatt slid a hand from his lap to hers, his palm spanning the entire width of her thigh. He squeezed, then turned his palm up. She took it, threading her fingers through his.

"Marissa has been working on a special menu for a while and I gave her the approval to execute it this weekend," he said. "So she's in charge."

"Yeah she is!" Jayce boomed, giving Marissa a high-five.

Joy bubbled in her chest. "So that means..."

Wyatt traced a thumb on the inside of her wrist. "That means I'm free all weekend," he murmured only to her.

She closed her eyes as a smile bloomed across her cheeks. He made arrangements so she wouldn't have to go about this weekend alone.

As if he read her thoughts, Wyatt squeezed her hand.

"And how will you spend your weekend of freedom?" Jayce asked, leaning into Daniel's side.

Wyatt smiled at her before looking at his sommelier. "Percy Chase is getting engaged. Bella invited me to the party."

"*Percy Chase?*" Marissa squeaked. "Like, the columnist from *Taster?*"

Bella nodded. "She's my best friend."

"Ahh. Now I see Wyatt's motivation."

She frowned. "Huh?"

Marissa leaned over the table. "Getting it on with the best friend so you can have an in with Chase, huh?"

"Watch your mouth," Wyatt snapped.

Marissa chuckled and waved him off, then turned to her. She didn't have to look in a mirror to know her face was now splotchy and red. "I'm kidding. Wyatt would never. He's one of the good ones."

Bella coughed in response, her gaze instinctively landing on Matteo. *Isn't that what I'm doing to Wyatt, though?* She shivered.

Shaking it off, she planted herself back in the moment. It was Wyatt's night, and apparently his first weekend off in a long time. She wouldn't ruin it. "Maybe you can help me find some kind of dessert for tomorrow. I forgot to put in an order and I'm in charge of bringing something."

"Good thing I know a pastry chef," Wyatt replied.

Benji perked up at the end of the table. "Is Asshole about to *recommend* me?"

He gave him a *stop shitting with me* face. "Why wouldn't I?"

"Oh, I don't know, I'm not fancy enough to work someplace like here," he bantered.

"You *could* be," Marissa added. "If you weren't so bloody set on that bagel spot of yours."

Benji leaned forward, his eyes menacing. "Remind me, little one. Who did *The New York Times* dub the best bagel spot in the city?"

Marissa's face went beet red. "Don't call me that."

"*Little one.*"

Marissa jumped at him, but Jayce pinched her coat from across the table and held her back before her hand met Benji's face. "She's little but fierce. Don't forget that she could beat you up."

Benji gave Marissa a devilish grin. "Oh, I'm well aware."

She huffed and turned to Bella. "I could make something *far* better than him. What do you want?"

"A cake?" Bella thought about it. "Actually, no, that's a pain to cut and serve. Something people can easily grab. Cupcakes? Cookies?"

Marissa's face brightened. "I've been messing around with a vanilla yuzu whoopie pie recipe."

"Chef," Wyatt said coolly. "Who's in charge this weekend?"

"Shit, right. Sorry, chef."

Benji cheekily clucked his tongue. "Looks like I'll be the one making whoopie pies."

Marissa frowned. "But they won't have yuzu."

"They won't. What's a flavor the couple will like?"

"Percy is a really big black-and-white cookie fan," Bella revealed.

Benji's eyes sparkled. "Oh, I'm about to have fun with this."

Marissa crossed her arms in front of her chest. "No fair."

"Says the woman who's about to take over the kitchen all weekend," Jayce quipped.

Marissa perked up. "You're so right. I'll be too busy preparing crudo and pansotti and branzino."

"Show off," Benji grumbled.

The group continued to debate about food and pastries

and kitchens as Wyatt slipped a hand around Bella's waist, his fingers tracing her hip bone. "I missed you, *mia bella*," he whispered.

She leaned back against his chest, her eyes still on the group as she whispered back, "You're so obsessed with me."

He hummed. "I'm assuming you're free this weekend?"

"Even if I wasn't, I would cancel all my plans to hang out with you."

She liked the way his chest rumbled when he hummed again. No one was watching them as Wyatt leaned in and kissed her neck. "Thank you for coming."

She placed a hand on his leg. "I wouldn't miss it."

Wyatt kissed behind her ear. Matteo turned his head and looked at them, then raised a brow in Bella's direction.

"Your staff is going to notice," she whispered to Wyatt from the corner of her mouth.

"Don't care," he said, nuzzling her neck.

She sat up and turned to him. His face was shining, his eyes half lidded, his smile big and borderline sloppy. "Uh oh," she teased. "Did someone have a little too much to drink?"

He tucked a lock of her hair behind her ear. "Maybe."

Matteo leaned forward. "Take him home, Bella."

Her eyes bounced between Matteo and Wyatt. "Yeah?"

Wyatt grinned. "Yeah. Take me home."

Matteo chuckled, clearly amused by Wyatt's state...and his out-of-character public display of affection. He ordered the group to move out of the way so they could slide out of the booth.

Marissa jumped up, frowning at Benji's neck. She licked her thumb and wiped at the flour behind his ear. "You should groom yourself before leaving your kitchen."

"Why would I do that when you do it so well?" Benji lobbed back.

She rolled her eyes. Wyatt stood up and mumbled a few words to Marissa about the weekend as Jayce handed Bella her coat and tote bag, and to her shock, Wyatt's knife roll. "Guard it with your life."

She took it, tucking it into her work bag. "Too bad. I was thinking about selling it for lots of money. Knives from an award-nominated chef have to go for a decent price, right?"

"Very funny," Wyatt added, slipping his hand in hers. He turned back to Marissa. "Call if there are any issues."

"Respectfully, no, chef. Take the weekend off. I'll only call if the kitchen is burning down."

He sighed. "Fine." He then waved to his staff. "Good night, everyone, congratulations again. I'm proud of all of you."

Cheers and *Thanks, chef!* echoed behind them as they made their way out of the restaurant and into the dark, chilly evening. The air was biting compared to Manhattan, the breeze from the water cutting into her coat and making her shiver.

Wyatt put his arm around Bella and tucked her close as they wandered down the cobblestone street. He dipped his head and began kissing her neck, first with small pecks, then with slow luxurious teases of his tongue.

"Someone's happy," Bella teased as they stepped up to his apartment's stoop.

"Yes," he admitted. "Really happy."

She turned to face him, holding out her hand. "Keys?"

He reached into the pocket of his slacks and handed them to her. She turned and began fiddling through the keys to pick out the right one, which Wyatt did not help her decipher. Instead, his hands slipped around her waist as he pulled her flush against him, his mouth kissing the soft spot behind her ear. Goose flesh pricked at the nape of her neck.

"You're making it hard to concentrate," she admitted.

"Black key," he grumbled before returning to her ear, nibbling the top of it.

Her hands trembled as she turned the black key and unlocked the door. They broke apart and stepped inside, climbing the stairs up into his kitchen. Wyatt stood help-lessly as Bella put her things down. She pointed to his bedroom. "Time for bed."

His hand curled around her wrist as he pulled her close. "Will you join me?"

She cocked a brow. "Only if you behave."

"I cannot promise that right now."

She huffed a laugh, taking charge and leading him to his bedroom. "Come on."

She pushed open his bedroom door, then turned and lifted her hands to his shoulders, guiding him to the bed. He dutifully sat down, eyes never leaving her face as she began unbuttoning his chef's coat.

A warm hand ran up the side of her leg as she worked at the buttons. Bella thought he would stop his pursuit before he hit the hem of her dress, but he surprised her by slipping his hand underneath the fabric and continuing his climb.

She smirked. "What are you doing?"

His hand was now at the top of her tights. Fingers dipped in playfully, caressing her skin. It made her go hot all over. She unfastened the last button of his coat, then looked into his eyes. They were a blazing, eager, greedy green.

"Is this okay?" he asked.

"Y-yeah," she breathed. "That's not exactly taking it slow, though."

His knuckles traced her hip, fingers still hooked inside her tights. "I'm done pretending."

Her eyes widened. "Pretending?"

In one swift movement, Wyatt grabbed the backs of her thighs and pulled her right on top of him. Her knees bracketed his hips as he sealed his chest to hers. "I'm done pretending like I don't want you all the damn time."

Everything inside her *burned*. Any coherent thought she had went completely fuzzy as she watched his chest visibly rise and fall. He was waiting for her to say something. *Do* something.

So, she did.

Bella wrapped her arms around his neck and kissed him. He groaned, letting his hands trail around the fabric of her tights and squeeze her hips hard. He sucked on her bottom lip, then softened his grip as he pulled back, his gaze on the front tie of her wrap dress. With shaking hands, he reached for it, then looked up at her.

He was waiting again. Waiting for her to say *no* or *yes*. Waiting for her to stop him if she didn't want to go this far, or to admit that she, too, was done pretending. That she, too, wanted him in all the same ways.

She nodded her head.

Wyatt kissed her slowly as he pulled the tie loose.

Chapter Eighteen

He opened up the front of her dress, the chill from his bedroom making her skin prickly. His hands brushed her shoulders and lowered her dress, the fabric dangling loose at her elbows.

"Wow," he breathed.

She smirked. "What does wow mean in this context?"

His eyes were on her bra, on the bits of black lace that matched well with the silk underwear tucked inside her tights. Bella didn't intend for him to see them today—she simply enjoyed wearing lace and silk because it made her feel beautiful and confident in a body that rarely made her feel that way. But she was proud she'd chosen this combination as his eyes trailed from the elastic strap down to the lace and sheer fabric, his fingers raking the back of her neck as he stared, the awestruck look he gave her doing plenty to quell her nerves.

"It means 'wow, I am such an idiot.'"

"Why are you an—"

He didn't let her finish, his lips hot on hers as he slipped off the sleeves of her dress and let it drop to the floor. She tugged him out of his chef's coat, then peeled off his white T-shirt. His chest was as she remembered, all toned muscle and hard lines. She let herself explore this time, dragging a finger down his sternum and across the divots of his abs. When she got to his pants, she pinched the center and flicked open the button.

Wyatt snatched her waist and maneuvered them around, laying her out on his bed. He pressed his body to hers as he trailed kisses from her chin, down her neck, between her breasts. His hands curled at the waistband of her tights, then he was peeling them off her. He tossed them aside and froze, his eyes almost disbelieving as they took in the sight of her.

He swore. "God, *look at you*."

She bit her bottom lip. "Like what you see, chef?"

"I feel unworthy."

Her nipples perked at the sound of his raspy voice, at the way he was unraveling in front of her. She shimmied down and grasped his hand, guiding it to her chest. He tugged on a strap and released it, the sting causing her breath to hitch, before moving down and palming her breast through the lace. He gently squeezed, and the pressure made her moan.

He swore again. "You are perfect. So...so perfect."

Both his hands were now on her breasts, hard and wanting. But her bra was still in the way. "Take it off," she demanded.

"Not so fast. I'm currently enjoying my favorite new piece in your monochromatic wardrobe." He pressed his body against hers as he sucked on her neck.

She smiled, wanting to mess with him a little. "My wardrobe isn't all black, you know."

"Right, the tank top." His teeth scraped against her skin. "How could I forget?"

"No, I mean...*this* particular wardrobe."

He lifted his head, looking confused. "Huh?"

She smirked, dragging a finger along the hem of her underwear. "I own a few red things as well."

Wyatt groaned so loud it made her laugh. He sat up, bringing her along with him, his hands on her back. With a swift tug and a flick, her bra was undone. He peeled it off her, then slowed his movements as he stared at her chest. He pulled her back into his lap.

"Touch me," she whispered.

He did as he was told, cupping her breasts as he kissed her hard, his thumbs brushing across her nipples. She leaned in to him, wanting more pressure. Wanting more of *him*.

Bella's hands itched to take off his pants, to touch him in the same ways. She reached for the zipper, but a hand wrapped around her wrist to stop her.

She froze, her lips breaking apart from his. Wyatt's eyes snapped shut, his breathing heavy and ragged.

She felt like a fool. "I-I'm sorry," she blubbered. "We shouldn't be doing this. You admitted to having too much to drink and I'm totally taking advantage of you—"

"*No.*"

She stopped speaking.

He loosened his tight hold and pressed his mouth to her wrist, leaving a trail of kisses up her inner arm. When he reached her shoulder, he stopped, brushing a finger under her chin so he could look her right in the eye. "You are not taking advantage of me, *mia bella*. It just...takes me a little time, okay?"

"*Oh.*"

He clutched her waist and laid down on the bed, pulling her on top of him. Bella's eyes were on his, but her mind was on the places of his body that were hard and the places that were *not*. She was so turned on by him, so distracted by how *good* he made her feel, that she didn't even realize what was missing.

He held her neck and kissed her while his other hand skimmed her spine, then dipped inside the fabric of her underwear. He cupped her ass with a firm hand and a moan tumbled from his chest. She bit his bottom lip and wiggled, hoping to feel hardness and friction but was met with nothing.

She broke apart from him. "What do you like?" she asked.

"I like *you*."

"No, I mean..." She dragged her nails softly down his chest, to his abs, stopping at the waist of his pants. "What do you *like*?"

"Trust me, Bella," he whispered. "I wish it were that easy."

She made circles over the dip at his right hip. "Can I at least...see you?"

The cadence of his breaths quickened, becoming even more intense and ragged.

"Please," she pleaded. "I want to see you, Wyatt. All of you."

He ran a hand through his hair as he sat up. Bella slipped onto the duvet beside him. The distant lights of the skyline pierced through the dark room from the window, streaks of orange and blue light illuminating his face.

She wondered if she'd really overstepped this time. This wasn't just physical intimacy. This was...*intimacy*. Emotional and raw. Everything about his behavior the past few weeks—the drawing close, only to push himself far away—now made sense. He was anxious about showing a side of him that was deeply personal. It made her want to grab on to him and say *Me too.* That she knew exactly how it felt to have a body that failed her.

He finally exhaled and surprised her with his response. "On one condition."

Her eyes widened. "What is it?"

Wyatt pinched the silk fabric of her underwear at her hips and pulled them down to her ankles. His hands grazed up her legs as he took *all* of her in, his eyes dark and hungry. "After you get your look, you're going to show me *everything*. What makes you moan and what makes you wet, what ways I should taste you that will make you scream my name."

Bella panted as his thumb dipped low, tracing the soft skin between her thigh and her...*oh god.* She squeezed her eyes shut and fisted the fabric of the duvet underneath her, wanting desperately for him to dip that thumb down the center.

"Y-yes," she gasped.

"Yes what?"

"*Yes, chef.*"

Wyatt hummed as he stood up and unzipped his pants. "Good girl."

She watched him as he let his pants fall, the sight of his tight boxer briefs making her mouth go dry. He reached to slip those off as well, but she bolted upright and crawled for him. "Wait." He stopped and held his hands up as she reached for his boxers. "It's only fair."

She watched his throat bob as she pulled his boxers down. Her hands skimmed his legs and his hips, and she took all of him in. Even without an erection, the man was undeniably sexy. She wanted to tell him that, to reveal how much she wanted him, even when he looked at her like he was broken. But she also knew how it felt to sit there in shame, to feel like you weren't good enough. Wyatt was baring himself to her—emotionally and *literally*—but the man wasn't asking for a conversation right now. Instead, she had a condition to fulfill.

The heat between her thighs throbbed at the thought. She shifted her legs, desperate for some friction. Wyatt noticed, and instantly his hands were on her, pushing her back onto the bed. His tongue teased one of her nipples as his hand moved lower and lower. When his fingers dipped into the soft wetness between her legs, she was almost seconds away from screaming his name.

Wyatt swore for the third time tonight. "*You* are effervescent. Like the best tasting wine. The juiciest fruit."

She whimpered at the way he drew slow, methodical circles.

"Talk to me, *mia bella*."

"Talking requires thinking and...that is not something I can successfully do right now."

"I need to know what you like," he breathed. He trailed his tongue between her breasts, then up her neck until he reached her mouth. "Teach me."

She slipped her hand low and gripped his teasing hand. She lowered it, deeper down, then pressed his fingers where she liked it. "There."

He smiled against her lips. "Yeah?"

His hand moved painfully slow, the feel of his fingers at her most sensitive spot making her back arch in response. "Yes. Right there."

His pace quickened, their breathing going ragged. He dipped a finger inside her. "God, Bella. I want to taste you."

Now she was the one smiling. "Do you think I taste like strawberries?"

He groaned when he pulled his hand away from her. Before she could complain, he crawled down her body, kissing down her stomach and hips, then to her thighs. He positioned his face between her legs, then looked up at her with those blazing emerald eyes and that familiar cocky smirk. "I think it's time to find out."

"Oh god," she moaned as his lips and his tongue made contact. She lost all concept of space and time except for the feel of his silky hair between her fingers, his tongue deep inside her, and the taste of his name on her lips.

Chapter Nineteen

BELLA WOKE to soft morning light on her face, the sky still pink from the sunrise. She yawned, tucking her hands inside the sleeves of the crewneck Wyatt lent her to sleep in. The hand around her waist tightened from her movements, then pulled her close, her body now flush against his bare chest.

Wyatt kissed the back of her head. "Good morning, *mia bella*."

She smiled as she shimmied closer, her legs now sealed against his underneath the covers. "Be honest, did you look up how to say beautiful in Italian and found that connection?"

"I think the phrase is common knowledge," Wyatt said. She felt his lips brush against her neck. "But also...yes."

She laughed, and his chest rumbled as he laughed along with her. She liked the sensation of his body against hers, pressed close, his lips on her skin first thing in the morning. It all felt like a dream. And last night...*Oh*. Her mind replayed the ways he studied her, learning every place to touch, like she was a test he needed to ace. He was so attentive with her, so *competent*. Capable. She shouldn't have been surprised; it was a theme when it came to everything in Wyatt's life.

Bella rolled over to face him, burying her face in his neck. He hummed as he pulled her toward him, a hand brushing the nape of her neck. "How'd you sleep?" she asked.

"Great," he replied, sounding a little surprised. "You?"

"Like a damn rock."

She could feel his grin. "That's what I like to hear."

The two of them lay there for a while, breaths going heavy, hands stroking softly as the sun rose above the skyline.

"Want breakfast?" he asked, his hand tracing lazy circles on her collarbone, fingers dipping inside the sweatshirt so he could touch more of her bare skin.

She kissed his chest. "Depends. What's on the menu?"

"It would probably be too cliché to say you, right?"

She rolled her eyes, a grin skimming her cheeks. "Definitely."

"How about omelets then?"

She nodded her head enthusiastically. "Still have my toothbrush?"

"It's in the holder on the counter, next to mine."

She arched back so she could look at his face. His wavy hair was tousled and sticking up in every direction, his cheeks pink from their cocoon. "You're such a sap."

He looked pleased. "There's also something for you under the bathroom sink."

"A *present*?"

"Something like that."

Bella jumped out of bed despite Wyatt's pleas to *wait* and *come back here*. She scurried to his bathroom and flung open the cabinet door. A miniature basket was placed underneath next to a clean set of towels. She lifted the basket to find it stuffed with all kinds of supplies: makeup wipes, mouthwash, deodorant, sunscreen, even a box of tampons.

She looked back at him in the bedroom, mouth agape. "You bought all of this? For *me*?"

Wyatt sat up and ran a hand through his hair in an attempt to smooth it down, which only made his bed head worse. "I didn't want you to feel like you weren't prepared if you stayed here again. I want you to feel comfortable in my space. Comfortable with me."

She squinted her eyes. "You sure you don't keep this in your bathroom for all the other women you have stay over?"

Wyatt scratched his cheek as he stood up and padded over to her. He took the basket out of her hands and placed it next to the sink, then braced both hands on the counter, caging her in. "Bella, I think by now you've probably figured out that I never have women over."

More visions from the night before popped into her head. His eyes slamming shut when she reached for him. The way he looked at her when she peeled off his boxers, how vulnerable and scared he seemed.

He stood up straight and handed her her toothbrush. They brushed in silence, eyes trained on each other in the mirror's reflection. He rinsed his under the sink as Bella tore open the package of makeup wipes and cleaned her face. Wyatt slipped a hand under her sweatshirt, letting it slide up her bare back all the way to her neck, then back down. When she finished washing her face, she turned to face him, his arm still tucked around her. "Should we talk about it?"

He sighed. "Yeah. Probably."

She walked two fingers up his bare chest. "I'm guessing

this is what you meant when you said you weren't good at physical things."

"Correct."

Her heart ached. "Women have really told you that before? Because of this?"

"Well, they aren't wrong, Bella."

"That's...but that's so mean."

"Is it? Or is it mean to lead them to believe one thing, only to be unable to give them what they want in the end?"

She shivered at his words, how *real* they sounded. How similar they sounded to her own thoughts. "Sex shouldn't be the only end goal, Wyatt. There's so much more to a relationship."

"Sure, but it's also a very important part of it," he countered. "If I can't show someone the way I feel in the most innate physical way..." His eyes dropped to her lips. "Then it's kind of hard to convince someone to stick around."

Her lips twisted as she thought it through. "Have you tried...medical treatments?"

"Of course. Some don't work, some I have these horrible reactions. For the few that do, they...don't last long." He sighed and hung his head. "Because I have *that* problem as well."

"What do you mean?"

He looked at her like he wanted to crawl in a hole. Bella wrapped her arms around his neck and pulled him close. "I'm not going anywhere, okay?"

He closed his eyes and nodded, his expression anguished.

"What does that mean, Wyatt?"

"I have a problem staying up," he admitted, eyes still closed. "And when it happens, I don't last very long."

They stood there, her arms wrapped around him, his hand frozen, splayed on her back.

"That's..." Bella started, unsure of what to say.

"Really fucking unlucky."

"I'm sorry," she whispered. "I'm so, so sorry you have to go through that."

He opened his eyes. "You're...sorry? Why? Bella, *I* should be the one who's sorry. I'm the one with a body that can't seem to function properly."

It was there, on the tip of her tongue. *Mine doesn't function properly, either.* But she couldn't get the words out, lodged somewhere deep in her throat.

Wyatt pressed himself up to her, her back digging into the cool countertop behind her. "Bella, I...god, I like you so much. But if this is too much for you and you want something *better*—"

"Stop that."

He did as he was told, his eyes on her lips again.

"The only thing I want is you, Wyatt."

He kissed her hard, the minty taste of toothpaste sharp on her tongue. Her body went pliant as his lips moved over hers with bruising ferocity, both of his hands tucked into her sweatshirt so he could explore every inch of bare skin.

He broke apart, but only millimeters away so he could say what he needed to. "On the other hand, there are many things I *am* good at."

She smirked. "Oh yeah? Care to enlighten me?"

"Oh, I'll do more than enlighten you." Wyatt dipped down and gripped the backs of her thighs, picking her up. She squealed and wrapped her legs around his waist, then kissed him square on the mouth as he carried her back to the bed.

An hour later, Bella sat at the table as Wyatt cooked her an omelet. His hair was even worse now, and he was only in his boxer briefs and a white T-shirt. She decided she liked this particular view as she tilted her head, watching his thighs flex as he stepped to grab a plate. He returned to the frying pan, carefully folding the omelet with a spatula, the sight of his corded forearms making her feel warm and gooey all over.

He slid the omelet onto the plate, then looked around the counter for something. "Crap," he mumbled, then went out to his porch. She watched in delight as he swung open the glass door and knelt in front of a line of potted plants, plucking a few herbs. He shivered as he stepped back in, a smile blooming on his face when he registered her amusement. "What?" he asked.

"You actually do grow herbs on your porch," she exclaimed. "I mean, of course you do. It's satisfying for me to know I was correct, though."

She watched as he lightly rinsed, chopped, and garnished her omelet with parsley.

"You've thought about this?" he asked.

"Your sweatshirts smell like herbs."

He beamed as he lowered the plate in front of her. "Which herbs?"

"You want me to decipher which herbs you're growing out there by the smell of your sweatshirt?" She took a bite of the perfectly folded French omelet in front of her, stuffed with a soft cheese. She groaned and shoveled in another bite.

Wyatt retrieved his coffee from the kitchen, then returned to the table, sitting down right beside her. She frowned when she realized he didn't make an omelet for himself. "Breakfast only for me?"

He picked up her fork and took a bite. "We can share."

She glared. "I don't like sharing when the food is this good."

"It's okay, I don't eat much in the morning anyway." Wyatt handed her fork back to her, then kissed her temple. "Herbs, Bella."

"Oh *my god*, so bossy."

"I'm kind of curious if you can identify them."

She squinted her eyes as she took a sip of her coffee. "Parsley."

"Cheater, you know there's parsley. What else?"

Bella buried her nose into the front of his sweatshirt, then sighed. "Rosemary. Basil. And...I think thyme and sage?"

He grinned.

"Did I get an A, chef?"

Wyatt ran both hands up her thighs and brushed his lips against hers. "You're amazing, you know that?"

"No, tell me again."

He grinned. "You're amazing, Bella."

Heat climbed up her arms and legs at his words, his lips caressing hers briefly before he leaned back in his chair.

"What time is this thing tonight?" he asked, sipping on his coffee from a mug with a logo that read *Institute of Culinary Education.*

"Oh shit," Bella bolted up from her seat. "Where's my phone?"

"Um, your bag, maybe?"

Bella ran for her tote bag near the apartment entrance

and rummaged through it. She relaxed when she realized there weren't any texts or calls. It was almost dead, but she had enough juice to type out a text.

BELLA

You are a badass woman capable of great things. I love you.

She didn't want to be too forward, knowing that Yaz might see the texts coming through.

Percy responded immediately.

PERCY

I love you too, babe. See you tonight!!

Bella sighed and walked back to the table. Before she could retake her seat, Wyatt caressed the back of her thigh and pulled her toward him, guiding her down on his lap instead. "All good?"

"Yeah," she said, placing her phone down on the table. "I wanted to wish her luck, make sure I wasn't missing anything in case she needed me."

"You guys are pretty close," Wyatt said. Not a question, but a statement.

She nodded, tracing her index finger along the line of his jaw, down to his lips. "She knows every side of me. The good. The bad. The peeling-me-off-the-floor-of-my-now-empty-apartment kind of ugly. And she's always been there for me. Even when I've been a crappy friend in return."

"I highly doubt you're a crappy friend."

She shrugged. "I am. Or at least I have been this past year. I want to make up for it."

Wyatt pinched her chin and drew her face down to his. "I want to know every side of you too, Bella."

Her stomach turned and her head started pounding, the

pressure almost too much to bear. She felt the over-whelming desire to jump and run. Which made no sense to her, especially after she told Wyatt that she wasn't going anywhere. Why the sudden need to flee *now*?

Then it all came to her, like autumn leaves softly falling from the trees, carpeting the sidewalk. There were things Wyatt needed to know about her, especially if she was about to take him to Percy's engagement party.

She fisted his white T-shirt. "Wyatt...I have things I need to tell you."

"Okay."

Bella kept a firm hold on his shirt. When she didn't let go, he softly pried her hand away and folded it into his, then squeezed. "Whatever it is, Bella, it's going to be okay."

She looked into his eyes. The man had shown her his deepest insecurity, the most personal side of himself last night. Why couldn't she do the same?

He drew circles on her palm with his thumb, waiting patiently.

"O-okay," she croaked. "So, tonight..."

He nodded. "Tonight."

"It's Percy's engagement party, but it's also..." Her chest tightened to an unbearable degree. She sucked in a long breath, then pinched her eyes shut. "Percy's brother is my ex-husband."

She didn't dare face his expression yet, so she kept her eyes shut as she continued. "I met Lon when I joined Percy one summer with her family in the Hamptons. Things progressed slowly and then...rather quickly."

Should I tell him why? She shook it off. One truth at a time.

"Clearly things...didn't work out," she explained, hoping her ambiguity surrounding the divorce was good enough for Wyatt. At least for now. Besides, he already knew a portion of the *why*; she wasn't being purposely evasive, she'd just never voiced the words out loud to anyone apart from her family, Percy, and a handful of doctors. "He'll be there. Tonight."

"With his fiancée?"

She exhaled and nodded, the pressure in her chest loosening, like the promising start of undoing a tight, impossible knot.

He squeezed her hand. "Hey. Look at me."

She finally did, blinking her eyes open. To her surprise he was smiling at her. It was a soft, caring, considerate thing.

"I'm guessing this is why you didn't want to go alone?" he asked.

"Yeah," she breathed. "It's the first time I'll see him since signing the papers. The first time I'll see them actually *together*."

He exhaled audibly. "That's a lot."

Her eyes widened. "It is. I'm sorry. I shouldn't make you do this—"

"*Bella*." His hands cupped her face, his thumbs moving across her cheekbones. "I mean that's a lot for *you*. I wish I'd known the context when you originally asked me. I wouldn't have said no so fast."

"You're an award-nominated chef now. You have a lot going on."

He shook his head. "None of that matters."

"Yes, it does. You *know* it does."

He didn't say anything in response, his thumbs moving to massage the backs of her ears.

"I want that to matter, Wyatt. You worked so hard to be where you are. You should never have to pick one over the other. Anyone who forces you to do that doesn't deserve you."

Visions of Matteo popped in her head... Of Claire. *Wyatt doesn't deserve you.* Bella wondered if there was more to that statement, if Claire knew how deep Wyatt's personal struggles went and how he'd been mistreated by women in the past. Did she really think Wyatt deserved better than her, or was she being protective after watching his past relationships fail over and over?

Wyatt pulled her face to his and kissed her lips softly. "Thank you for telling me."

She hesitated, wondering if she should tell him *more*. But something made her stop, made her hold back the rest of it. So, she simply nodded.

His hands trailed down her shoulders to her forearms. "Do they know I'm coming with you?"

"Percy said I could invite you, but I'm not sure if that was, um, communicated..." She thought about Katie at the Dreamscape location the night before. "Although, I think Katie might suspect something."

"Who's Katie?"

"Lon's fiancée."

He nodded, his eyes looking past her and through the porch door, thinking it through. "Your employee."

"Yeah."

Wyatt sighed. "Do I have permission to punch this guy in the face when I see him?"

"*Wyatt.*"

He chuckled, finally looking at her. "Okay, fine. But do I have permission to hold your hand the whole time, and squeeze your butt when no one is looking?"

She wrapped her arms around his neck. "Permission granted."

He grinned before he kissed her, his hands slipping underneath the fabric of her underwear at her hips. "Should we head to Park Slope and see whatever crazy thing Benji has made for you?"

She perked up. "Did he really make something?"

"I would assume so based on the thirty-four text messages I woke up to. I think he sent some pictures while he was working on it."

"Don't show me, I want to wait for the big reveal." She twisted her lips. "We'll need to stop at my place so I can change clothes. Maybe shower."

He gripped her hips. "Or...you could shower here."

She smirked down at him. "Yeah?"

Wyatt nodded, looking positively giddy.

Chapter Twenty

The two of them stood outside of a packed Gran Via. Stone Street was buzzing, tables crowded with fresh-out-of-college city goers, taking advantage of the two-for-one drink deals and shared fish bowls full of potent, cheap tequila.

"I can't believe this used to be my *place*," Bella grumbled.

Wyatt snaked an arm low on her waist and kissed her temple. "You okay?"

She let out a long exhale. "Have I mentioned how glad I am that you're here?"

He smiled and leaned down to kiss her again, this time on the lips. She froze, her lips barely moving, nervous about who might see them. The bar in front of them was packed with people from her old life, and for the briefest moment, she panicked, wondering if bringing Wyatt inside was a smart idea.

But he made the decision for her as he reached for her hand and led her through the doors of the bar.

Music blasted from the speakers. Friends of Percy and Yaz talked animatedly, the occasional cheer ringing above the constant chatter and noise from cocktail shakers, clinking glasses, and forks on plates.

"*BELLS!*"

Percy rushed over in a posh all-white getup, her low-cut sheer blouse tucked into stylish pleated trousers. Yaz was dressed in a matching white gown, with romantic off-the-shoulder sleeves and a sweetheart neckline. The sight of the two of them brought fresh tears to Bella's eyes as Percy threw her arms around her.

"Oh my *god*," Bella bellowed. "Congratulations. I love you both so much."

Yaz joined in, the three of them huddled in a tight hug. When they broke apart, Bella held her tears with the back of her hand in an attempt to not totally ruin her makeup.

"Let me see it," she demanded. "The ring."

Yaz held out her hand, a Toi Et Moi double diamond set in a rose gold band. "Two diamonds in the rough," she said wistfully, her eyes meeting Percy's.

Percy grinned and kissed her fiancée square on the mouth, then held up her hand to reveal a gold ring of her own, tiny diamonds dotted around the band. "Yaz insisted I need one, too. We picked this out after khastegāri with our families."

"Well, you do," Bella exclaimed, holding both hands as she examined the rings. "These are perfect for you both."

Percy kissed Yaz again before cocking her head, eyes flashing with muted excitement. "Chef Henderson?"

Bella felt his hand on her shoulder. "Call me Wyatt," he said. "Congratulations to you both. This is for you, compliments of one of my friends." He set down the box that he carried, vanilla whoopie pies half dipped in chocolate and vanilla tucked in neat rows inside.

Percy squealed. "No fucking way," she said. "Are these stuffed black-and-whites?"

Yaz's eyes went wide. Not at the box, but at Wyatt. "Oh my god, is this *hot chef*?"

Wyatt looked at Bella, amused. "Hot chef, huh?"

Bella's face flushed as she looked from Wyatt, to Percy, then back to Wyatt. "A nickname between the three of us."

His hand moved from her shoulder down to the small of her back. "And I thought I was the only one with a nickname."

Percy's eyes widened at their closeness, at his comfortable way of presenting the fact that *he had a nickname for her*. She grabbed Yaz's hand. "Drinks?"

"Yeah," Bella agreed. "Drinks would be good."

They squeezed their way to the bar and ordered blood orange mezcal margaritas. Bella scanned the crowd, looking for a particular tall figure with blond hair neatly slicked to the side. She doubted Lon's insistence on looking poised and put together had changed at all in their fourteen months apart.

Chilled drinks rimmed with chili lime salt were placed in front of them. They clinked glasses, but before Percy or Yaz could take sips, a couple Bella did not know interrupted them to share their well wishes. The women glowed as they retold the story of the proposal in the park.

"Settle a debate with us, will you?" the man asked Percy.

"Sure, I love having a strong opinion," Percy answered.

Yaz rolled her eyes and slapped her arm playfully.

"Whose last name will you take? Hamilton or Kashani?" asked the woman as she tapped her six-inch Louboutins.

"Hamilton?" Wyatt murmured. The bar was loud, but

Bella heard his unmistakable confusion. She pretended not to, her breathing growing thicker.

"We haven't even discussed it yet," Percy answered the man, completely unfazed. She slipped an arm around Yaz. "Besides having a sofre aghd, we have no other plans yet."

Satisfied, the couple walked away.

"Hang on," Wyatt spoke out loud to Percy. "I thought your last name was Chase?"

Bella gripped her glass tight.

"That's my pen name," Percy answered with a flick of her hand. "Not important. What is important is the fact that you just got nominated for a James Beard Award."

"No work talk tonight, you promised," Yaz insisted. "I'm sure hot chef will fill you in on whatever you want to know later."

"*Fine.* But later better come soon. I want the interview before everyone else."

"The interview is yours; I won't talk to another publication before you," Wyatt promised. He gently set down his drink, turning slightly to Bella. "Can we talk?"

"Bella! Darling!"

She felt like she was going to puke as Janice, her former mother-in-law, pulled her in for a tight hug. Bella patted her back a couple of times before stepping out of her grasp. "It's good to see you, Mrs. Hamilton."

Wyatt stiffened, then picked up his drink and took a long sip. Bella wanted the ground to crack open beneath her feet.

"Sweetheart, we are *family*. There is no need for pleasantries." She ordered a glass of Chardonnay with the bartender. "We missed having you at the house this summer! It didn't feel the same."

"R-right," Bella sputtered. "I missed you guys, too."

"Oh, do come next year," she pleaded. "There's no need to be afraid, we can all move past it—"

"*Mom.*"

Janice stopped mid-sentence at Percy's interruption.

"Leave her alone, she doesn't want to travel all the way to Amagansett to be traumatized," Percy said through gritted teeth.

Janice looked confused. "Traumatized? Why—"

Metal against glass chimed from a few feet away and disrupted her questioning. Yaz's parents stood at the front of the bar, their arms linked as they held up champagne flutes. Mr. Kashani began to speak, his thick Tehrani accent filling the space with a pleasant charm. Bella could barely concentrate though, her breathing ragged as she replayed the exchange over and over in her head.

Wyatt slipped a hand underneath the back of her navy-blue tank top. He pleaded for her to wear it after a not-so-quick, distracted visit to her apartment. "Take a deep breath."

Her eyelids fluttered shut.

"You're okay," he reassured her. His gaze flicked behind her, and in a flash, his grip tightened around the curve of her hip. "What does your ex look like?"

"Tall. Blond. Blue eyes. Like he was produced in a factory of finance bros."

He drummed his fingers against her skin, the feel of it grounding her. "Sounds like the guy who is currently glaring at me like he wants to throw me in a dumpster and set it on fire."

Bella stiffened and began to turn her head. But Wyatt caught her chin and tilted it up toward him instead. "Don't give him the satisfaction."

"It needs to happen eventually, Wyatt."

He hummed. "That doesn't mean we can't make him squirm a little."

To her shock, Wyatt dipped down and kissed her lips. It was chaste, quick, and polite. But it sent a clear message.

"I didn't think you were the petty type, chef," she teased. Her gaze remained locked on his, even though she desperately wanted to turn and catch Lon's expression.

"You're not letting me punch him, so this felt like a nice trade."

She rolled her eyes. "How are you doing? You okay?" she asked in return.

His brow creased. "Fine, but...I thought you told me you didn't end up changing your last name when you got married. But now I'm wondering if I imagined that."

Oh god. She was really, truly digging herself into a hole. Actually, scratch that. The hole was dug. If anything, she was surprised she didn't have blisters to show for all her work.

The applauding crowd and the happy couple's blissful kiss saved her from responding.

She downed the rest of her drink as the commotion died down. "I think I need to use the bathroom. Grab a plate of snacks?"

"Of course."

Bella pushed through the packed bodies and weaseled her way to the bathrooms. The line for the women's was long, but she didn't feel like waiting. She stepped into the men's and closed the door, sliding the lock in place. She leaned against the cool metal door and closed her eyes, taking sharp, ragged breaths until her inhales and exhales steadied.

After dabbing cold water on her face, Bella squared her shoulders and stepped out of the bathroom. She must have been in there for quite some time, because the line had already thinned except for one lone, tall figure.

Lon leaned against the opposite wall, arms crossed tight at his chest. His piercing blue eyes bore into her as she closed the door. His jaw ticked as he shifted, crossing a foot over the other as he took her in. "Bella."

Somehow in the stuffy, humid bar, she felt cold. She rubbed her forearms, not looking him directly in the eye. "Lon."

Fourteen months hadn't changed Lon much, as predicted. His physical appearance remained the same, but it was the other details she couldn't help noticing. Same button-down from Ralph Lauren. Same jeans. Same loafers and watch. Same broad shoulders and clean-shaven face and slicked-back blond hair.

"I see you still have a penchant for using the men's bathroom," he said, tipping his chin to the door behind her.

"There's no reason to have an empty bathroom sitting here when there's a line. We're New Yorkers, we're not built to be patient."

He didn't laugh at her attempt at a pithy joke. He simply stared at her, his jaw locked in place. She wondered if it was polite to wish him well on his engagement, then thought better of it. There was no reason to lie.

Instead, she blurted, "Where's Katie?"

"Chatting with my mother about floral arrangements." He exhaled. "Only so much of that I can take."

"Well, thankfully you didn't have to do that the first time around. Shotgun wedding and all that."

She regretted the words as soon as they came out of her mouth. But Lon seemed unaffected, especially when there was something else clearly on his mind.

"Who's the asshole?"

Bella frowned, no longer feeling cold. "Don't call him that."

"Fine. Who's the prick?"

"Dammit, Lon." She made a move to leave the hallway, but he blocked the entrance back into the bar, his six-foot-three build towering over her.

She stepped back. "Let me through."

"Who is he?"

She huffed. "A very nice guy I'm seeing."

"*Very nice*, huh?"

Bella felt her face flush. "Yes. He's...kind."

Lon grinned, but he didn't look happy. No, this was something nasty. Victorious.

She glared at him. "Enough. Don't you have a fiancée to get back to?"

"She's the one who told me to come back here."

Bella cocked her head. "Oh yeah?"

He pinched the bridge of his nose. Bella knew that look well. Lon was tired, likely from all-nighters at the office crunching numbers and dealing with clients. It was the reason for the dark circles under his eyes. Or at least that's what he used to tell her.

"Katie wanted me to check on you," he said, dropping his hand. "She said you don't talk to her at all besides work stuff, and she's worried."

"Of course I only talk to her about work stuff, it's awkward," Bella huffed out. "Also, why is she worrying? Why does she care? Why do *you* care?"

"Do you really think I ever stopped caring?"

"Yeah, I do." Bella took a deep breath, thinking about Percy and how she promised her she wouldn't make a scene. "Look, let's not do this, okay? Not here. You're...happy, or whatever. And I'm happy."

"Seriously? You're *happy*?"

"What's that supposed to mean?"

"With this guy? Come on, Bella. He's a rebound. You know you can do better."

"Oh yeah? With whom, someone like you? Look how well that turned out for me the first time."

A different voice from behind Lon broke the silence. "Everything all right back here?"

Lon straightened as he made room, then slumped when he saw who it was.

Wyatt shuffled around him and up to her, his hand curling around her wrist. "You good?"

"Y-yeah," Bella lied. "All good."

Wyatt nodded, then turned to face Lon, who looked at the chef like he was truly about to hunt for a container of lighter fluid. Wyatt held out his hand to her ex, his face expressionless. "Wyatt Henderson."

"Pleasure," Lon said, not returning his greeting or his handshake.

Wyatt lowered his arm to his side.

"And how'd you two meet?" Lon inquired.

Bella felt faint, or at least like she was about to cry.

"She came to my restaurant a few weeks ago with Percy," Wyatt explained.

Lon's brow raised. "Your restaurant, huh? Are you the cook?"

"I'm the executive chef."

Lon chuckled, looking amused, as if the title "executive chef" meant absolutely nothing.

"Wyatt worked as a chef at Hyacinth before he opened his restaurant," Bella blurted. "And he was just nominated for a James Beard Award. He's kind of a big deal."

Wyatt squeezed her wrist tight.

Lon looked unimpressed. "So you're not completely broke then."

"The twenty-five-hundred-square-foot apartment I own would have to agree with you," Wyatt replied, not missing a beat.

Lon ran a hand down his face, then let out an exasperated wheeze.

Wyatt angled himself toward her, sliding his hand from her wrist and down to her palm. "I think Percy wants to open the dessert, but she said she won't do it without you."

She interlaced her fingers with his. "Okay."

The two of them made their way around Lon, who stood there silent for a beat. But the silence didn't last long.

"You may enjoy screwing her now, but trust me, man, that will fade fast."

Wyatt's back went ramrod straight. He turned slowly, pulling Bella's hand to make sure she was standing behind him. "I don't know what the hell that means, but I would prefer you didn't talk about my girlfriend's sex life."

"*Girlfriend,*" Lon squawked. He attempted to move around Wyatt to get a look at Bella, but Wyatt took a side-step to block him. "Bella, are you out of your *fucking* mind?"

Conversations hushed around them as people stared at what was unfolding in front of them.

Lon's eyes narrowed at Wyatt. "I will talk about *my ex-wife's* sex life as much as I goddamn please. And while you clearly don't deserve my help, I'll do you a solid and let you know that it might be all fun and games now, but eventually she'll stop letting you in her bed. So you might as well cut ties before you regret it later."

"*LON.*"

It was Katie shouting at the other end of the bar,

standing next to a horrified Janice. The entire party was watching them now, no more merriment to drown out the noise.

Bella couldn't breathe. She searched the crowd for Percy, which didn't take long. The two figures in white stared back at her from the bar. Yaz rubbed Percy's arm in comfort, looking frightened. But Percy looked far from it. Her face was red with fury. And Bella couldn't tell if it was anger toward her brother...or the scene Bella promised wouldn't happen.

All eyes were on Wyatt as a small smirk inched up his right cheek, but he spoke so low only she and Lon could hear. "I guess if you're so invested, you'll be pleased to know who's name she screamed all last night."

Bella felt her face go hot, but certainly not as red as the color coming from her ex, whose cheeks were a startling shade of purple.

Wyatt tugged on her hand, the one he'd kept a firm hold on throughout all of it. "Want to get out of here?" he whispered only to her.

She nodded. The party watched in stunned silence as they made their way to the exit without a backward glance.

Chapter Twenty-One

He didn't say anything as he hailed a cab, except for listing off her address to the driver. She kept her gaze out the window as tears trickled down her face, angry at herself for plenty of things but mostly for letting Lon bait them and causing a scene. *Oh, god.* Yaz's parents' faces... *Percy's* face...

Wyatt slid across the seat, his thigh pressed to hers as he reached for her hand and folded it in his.

"You called me your girlfriend." The only words she could think to say came out wet and throaty.

"Because that's what you are."

She looked up at him. Shadows hooded his face, but she saw enough of him to know that he meant what he was saying.

"Are you sure?"

Wyatt wiped the tears from her cheeks with the sleeve of his sweater. "Yes. There's no way I'm letting you go."

"Even after everything Lon said?"

"It's obvious he's still in love with you, Bella. And he's hurting from whatever happened between the two of you."

She leaned her head on his shoulder and exhaled. She

wanted to say *he doesn't deserve to hurt*, especially after leaving her the way he did. But she also knew it was valid for him to feel that way, because in the end, she'd shut him out. Shut the world out.

Wyatt didn't push the matter further, not even after they made it to her building and climbed the three flights of stairs to her apartment, or as they got ready for bed and tucked into her sheets. The only other words he spoke were his whispers to *sleep well* against her hair as he cuddled her close. And despite everything that had happened that night, how much she'd disappointed her best friend, how angry her ex was, how humiliated she felt that Wyatt had to witness all of it... In his arms, she did sleep well.

BELLA WOKE up to a text from Percy.

PERCY

Joe's. 10am.

She sat up in bed and stared at it, wondering if she should say anything back, but there was no time. It was already nine-thirty, and if she wanted to get to the coffee shop in time, she needed to leave immediately. There were a number of Joe's locations across the city, but Bella knew which one Percy meant. It was *their* shop, the one across from their old apartment in the Village.

Wyatt sat up next to her. "Everything okay?"

"Percy wants to meet, I need to leave."

He nodded. "Okay. I can head home."

The *no* tumbled out of her fast. She was surprised by it. Embarrassed, she bit her bottom lip.

Wyatt smirked. "Then I'll stay. You go. I need to call Marissa and check in anyway."

She jumped out of bed, then threw him her apartment keys. "There's a bodega around the corner with decent coffee."

He tossed the keys back and forth in his hands. "When will you be back?"

She hobbled into a pair of jeans, then rummaged for a sweater. "Um. I'm not sure. I don't want to rush her."

She slipped her arms into her coat, then bent down to kiss him on the cheek.

He caught her chin and moved her lips to his instead. "It's going to be okay," he said, then gave her a lingering kiss. His touch calmed her. Made her want to hop right back in bed and never leave.

But...*Percy.*

She pulled herself away from him. "Be back soon."

PERCY SAT at their usual table, frowning at the untouched iced latte in front of her.

Bella slumped down in the seat across from her. "Hey."

Her friend looked up and seemed far from happy. "What the hell, Bells?"

"I'm so sorry, I didn't mean for us to cause a scene..."

"Yet you did. Don't get me wrong, my brother is *such* a dickhole," she continued. "But the way you guys just *left.* It set a damper on the rest of the night. Yaz was really upset."

Bella's face twisted with anger. "What was I supposed to do, Percy? Your brother was openly talking about my sex life to a crowd of people. You expected me to, what, stick around after that? Act happy?"

"Ugh, *I don't know*," Percy said, dropping a fist to the table with a dramatic *thump*. "All I know is that it ruined the night, and I'm really fucking pissed. But I don't know who to be pissed at. You're my best friend. He's *my brother*. He's hurt that you came with Wyatt."

She felt like she'd been punched in the gut. "You told me I could bring him."

"Yeah, because I thought you guys could act like adults, but clearly—"

"Clearly your brother can't be an adult," she interrupted. "I told him to let it go, but he kept..." She pressed the heels of her palms into her eyes.

Percy finally picked up her coffee and took a sip. "Bells, have you still not told Wyatt the truth?"

She dropped her hands. "What?"

"He seemed confused last night that my name was Hamilton."

Bella shifted uncomfortably in her seat.

"God, you still haven't told him?"

Heat crawled up her neck. "N-no. I...I am going to."

Percy huffed and shook her head in disbelief.

"I don't want to hurt him with the truth, P."

"Is that *actually* how you feel?"

Bella's eyes widened. "What does that mean?"

Percy crossed her arms. "Do you want to know what I think?"

She held out her arms, frustrated now. "*Please* enlighten me."

"I think you keeping things from him has nothing to do with Matteo or your grandfather or your family, and everything to do with the fact that you are too scared to let someone in again."

Bella looked down at her stomach, checking to make sure there wasn't actually a fist there, because the pain made her want to double over.

Percy carried on. "Wyatt honestly seems like a decent guy, Bells. He seems levelheaded and confident enough in himself that even a shit storm from my brother didn't faze him. I think he would understand if you told him the truth, but the fact that you haven't yet—that you kept *so much* from him—is really freaking strange. Why is that? Why can't you be honest with him?"

Tears trickled down her cheeks. Percy's sharp words exhausted her too much to wipe them away.

"I think you're scared that if he learns the truth...*all* of the truth...that he won't stick around. That he won't like what he sees."

"Percy..."

"Am I wrong?"

Bella looked down at her hands, Wyatt's words from last night playing out in her head. *There's no way I'm letting you go.* But what if he did? What if she finally told him everything about herself, and he decided it was too much? That *she* was too much?

"Whatever." She picked up her latte and stood up. "For one night—*one night*—I ask you to put aside your shit and be there for me. And you couldn't even do that."

Her chest burned as she watched Percy charge out of Joe's. Bella jumped up, giving zero thought to the people staring as she chased after her friend.

"You're not being fair," Bella bellowed after her once she'd cleared the door and stepped onto the sidewalk. "You knew last night was going to be hard for me. Having Wyatt there made it better."

Percy spun around, her face red. "I know, Bells. But still—"

"And everything would have been completely fine if your brother didn't say all that he said. He was vile."

"*I know!*" Percy's voice was louder now. "But he's my brother!"

"So that gives him the right to be awful to *your best friend?*" Bella yelled back, not caring if she was catching eyeballs. It was New York. No one knew who they were. "To tell the guy I'm seeing that I'm not worth the effort?"

"Well, if you keep *lying* to him, maybe you aren't worth the effort."

Bella froze. She felt the blood drain from her face.

Percy's face went white as well. "Bells, wait, I didn't mean that."

Tears welled in her eyes. "Fuck you."

Then she turned away from her best friend and left her on the sidewalk.

Bella took her time getting back to the apartment, anger bubbling in her chest. The two of them had fought before, but this felt monumental. Cruel.

She riffled through the thoughts swimming in her head, and by the time she approached her stoop on Ludlow Street, she'd made up her mind. She rang the buzzer of her apartment building. No one answered. She frowned, reaching for her phone to text him.

"Bella."

Wyatt walked up her stoop, two cups of coffee in hand. He was bundled up in the sweatshirt she commandeered weeks ago, tucked into his corduroy jacket, his hat covering his bed head. "Wasn't sure if you needed another one. I noticed you have quite a few of these in the morning."

She nodded but didn't say anything, eyes remaining on his chest.

He frowned. "Everything good with Percy?"

Bella fisted his sweatshirt in her hands and pulled him to her, kissing him on the lips. Wyatt let out a surprised hum, then melted into it.

"Wyatt," she whispered, her lips brushing his.

"Yes, *mia bella*."

She looked up into his eyes. "Come with me to supper tonight. Come meet my family."

He scanned her face. "Are you sure? I don't want to intrude."

"*Please*." She was not above begging right now. She intended to peel back the truths one layer at a time, her real last name being one of them.

"Okay," he agreed. "Should I pick up a bottle of wine?"

Lon was the only guy Bella had ever taken to a Sunday supper. It was two days after he proposed, and she'd wanted him there when she told Nonna. Mom and Dad already knew, she called them after she and Percy screamed incoherent sentences at each other on FaceTime. Lon had met her parents a handful of times, the occasional dinner or weekend brunch. But she had yet to bring him to a Sunday supper. Inviting him into their sacred family tradition felt *official*. Something he made sure of when he placed a three-carat diamond on her left hand.

The dinner had gone well. Nonna seemed pleased

about the engagement and the baby, pulling Bella into a fierce hug and pinching her cheeks lovingly. And yet...deep in her marrow, she'd suspected her grandmother didn't approve. Their meeting felt stilted and formal. Lon looked uncomfortable in his wooden chair at the small table, answering Nonna's questions politely but not offering much else. Later that night, after Bella spent a majority of the evening puking up her meal from the nausea, Lon held her tight and confessed *I love you, but maybe I shouldn't go with you on Sundays.*

It broke her heart, but she put on a smile and agreed, thanking him for trying. His world was so *different* compared to hers—chilled Sancerre shipped from France and meals cooked by private chefs versus cheap Italian red blends and bowls of grandma's homemade meatballs. She hadn't wanted to force him to commit to every week, and told him he could join her whenever he felt up to it.

That dreadful night played in Bella's head as she and Wyatt turned the corner onto Mulberry Street. The tourists from previous weeks had quieted down, the streets not as packed as the city rested before the chaotic holiday season ahead. Manhattan was always a zoo for the holidays, with throngs of people at Rockefeller and the markets at Bryant Park and Union Square. But it was a zoo she would happily step into again and again. Especially if it meant she would always end up back *here*, the colorful *Welcome to Little Italy* sign sparkling brightly above her.

She pulled on Wyatt's arm as she made her usual way down the street. If he was at all confused as to why she was taking him down this particular road, he didn't show it as he followed her. She peeked back at him, noticing the way he was eyeing the plates of pasta waiters brought out to guests sitting at enclosed patio tables.

They reached a vacant-looking Russo's. The pounding sound of her heartbeat increased to an insufferable decibel as she paused in front of it.

"You know, I never understood this place," Wyatt started.

"Oh yeah?" Her voice came out squeaky and unsure. She coughed to force it back to normal. "Why's that?"

"Weekends are always best for a restaurant. Sunday might not have as much traffic as Friday or Saturday, but it's still a lot more than usual. Especially for a tourist attraction like this place." He pointed to the dark deli through the glass. "People make weekend trips all the time to the city. Why close on one of the best days for business?"

Bella curled their joined hands up to her chest and shuffled closer to him. "Maybe because she wants to spend her Sundays making dinner for her family."

He frowned. She waited.

Realization slowly dawned on him. His face slackened, his jaw falling open.

"You were right last night," she admitted. "I didn't change my last name when I got married. It was supposed to be Hamilton, but...I couldn't bear the thought of changing it. Not when my family name meant so much to me. *Means* so much to me."

He blinked once. Then twice. "What's your last name?"

Her pulse skyrocketed. No matter what he said or what happened next, Bella knew there was no turning back.

She swallowed. "Russo."

Chapter Twenty-Two

BELLA FELT like centuries came and went as she waited for Wyatt to respond. Wyatt stared at her, bug-eyed, but no words sputtered out. She waited and waited, growing impatient. Desperate.

"Say something," she pleaded.

He blinked. "I knew I'd tasted those meatballs before."

She covered her mouth with her free hand. "It couldn't have been that obvious."

"I thought I was imagining it." Wyatt shook his head. "Mind you, I haven't had a Russo's meatball in years. But that's a taste you can't really forget. I was genuinely shocked at how similar they were."

"Because it's the same recipe," she whispered.

"Y-you know it," he said, bewildered. "Of course you know it."

"Only the Russo women know it. Nonna, Mom, and me."

"*Jesus.*" Wyatt dropped her hand and stepped back, raking a hand through his hair. "I said all that shit at the restaurant about your nonna..."

She chuckled. "Yeah. You did."

"Is that why you didn't tell me?"

Her stomach twisted. "Partially." Bella fisted and released her hands. "I wanted to see if Russo's meatballs lived up to the hype for a chef."

I also wasn't sure if you knew my family drama. She would get there eventually. Preferably not when she was about to take him into a den of Russos, where more than half of them didn't know the full extent *of* the drama.

"Well, they did." His eyes landed on a spot above her shoulder.

"Are you mad?"

He shook his head, his gaze now down at his feet. "No. I'm...taking it in, that's all."

She waited for another beat. The cold wind cut through the street, making her shiver. She crossed her arms. "Shall we..."

Wyatt's eyes shot up to her, even wider than before. "Go *in* there?"

"Yes. Well, kind of. Her apartment is above the deli."

His mouth fell open as he looked at the side door, then up at the warm lights coming from the apartment she'd visited all her life. "Holy..." Wyatt shook his head again. "I don't think..."

She felt her stomach turn violently, her mind on the last time she brought a man to Sunday supper. She shouldn't have forced him. She should have known.

Instead, he coughed, then looked down at his baggy sweatshirt. "I am not dressed properly for this."

A cackle escaped her chest. "For *Nonna*? She's probably wearing her slippers!"

"I should have put my button-up back on," Wyatt mumbled. He finally looked into her eyes, and she melted.

His gaze didn't look at all irritated or burdened. No, he looked...adorably frightened. Embarrassed. Like he wasn't worthy.

Bella grinned as she threw her arms around his shoulders. "Wyatt, it's going to be great. And she's going to love you."

Wyatt wrapped his arms around her waist, the tote bag holding a fresh loaf of ciabatta and a bottle of wine dangling on his shoulder behind him. His lips brushed against hers, then he pressed in again and lingered. He kept her firmly in his arms when he angled his head back.

"Bella?"

Her lips were humming, her brain fuzzy except for the singular awareness that this man had a way of obliterating all of her anxious thoughts with a single kiss. "Hmm?"

"She's...she's cooked for the *president* before."

Bella threw her head back and laughed, not caring that her voice rang through the surprisingly quiet street, harmonizing with the distant sound of music playing over at Cannoli King.

Wyatt chuckled along with her. "I'm not gonna lie, I'm really fucking nervous."

Bella nuzzled her nose with his. "Don't be. Sure, she's cooked for the president and her meatballs have been served at the Oscars—"

He groaned, tilting his head to the sky. "I did not know that. That's even *worse.*"

She poked his cheek. "She's also the most normal grandma in the world. Not pretentious. In fact, she's so protective of her recipes and her legacy that she won't expand or share it with any grocery chain. She's the most stubborn woman I know, but also the fiercest."

His eyes twinkled. "I see where you get it from then."

She pursed her lips. "The stubborn part?"

"The fierce part." Wyatt released a hand and pinched the air between them. "But maybe a tad stubborn sometimes."

"Fair. I should warn you, though."

His brow furrowed. "Warn me?"

"When she's faced with an attractive man like yourself, she pretends to be super Italian so she can kiss you on both cheeks."

Wyatt gave her a mischievous smirk. "Are you calling me attractive, *mia bella*?"

"I do call you *hot chef* behind your back." She felt a pang of despair when she said it, her mind on her best friend and their disaster morning, the screaming words they exchanged.

He swooped in and nibbled on her bottom lip. "I like when you call me that," he confessed.

"What? Hot chef?"

"No, just...chef."

She hummed. "Kinky."

He grinned.

She pushed out of his grasp. "All right, *chef*."

Wyatt moaned. "You're not playing nice."

She took his hands and walked backward toward the apartment door. She fished for her keys, eyes on him. "Ready?"

He whooshed out a breath. "Absolutely not."

Bella froze. "Do you—"

He cupped her face to stop her, closing her lips with his thumb. "No. I mean I'm not ready to meet one of the most iconic chefs in New York, but I am absolutely ready to meet your grandmother."

Melting. She was somehow melting again at this

precious man in front of her. Why had she been so afraid to tell him?

With that small kernel of bravery, she unlocked the door and dragged him inside.

"*PICCOLA!*"

Bella grinned as she stepped into the apartment, propped open as usual with a wooden chair. Nonna was by her place at the stove, feet tucked into slippers, the pink apron tied at her waist faded from years of use. Mom and Dad were already about their tasks, tossing the salad and setting the table. But both of them froze when they saw Bella wasn't alone.

Mom sucked in a breath. "Oh...my."

Flurries of panic trembled in her stomach. "I should have warned you first. I'm sorry. I—"

Nonna dropped her wooden spoon and scurried her way around the table. "Nonsense, my sweet. There's always room for another at my table."

Bella moved aside to make room for Wyatt as he stepped through the doorway. His neck was red and his cheeks flushed as he took in the tiny space and the tiny woman with poofy gray hair in front of him. "H-hello," he stammered.

Mom and Dad had yet to move from their spots, the two of them clearly still in shock.

"This is Wyatt. He's my, um..." Bella turned to look at his face while she said it. "My boyfriend."

Wyatt's tense shoulders relaxed.

Nonna clapped her hands together. "*Bellissimo.*"

"Oh thank god," Mom huffed, not even pretending to feign indifference with the goofy grin sliding across her face.

"Boyfriend?!" Dad squawked. "Since when?"

Bella tilted her head. "Since rather recently."

Wyatt squeezed her hand.

After discarding their coats, Nonna swung up to her tiptoes and grabbed Wyatt's cheeks. Then, predictably, kissed them both. "Welcome, handsome."

The color of Wyatt's cheeks saturated to an even deeper shade of red. "Thank you," he mumbled, looking adorably flustered.

She patted his cheeks with her hands, then hooked her arm with his and dragged him to the bubbling pot on the stove. "Come. Taste the sauce."

Bella unloaded the fresh bread and bottle of wine from his bag, watching in fascination as Nonna snatched a spoon from the silverware she kept in the empty tomato can on her counter. She dipped it in the sauce and lifted it to Wyatt, eyes expectant.

He delicately took the spoon from her and tasted the sauce. His brow furrowed as he thought about it for a moment. When it dawned on him, his face brightened.

"Wait—" Nonna stopped him with a hand. She dipped another spoon in the pot. "Bella?"

Bella made her way around the table and took the spoon, tasting as well. She knew it in an instant. Nonna had made this variation before.

She looked at Wyatt, then they both said it at the same time. "White balsamic."

Nonna clapped her hands again, then handed Wyatt her wooden spoon. "Stir. I'll help with the bread."

Wyatt nodded once, carefully inspecting the sauce he stirred like he was trying to decode it.

Bella slid the bread out of the bag and chopped it as Nonna minced the garlic. "You never help me with the bread," she murmured only to her grandmother.

"Hush, I'm watching," she teased, her eyes on Wyatt.

"When were you going to tell me she had a boyfriend?" Dad mumbled behind them. Mom chuckled, promising him that she would explain later.

Bella smiled, very much enjoying how flustered her family was at this interaction. How taken Nonna was with her chef.

Once the bread was in the oven, she opened the bottle of Montepulciano Wyatt purchased and handed him a glass.

His eyes were tense as he dipped another clean spoon in the sauce and brought it to his lips. "I want to know how she made this."

Bella shook her head. "Not the meatballs. Not allowed."

"No, I get that," Wyatt confirmed. "I mean the sauce."

"I roasted the tomatoes fresh this morning, drizzled in a white balsamic with oregano and basil," Nonna shared. "I usually use canned, but something about today felt...*special*."

She shook her head, bemused at how forthcoming her grandmother was being with him.

"You couldn't have possibly known this was going to happen, *Mamma*," Mom chimed in.

Nonna winked at Bella. "Call it intuition."

After serving up bowls, they settled down for supper, legs pressed against one another with an extra chair at the table. Wyatt didn't hesitate as they all joined hands, taking Mom's in one and Bella's in the other. Bella dipped her head with her family as Nonna recited her prayer, but she couldn't help a peek at the chef. His eyes were open and on her, his expression full of curiosity and admiration.

Nonna finished with an *amen*, the four of them signing the cross on their bodies as they always do. Wyatt watched her, then slowly repeated the action. Bella's eyes flicked toward her grandmother whose smile was so wide, she almost expected her to burst into song.

Dad cut right through the moment with a cough. "So, how did you two meet?"

"I made fun of his sad excuse for meatballs at his restaurant," Bella teased, bumping Wyatt's knee under the table.

Mom's brows shot up past her bangs. "Meatballs?"

"Restaurant?" Dad asked at the same time.

Wyatt looked back and forth between them, unsure of who to answer first. "I'm the executive chef at Tri. And my meatballs are...nothing like these."

"Because they're not even meatballs," Bella quipped.

He shook his head with a smirk as he picked up his fork.

"Second in the city, I hear," Nonna said.

Wyatt's brow furrowed. "You knew that?"

"Of course, my sweet. I like to stay informed about the competition."

"Competition? *What* competition? These are unmatched." He looked down at his plate. "These are the same meatballs, right?"

Bella cut open her meatball with her fork, the unmistakable steam swirling in front of her. "One and only."

If she wasn't mistaken, she heard a soft "*Jesus*" come from his mouth.

Mom laughed. "Somebody is starstruck."

Nonna leaned her elbows on the table. "I feel like we should be starstruck by you this weekend, Chef Henderson.

If I heard correctly, someone was nominated for a James Beard Award. Outstanding Chef, wasn't it?"

"You saw that," he drew out, sounding like he was in complete disbelief.

Nonna rolled her eyes, bemused. "A little birdie might have told me."

Wyatt smirked at Bella.

She raised a timid hand. "Guilty."

His smirk widened. Having him *here*, at this table, felt inconceivable to her. And yet, it felt like the most natural thing in the world.

He also knew what he was doing and, in a few moments, was able to pick up on the family dynamic. Nonna was nosy but also loved to talk and tell stories. Mom and Dad were anxious; Dad flustered that his daughter brought a man to dinner, Mom worried that Nonna was always doing too much. Wyatt eased in and out of conversation, asking questions about Russo's and the family.

"So, you do this every Sunday?" Wyatt asked. His plate was almost empty. He devoured it.

"Sure do," Mom replied.

"Except for the time Nonna was so sick with food poisoning from an event that she actually wouldn't let us in the apartment," Bella teased.

"We never talk about that dark day," Nonna grumbled.

"Otherwise, yes, we're always here," she continued. "Every Sunday."

Wyatt smiled softly. "That's really sweet."

Nonna leaned back in her chair. "I like him."

Her heart swooped at those words. Wyatt had been in Nonna's apartment for less than an hour, and already she was declaring she liked him. Bella was in a relationship with Lon for five years and he never got the same courtesy.

"*Mamma*, you just met him! Don't scare him away," Mom pleaded.

Nonna tilted her head, eyes on Wyatt. "Are you easily scared?"

"No, ma'am."

Bella was a puddle again.

Her grandmother gave him a sly smile. "Good. That's what I like to hear."

Wyatt slid a hand across her lap and squeezed her thigh, then traced his thumb along her tights. She placed her hand on his and sketched swirls and circles with her index finger, her lazy smile stretching with every dip into the soft skin between his knuckles.

"Have you always run Russo's on your own?" Wyatt asked Nonna.

"Until Angela started helping me, yes. I was married for a brief period of my life, and at the time I thought my husband would want to become my partner in all of this. But alas..." Nonna sighed, placing her fork down on her empty plate. Her eyes locked with Bella's across the table. "Some people aren't meant to be."

Wyatt asked more questions, how Russo's was started by Nonna's parents, what the kitchens were like at the White House, why she never wanted to franchise.

"*Blech*, it turns my family store into a business transaction. I'm not doing it for the money, my sweet."

He nodded. "That makes sense. I would have a hard time franchising as well."

"Really?" Bella asked.

"It changes things," he explained. "When it's one restaurant, you can focus on the staff and the space. You can play around with the menu without having to hold executive meetings or have to wade through corporate red tape with marketing and branding. The restaurant can also be helpful for the community around it, like working with the vendors we do or participating in events. Franchising changes all of that."

Nonna lifted a finger to Wyatt, but her eyes landed on Mom. "See?"

"It would be nice to take things off our plates, *Mamma*."

"Have you guys considered joining a restaurant group?" Wyatt asked.

The table went silent.

"Sorry," he rushed out. "I don't mean to pry..."

"What does that mean, exactly?" Nonna interrupted.

"Tri is part of this small restaurant group owned by a good friend of mine," Wyatt started.

Bella's throat felt like a tight fist was around it.

"The group can help with managing the business, so the chef"—he pointed to Nonna—"can focus on the food and the service."

"But we're not exactly a restaurant." Mom was understandably flummoxed.

"Sure, but a place like Russo's is established enough that I think any group would be willing to consider it in their portfolio. I know Matteo would probably hop on the opportunity."

Her palms started to sweat. She removed her hand from where she traced his and wiped at them with a napkin.

"Matteo?" Mom asked, brows bent.

"The owner of Metro Gastronomy Group, the one Tri is a part of."

Nonna squinted her eyes as she concentrated. Bella watched her carefully, aware that her mother still did not know about Matteo, that Nonna had yet to divulge any of that information. She wished she could knock that brain open and know exactly what she was thinking.

In a flash, Nonna's thoughtful expression shifted to something playful as she clapped her hands. "Definitely something to consider. Now, should we eat this tiramisu Bianca brought me today? She's testing out a new hazelnut flavor for the holidays."

They began to clear plates from the table.

Wyatt turned, his knees knocking against her legs. "Who's Bianca?"

"She owns the bakery next door," Bella answered with a wobbly smile. "Nonna always sells her treats at the store. Her Italian cookies are a wonder."

He leaned in close, his expression faltering. "Did I over-step?" he asked in a whisper.

She eyed her family. Her mother's shoulders were tense, but Nonna seemed completely unfazed as she loaded the dishwasher.

"No," she whispered back. She curled a hand around his wrist to reassure him. "Conversations about the deli always end this way. But you gave her something new to consider, and she didn't immediately say no. Honestly, that's huge for her."

"Are you sure?"

She nodded, then brushed a thumb across his pulse. "So, were the meatballs as good as mine?"

"Will you be offended if I say they were better?"

Bella laughed. "Not at all. I don't have the magic touch like she does."

"*Nonsense,*" Nonna butted in as she set down heaping serves of tiramisu in front of them. "You are magical, *piccola.*"

When her grandmother padded away to dish up more

of the dessert, Wyatt leaned over to her. "You *are* magical," he whispered.

Her face flushed as he kissed her cheek and pulled away.

"So, Wyatt, will you be joining us for more suppers?" Dad asked. "It would be nice not to be the only male at the table."

Mom nudged him. "You love it."

"Sure do, but it would be an added *bonus*."

Wyatt sighed. "Unfortunately I have to be at the restaurant Sunday nights. But..." He eyed Bella. "I don't know. I'll see what I can do."

She almost fell off her seat. Her stomach did all kinds of gymnastic tricks as she thought about how different this man was compared to what she had before. He genuinely *wanted* to be here. He said things like *you are magical* and continued on like it was completely normal to make her feel so cherished.

As they finished their desserts and said their goodbyes, after Nonna forced Wyatt to promise he would come see her at the deli on Tuesday during his day off, Bella wondered why she'd been so afraid to tell him who she really was. And why, even after everything that happened that night, she *still* felt incapable of telling him the rest.

Chapter Twenty-Three

Having to say goodbye after being in each other's pockets was a lot harder than Bella anticipated. Monday felt as gray as it was outside, and after a weekend away from the restaurant, she should've been more prepared for the near radio silence from Wyatt. They were back to quick calls before she fell asleep, the warm tone of his voice soothing enough to help her relax, even though she would do anything to hear the real thing. Rough, whispered in her ear, heat radiating from his chest as he tucked his body behind hers.

Wyatt fulfilled his promise on Tuesday and visited Nonna and Mom at Russo's. He sent her a picture of Nonna behind the counter, then another selfie of him with her. Bella set it as her phone background.

She sat at her desk and clicked through emails, trying to get a grasp on her reality and *focus* on all the work she had to get done, even though her mind and her heart were fixated on what was happening at Russo's. She needed to approve the videos for Dreamscape. Arrange a meeting at the office with a potential new client for a luxury spa in

Brooklyn. Schedule one-on-one meetings with her employees. But she couldn't concentrate on any of it.

Her door creaked open as Katie took a tentative step into her office. "Have you looked at the files yet?"

"No," Bella answered abruptly, not taking her eyes off her computer screen. "Still catching up on a few things. I'll let you know my thoughts by the end of the day."

"All right," Katie said, her voice timid.

She noticed the way Katie shuffled back and forth, still lingering in the doorway.

Katie coughed. "He's cute."

Bella finally gave Katie her full attention, but with daggers in her eyes. "Excuse me?"

"Your new guy," Katie rushed out. "He's...he's pretty good looking. And he seems nice."

Fury blazed in her chest as she bolted out of her seat, her hands fisted at her desk. Before she could think clearly about what she was doing, her words came out like a slap. "Do not speak about Wyatt, or look at him, or *anything* with him. Stay far out of his life, and out of mine. Do you understand?"

Katie's face went ghostly white.

"*Do you understand?*"

"Yes. I...I'm so sorry." Katie scrambled out of her office like a spooked cat.

Bella settled back in her desk chair and waited for the guilt to drown her after what she had done. Yet after seconds, then minutes, she felt nothing. She instinctively picked up her phone and tapped on Percy's name, then thought better of it, placing the phone screen-side down on the desk. Percy's words were still ringing in her head after that weekend, and she wasn't ready to talk to her. Even though she knew her best friend would have loved the way she finally stood up for herself.

So it was quite the surprise when a text from Percy came through hours later. It was an image of a box of black-and-white cookies from Zabar's.

PERCY

Your man came in for his interview and gave me these. He sure knows what he's doing.

Bella ignored Percy and texted Wyatt instead, but didn't hear back from him the rest of the night. He had a meeting with Matteo and Marissa to discuss the impact of the nomination. Restaurant-goers had been quick to snap up reservations following the announcement, and Wyatt was looking at a two-month-long reservation list on top of perfecting the winter menu. He seemed calm when they talked on the phone the next evening, but Bella wondered if he was downplaying how he felt. Was he protecting her from the truth of their reality? That despite the incredible weekend they shared, she might go without seeing him for days, maybe weeks?

When Friday rolled around, she felt the impulse to text Percy and ask her to meet for happy hour drinks at Dante. Yet each time she opened up their text thread, her friend's words played back in her head. So, she left the office late and grabbed takeout green curry at her favorite Thai spot on her way home. She ate it in front of her laptop as she binge-watched a show that she half paid attention to, the other half fixed on her phone and the call that never came through from Wyatt. She put on his sweatshirt, the smell of his herbs faded after wearing it almost every night to bed, then curled inside the covers and passed out.

The sound of persistent knocking on her front door woke her up at eight o'clock the following morning. She grumbled as she trudged out of bed, then hesitantly opened the door to find Wyatt on the other side. His hair was neatly tucked into a hat, but the rest of him looked disheveled.

"Wyatt?"

He burst into her apartment and grabbed her, dropping the bag in his hand to the floor and claiming her mouth with a hunger that couldn't wait. The door slammed behind him as he backed her up against the wall, hands roaming over her body, mouth trailing from her lips and down her neck.

"Hi to you too," she teased.

His lips made their way back up to hers with a sweeping intensity that had her gasping for air.

"That was the longest week of my life," he admitted once he finally pulled back.

"Me too," she whispered.

He tore the sweatshirt off her body and carried her to bed, then showed her how much he missed her with his hands and his mouth. She slipped her fingers into his joggers, desperate to reach for him. But he slowed and removed it, kissing her wrist. "Not today."

Would the day ever come? The invasive thought didn't last long as his fingers returned to all of the spots she taught him, all the places that made her cry for more. Later, when she was slack and spent, they remained in her bed, except for the couple of minutes Wyatt padded to the kitchen in his boxer briefs to make coffee and retrieve the food he brought. They munched on pumpernickel bagels with veggie cream cheese and shared about their weeks, skin touching skin, wrappers eventually discarded to the floor, coffee mugs left on the nightstand. They didn't bother moving from their cocoon the rest of the morning.

Wyatt held her close to his bare chest, a hand lazily running up and down her arm. "You haven't spoken to Percy yet?"

She shook her head. Bella had briefly mentioned to Wyatt about their fight, but didn't give him too many details. Thankfully, he didn't push for them either.

He kissed her temple. "I can't believe you told Katie off like that."

Bella sighed. "I know. It wasn't polite or professional of me. But I felt so *angry*. It all came tumbling out."

He kissed her forehead. "Sounds like someone got protective."

That fury burned in her chest again. "I..."

Wyatt curled a hand around her neck, then angled her to him. He scanned her face. "Bella."

Her throat went dry.

"I meant it, you know. I'm not letting you go. Not seeing you this entire week was madness. I spent every night cooking for customers who fawned over our nomination. But the entire time, my mind was on you."

He kissed her shoulder. "I thought about the twin freckles you have on this shoulder." He cupped a hand underneath her left breast. "I thought about how these feel in my hands." His other hand slipped from her neck and down her back. "I thought about the way your back arches when I touch you."

Desire clung to her, but he didn't continue. Instead, he tucked her even closer to him. "I couldn't stop thinking about your family and if I could somehow finagle my way out of work on Sunday nights so I can watch you decipher the ingredients in your nonna's sauce. I thought about your witty comments and how kind and patient you are with everything I'm going through. I thought about the satisfied little smile on your face when you cut open a meatball, and the little crease that pops up in the center of your forehead when you're thinking hard about something when you think no one notices."

He kissed her lips softly. "I notice. I notice everything about you, and I'm greedy for it."

She rolled on top of him and kissed him with enthusiasm. He kissed her back in earnest, hands on her backside, one dipping between her legs. She let him explore her again, blissfully unaware of the time and how much longer she had with him before he was due back at the restaurant.

But that time eventually came, and at a painstaking slow rate, Wyatt got dressed. "I know it's three weeks away, but are you free on November 16th?"

"Let me check my empty calendar," she chaffed, snatching the sweatshirt he came in and putting it on before he could, enjoying the fresh scent of him.

He smiled, reaching for the one he peeled off her body earlier. "Want to be my date to the awards dinner?"

She sat up, eyes like saucers. "You want me to come with you?"

"That's kind of the whole point of asking someone, right?"

She playfully slapped his arm. "Smart-ass."

He chuckled. "Of course I want you there, *mia bella*."

"Will Matteo be there?"

"Yes," he responded with a nod. "Claire, as well."

She swallowed. "Oh?"

"Marissa, too," Wyatt continued, unaware of her change in demeanor. "I think she invited Benji."

"Are they..."

He rolled his eyes. "*Oh* yeah. They try to hide it from me, but I'm not dumb. It's been going on for years."

"Why do you think they're hiding it?"

"Could potentially make things messy, or maybe that's what they think. I don't know. At some point I should probably ask him about it."

Bella tugged on the hair tucked behind his right ear. "Why does he call you Asshole?"

He sighed. "Because during my time at Hyacinth, I kind of was. I had one goal, and nothing else mattered. I'm surprised he still wanted to be my friend after all of that."

"Is it so bad to have goals?" she whispered.

"No, but neglecting friendships? Relationships? At that point, I don't think any goal is worth it." He shimmied closer to her. "I want to do things differently this time. I want to be everything you deserve."

Panic built up in her chest as he dropped kisses down the line of her jaw to her neck. "Wyatt."

"Hmm?"

"I don't want you to feel like you have to give up your goals for me."

He stopped his pursuit and sat up.

"You worked so hard to be where you are. You were nominated for this really big award, and I would hate for you to feel like you can't prioritize it because of me."

Wyatt looked down at his hands.

"I don't think that makes you an asshole," she continued.

"Stop," he said curtly.

She inhaled, sucking in her lips.

"I used to be...*obsessive*, Bella. Nothing or no one would stand in my way," he explained. "But now? Everything about my life is different. This type of award is a different caliber of achievement. The restaurant culture I'm trying to create promotes a healthier work-life balance. I do my best to set boundaries and not obsess over all of the details like I used to, and instead focus on the people and the culture. I worked hard to repair my damaged relationship with Benji. And I will keep working hard to make sure I never do that to a relationship again."

His expression when he finally looked at her was one of clarity. "The fact that you're forcing me to prioritize myself and my goals is proof enough that you are worthy of my devotion. You know me on a level that very few actually understand, and yet you still choose to spend time with me. Some days I feel like I'm going to wake up and discover all of it was somehow a dream, a glimmering hope of something that I never deserved."

Bella hugged her knees and let out a breath, unsure of what to say. He was right; he let her in on the deepest parts of himself, trusted her to hold them carefully and to care for him. He felt like he didn't deserve her because of his earlier actions? Well, she knew that deep down, she wasn't deserving of *him*. He took the news of her real last name and her famous-adjacent life with reverence and grace. But would he be the same with the rest of it?

Wyatt dipped his hand into the pocket of his jacket. A flash of silver caught her eye as he opened up his palm, revealing a small key.

"It's for my place," he confessed. "Things at the restaurant are about to get nutty, and I know it would be a lot, but if there's ever a night you want to crash at my place so we can see each other, I would..." He trailed off, his eyes on her lips. He sighed. "I would really, really like that."

Before she could respond, he dropped the key in her hand, then asked for her phone. Her body moved of its own volition, watching, bewildered, as he entered his credit card information into her Uber app. "Order a car on me whenever you want to come."

He kissed her forehead and stood up, tucking his hair back before putting his hat on.

"Wait."

He froze.

"Will you still call me and wish me a good night? Even if I'm at your place." She felt her cheeks flush. "I know it's silly, but I like hearing your voice and..."

Wyatt cupped her face in her hands, a smile traced across his lips. "Of course, *mia bella*. Of course."

Chapter Twenty-Four

THE FIRST TIME Bella took him up on his offer was the following Wednesday night. She texted him to make sure it was okay at first. His reply was immediate and simple.

So she packed an overnight bag and headed for his place, where she let herself in. After changing into her sweats and her favorite Russo's T-shirt, she made her way to the kitchen to see what she could scrounge for dinner. When she opened the fridge, she found containers of her favorite takeout orders. Thai green curry. Vegetable lo mein. Mattar paneer.

I shouldn't even be surprised, she thought to herself as she popped a piece of naan in the toaster, the mattar paneer heating up in the microwave.

He fulfilled his promise and called her to wish her goodnight. Four hours later, cozy and tucked into his bed, she felt the duvet move as his body pressed up to her, smelling of soap and minty toothpaste. Wyatt folded her into his arms and kissed her cheek, droplets of water from his wet hair trickling down her face.

"I could end every day like this," he whispered in her ear.

She hummed, too exhausted to respond as she slipped into a dreamless sleep.

Her alarm went off on her phone at six-thirty, the sky still dark and waiting for the sun to wake up, too. She reached to silence it.

Wyatt's grip on her waist tightened. She grinned and turned toward him, running a finger down his cheek. "Morning, chef."

He smiled back, his eyes still closed. "Hi."

They remained there for another half hour, talking about his night at the restaurant, the clients she was working with, the awkward silences between her and Katie at work, his winter menu that he still didn't have down. She took a shower and got ready for work as he made her coffee. They bundled up in their coats and scarves and hats, the weather in New York finally cold enough for necessary layers. He handed her a to-go mug of coffee, another in his hand as they made their way to his car so he could drive her to work.

Their nights quickly evolved into a routine, and soon she found herself sleeping in Wyatt's bed more often than her own. Tuesdays he cooked her dinner, the two of them staying up well past midnight as they ate, drank wine, and spent their evenings cuddled on the couch watching classic New York rom-coms—*You've Got Mail*, *27 Dresses*, *When Harry Met Sally*—or tucked under warm blankets as they sat out on his back patio, their faces illuminated by the soft lights of the skyline. Originally she told herself she didn't need to go every night. But after waking up in her bed and not in *his* arms, she crumbled. Soon, she was spending every weeknight at his apartment.

They continued on like this for weeks, waking up early in the mornings so they could have moments together before he took her to work, then Saturdays for days out in the city. He took her to the Brooklyn Botanical Garden to see the fall foliage and a food truck tour at Smorgasburg in Williamsburg. She slowly started leaving some of her clothes at his place to make things easier. Sweaters, jeans, work dresses, and pajamas took residence in his closet and dresser. Extra hats and scarves he gave her to borrow ended up at her place, their apartments a comical mix of mismatched clothes. Keeping track of what was where didn't matter much when they spent a majority of their time rarely clothed at all.

Wyatt became the expert at mastering her needs, knowing exactly what made her feel good and executing it with enthusiasm. She was consumed with giving him that in return; he even let her explore and touch him, hoping her hands would spark that arousal. But her exploration never lasted long before he was shaking his head and telling her they would try another night. She didn't push it further... but she really wanted to.

Sunday suppers were always the hardest. Wyatt was unable to find an easy way to make it back to dinner with her family, so Bella went alone. She told herself that she should be used to this after years of going without Lon, and then again when there was no Lon. But being with Wyatt felt different to her, and for the first time in her life, she sat at her nonna's table on Sundays and wished she could be elsewhere.

She was shocked when it first dawned on her. Her family's words sounded muffled in her ears as her mind drifted to thoughts of Wyatt at the restaurant, wishing she could be back in his bed and in his arms. The pang in her heart from that vision felt completely foreign, and she poked at it for days, wondering what it meant.

Could it be love? She thought about what Nonna had said to her weeks earlier. *You are in love with the chef, I can see it.* Yet this deep feeling she had for Wyatt felt like something different. Or at least something new compared to how she felt for Lon. Was it possible for love to have a different kind of feeling for different people? With Lon, she'd felt comfortable. But with Wyatt? She felt a burning need to be around him, to hear his voice, to touch his skin.

"I don't like being apart from you," she admitted to him one Thursday night. It was late, and she should have been fast asleep, but she was too anxious to see him. It was one in the morning when he'd finally crawled into bed.

"I don't either." He kissed the corner of her mouth. "I know it would be crazy to ask you to move in, but you make me crazy, Bella."

His confession didn't quell her anxiety the rest of that night or the following morning. Unable to focus on work and exhausted from constantly evading Katie, Bella decided she was done with the distance between her and her best friend. So she took a long lunch break, made a pit spot to grab something at her apartment, then took the train up to Union Square to the *Taster* offices.

Percy emerged from the elevator ten minutes later. Her approach was timid as she made her way across the lobby. "Bells?"

Bella opened up her tote and pulled out a stack of magazines, then held them out to her friend. "Remember these?"

Percy's mouth twitched.

She took that as a good sign, so she continued. "Blue

tabs were for you, yellow for me. We picked out everything we wanted for our dream weddings. Gowns and bridesmaid dresses, floral arrangements, swanky New York weddings on rooftops and big beach celebrations on the sand. We dipped into our grocery budget that week and lived on instant mac and cheese, all so we could dream up our future weddings. You were going through that horrible breakup with Carly, and I was in this weird place with Lon because he kissed me for the first time after visiting us that weekend. We wanted something that felt concrete. A *plan*."

"I remember," Percy murmured, taking the stack of magazines from her.

"I don't know if you want any of these anymore, I mean it's not like my wedding followed any of these ideas." She shrugged. "But we can dive through them, maybe even see if there's anything worthy in our cringy Pinterest boards. Whatever you want."

Percy placed the stack of magazines down on a bench beside them, then looped her arms around Bella's shoulders. "Bells. I'm so sorry. I shouldn't have said what I said, and I should have been kinder to you. I knew that night was going to be a lot after everything that happened."

"I know," she whispered back. "I'm sorry all of my messy drama keeps getting in the way."

"I'm sorry my brother is a trash bag of a human who made things messy."

"I'm sorry that I ignored you for weeks."

"Yeah, I hated that. Let's never do it again."

"Never." Bella's shoulders drooped. "Wyatt told me he wants me to move in with him."

Percy pushed back, her eyes like saucers. "*What?*"

"He said it would be crazy to do it, even though he wants to. And I realized I can't make this big decision to move in with my boyfriend simply because I'm lonely. I need you."

"I need you, too, Bells."

"Are you free for lunch?"

Percy looped her arm through hers. "Only if you're buying."

Bella grinned.

"But I do have one stipulation," her friend added.

"Literally anything."

"I require every juicy detail about the fact that your *boyfriend* is officially New York's hottest chef."

She burst out laughing. "Hottest chef?"

"Yeah, some chick from *Taster* wrote an article about his nomination and it went viral online."

Bella held a hand in front of her face.

Percy smirked at her deviously. "Oh, we have *so* much to catch up on."

PERCY WASN'T KIDDING. Her feature on Wyatt was sweeping, from his days at ICE to his past at Hyacinth, leading up to his relationship with Matteo and opening the restaurant. She used phrases like "short king" and "yes, chef" and the internet ate it up.

"What's a short king?" Wyatt mumbled to her when they met up for coffee. He journeyed to her office building on a Monday afternoon after he met with Matteo to discuss their hectic new schedule. They were less than a week out from the awards ceremony, and the article launched them into a whole new kind of frenzy.

She kissed his cheek. "A man who is so sexy, even his height couldn't change the appeal."

He frowned.

Bella laughed and kissed him again. When the barista announced their order—flat white, pumpkin spice latte—and Wyatt stepped up to the counter, Bella noticed a giggling group of women in the corner of the shop, sneaking pictures of him on their phones.

Her stomach twisted as he handed over her latte.

"You okay?" he asked, unaware of the pictures and the attention he was getting.

She squared her shoulders to him. "If things are about to get really crazy at the restaurant, what will that mean?"

He frowned. "For you and me?"

She nodded.

Wyatt banded an arm around the small of her back and pulled her close. Bella heard soft sighs and swoons from the corner.

"I don't know," he whispered. "But we are going to make it work, okay?"

"Promise?" she whispered back.

He nodded, kissing her cheek.

Pictures of them went viral on Instagram an hour later.

BELLA SLICKED her hair back into a low ponytail, then twisted it into a knot, giving the teardrop pearl earrings she wore the attention they deserved. Her black silk dress clipped at her neck in a halter, hugging her waist and draping down her legs, a slit running up her right thigh. The back of the dress was low, dipping below the small of her back, making it impossible to hide any kind of bra. So she decided to go without.

Her buzzer sounded for the front door. She slipped into her black suede pumps as she pressed the talk button. "If this is the paparazzi, go away."

"Ha ha, very funny," Wyatt said back, his voice gravelly through the speaker.

She let him in and unlocked her front door before making her way back to the bathroom. She swiped a soft pink gloss on her lips, then smiled as she turned to examine her handiwork.

He knocked on the door.

"It's open!" she called, heading into her bedroom to grab her purse. When she stepped into the living area, she froze.

Wyatt was every bit deserving of the title of New York's Hottest Chef. His black tux was cut perfectly to his lean build, a black bow tie loosely tied at his neck. His hair looked soft, tucked back smartly behind his ears.

He didn't seem to notice her ogling, because he was too transfixed himself. His gaze roamed slowly over her dress, his green eyes dimming as his pupils grew wider and wider. He sucked in a breath and covered his mouth, shaking his head.

Reveling in his reaction, she slowly spun. When her back was in his view, she gazed toward him and blinked.

A curse slipped from his mouth, the word too raspy for her to make out.

"Is this good enough for you, chef?" she teased.

"*Fuck*," he cursed again. He placed his hands on his hips and looked down at his pants. "This is the most inconvenient time to have a boner."

Thrill zipped down her spine. She stole a glance at his suit pants, then to the time on her microwave. "I think we'll be fine for ten minutes," she rushed out with a breath.

His car keys clattered to the floor as he crossed the room, removing his tux jacket and tossing it to the couch as he made his pursuit. "Make that fifteen."

Chapter Twenty-Five

She grinned as he closed the distance between them. Wyatt slid his hands down her back and cupped her ass, squeezing hard as he consumed her. His kisses were languid and deep, his hands moving up her waist as he guided her back into her room. He tipped her down and placed her gently on the bed, then climbed on top of her.

"I want you to know," he breathed, running his hand along the silk of her dress, up to her stomach and to her ribs. He cupped her breast, brushing his thumb across the peak. Her back arched in response. "I feel this deeply for you, all the time. Even if I can't show you..."

"I know," she whispered. She reached for him, palming him over his suit pants, humming with satisfaction at *finally* being able to feel his length.

He slammed his eyes shut and dipped his head, taking a shaky breath as his lips brushed her shoulder.

She smirked. "Does that feel good?"

He huffed a laugh, and it warmed her skin. He sketched a line with his lips from her collarbone up to the clasp of her dress high on her neck. "Yes. So good."

She ripped off the suspenders on his shoulders and unbuttoned his pants, sliding her hand into his boxer briefs, then ran her palm up and down before gripping him tight and tracing her thumb over his tip.

"*Bella*," he moaned. He propped himself up with his elbows, looking into her eyes. "I'm...not going to last long."

She twisted toward her nightstand and tugged the drawer open. "Then let's make it count."

Wyatt slipped a hand underneath her dress and trailed up her thigh, his fingers finding the lace she specifically chose for tonight. He muttered something unintelligible as he peeled it off her. He held her thong up to inspect it, his cheeks flushed.

"They're red." He swallowed. Pocketed it. "I will never stop thinking about this."

She giggled, then ripped at the wrapper in her hand with her teeth. She slowly rolled the condom on him, relishing the way his muscles tensed with each touch, how his veins popped in his neck.

"*Mia bella*," he breathed. He pushed her dress up past her waist as he kissed her temple, his thumb drawing a line up her inner thigh, then brushing slowly up her center. He pressed his fingers low, right at the spot he knew *well*.

She was already wet, her desire a needy thing. "Faster," she demanded.

The pace of his circles sped up, the pressure of his thumb making every nerve in her body throb with *want*.

"You are exquisite," he whispered. He dipped one finger inside her, then two, pumping at an excruciatingly slow pace that made her want to scream, his thumb still circling her clit and making her tremble. "Every single inch of you is a work of art."

"*Wyatt*," she sighed. "I need—"

She didn't finish her sentence as he removed his fingers, then *finally* slid into her.

Wyatt froze, his jaw clenched. The stretch of him inside of her made her feverish and impatient. She gripped his shoulders and rolled her hips against his, and he let out a guttural moan.

"I won't be able to—I'm not—" he stuttered.

She paused to look at him, understanding what he was saying. They were finally together in the ways that she hadn't stopped thinking about for weeks now, yet he looked at her like he was about to let her down.

Bella wrapped her arms around Wyatt's shoulders. "Don't think too hard. Just be here with me."

He brushed the back of his hand down her cheek, then reached down to lift one of her thighs, positioning it around his waist. He slipped his other hand underneath her back, moving it up so he could cradle her neck.

Then he moved a steady, slow, delicious rhythm. Every press. Every pull. His movements were unhurried and thorough as he pressed deep into her.

A muffled *"Yes, more"* tumbled from her lips. His rhythm moved faster, his grip on her thigh bruising as he finally let himself go.

She opened her eyes and watched him as he took her, entranced by the relief and the pleasure on his face, the burning in her belly building and building with each stroke. She slipped a hand underneath his shirt, needing to feel his warm skin against hers as she gripped his back. He dropped his head and grazed his teeth along her neck, licking the soft spot underneath her ear.

"I love you," he whispered.

His confession had her losing all train of thought as the burning grew powerful. She closed her eyes and moaned, right on the tip of her orgasm, waiting to crest over.

The sound of her noises sent him over the edge. He cried out, slamming all of his weight into her with one last thrust. She clenched to give him more pressure, and he groaned again, his hands tight on her skin.

She blinked, looking up at Wyatt and his flushed cheeks. He leaned in and kissed her forehead, trailing kisses down her face to her neck. He wouldn't look at her.

"Did you...?" he asked.

"No," she whispered.

He exhaled audibly. "I would keep going if I could, but I don't think...I could maybe help you out another way?"

She shook her head, then kissed his cheek. "Tonight is about you."

His lips were back on hers. Not hot or wanting, but slow and methodical. Loving. Giving.

Chapter Twenty-Six

Bella stepped out of the bathroom then paused. Wyatt had his suit jacket back on, but his hair was ruffled from her hands. He sat on the edge of her bed, eyes cast out the window.

Tears streaked his cheeks.

She took a seat close to him, tucking a foot underneath her as she placed her knee against his leg. He didn't move to touch her back, his hands still clasped in his lap.

He sniffed and wiped his tears with the back of his hand. "This is why I don't get intimate with anyone."

He still wouldn't look her directly in the eye after what they did.

"Are you embarrassed?" she whispered.

He nodded his head, his gaze still out the window. "It's really fucking embarrassing, Bella. It's emasculating to not be able to give the woman I love the intimacy she deserves, watching all of my failings happen in real time."

There it is again. Love. Those three words slipped out of him at the peak of his passion, a soft confession in her ear. *I love you.*

She took a deep breath. "I think there are many ways to be intimate, Wyatt. Sex is one of them, but I don't think it's fair to say that's the only way. You have shown me intimacy in deeper, more meaningful ways than I have ever experienced in my life. You don't have to take me to bed to make that happen."

He *finally* turned his head and looked at her. She brushed the tears from his red-rimmed eyes.

"Did you mean what you said?" she asked, her voice soft.

He nodded. "I have felt that for you since the night I first cooked you dinner, the night that I kissed you. But I could never get the words out. I was afraid it was too soon to feel this way, and that I might scare you off."

She hooked her arms around his neck, giving in to the feeling she could no longer pretend didn't exist. "Wyatt, I love you too."

He brushed a hand along her thigh, his gaze following his trail. "You promise you're not just saying that to make me feel better right now?"

"On my honor," she said. She snatched his hand and placed it on her heart. "You may think this moment wasn't right to say you loved me, but for me, it was perfect."

He pulled her into his lap and kissed her neck, then her temple, then pressed his nose to her cheek. "Every woman I've been with has given up on me by this point."

"I won't give up on you," she confessed to him. "I don't want to give up on us."

"*Mia bella,*" he whispered, dropping soft butterfly kisses on her jaw. He massaged the back of her neck as he checked the clock by her nightstand.

"We better, um—" He reached into his pocket and pulled out her underwear. "Do you want this back?"

She hopped off his lap and grabbed his free hand, pulling him up. She plucked the red, lacy thong from his grasp and slid it back into his pocket. "Keep it." She winked. "It can be your good luck charm."

SNOW BEGAN to trickle down as their Uber pulled up in front of the Whitney Museum. Wyatt stepped out first, holding out a hand to help her climb out of the car in her heels. He swept her up into his arms and kissed her on the mouth. A smile traced her lips as she reached for his bow tie and straightened it, then smoothed his hair. "You ready for this?"

He kissed her again. "I am, but only because you're here with me."

"You're *obsessed* with me."

"You have no idea."

Her heart fluttered as he took her hand and led her inside. The entrance was abuzz with guests in tuxedos and gowns, lingering scents of cologne and Chanel No. 5 in the air. Wyatt kept a firm grasp on her hand as they made their way to the coat check. Once her coat was tucked away, he slipped a possessive hand low on her back as they beelined to the elevator bank that took them to the banquet hall on the third floor. She hoped the rest of their group wouldn't give them too hard a time for being late.

The space was covered with circle tables lined with satin, each one adorned with romantic floating candles and yellow chrysanthemums in bowls of water at the center. Soft jazz trilled from a band in the corner as high-brow guests mingled with flutes of champagne in hand, sauntering over to their assigned tables.

"Chef Henderson!"

Wyatt grinned at the familiar booming voice. Matteo wore a navy tux with black lapels, his dark hair cut shorter than the last time she saw him, his beard freshly trimmed. His caramel eyes danced with delight as he held out a palm to Wyatt, the two shaking hands in a move that felt too formal at first. Matteo nimbly fixed it by pulling Wyatt in for a quick hug.

Bella's throat tightened as she scanned the crowd, noticing Matteo was alone. "Is Claire not here?"

"Haley Jo left school early today with a nasty cold, so she stayed behind."

Sweet relief warmed her chest, reminding her that at some point, she would have to face Matteo's wife...and the rest of it.

"I decided to invite someone else to take her spot, though," Matteo continued. "A new business partner, so play nice."

Wyatt raised his brow. "You invited a new partner to an award's ceremony?"

He scratched his beard. "Let's just say she's a *big* client. I need to impress her."

Before Wyatt could ask another question, Matteo turned his smile on her. "You look radiant, Bella."

She blushed. "Thank you."

Pleased, Matteo stepped away. "Champagne?"

They nodded and watched him leave. Wyatt tucked his thumb inside the fabric of her dress at her lower back and kissed her shoulder. "You do look radiant."

"Be careful," she teased. "There's nothing underneath there."

She felt his smile on her skin. "Oh trust me, I'm well aware."

A firm hand to Wyatt's back made him jump upright. Benji howled in response, his white suit making the red in his burly beard even more prominent.

"Enough PDA, love birds," Marissa said, slinking around him. "It's making me sick."

Marissa looked completely transformed from her chef getup, her svelte figure tucked into a tight cornflower blue dress that drifted out at her knees like a mermaid. Her eyeliner was even more prominent, but this time there were brushes of sparkling glitter at the corners of her eyelids. She tucked her hands behind her and stood up straight. "How are you doing, chef?"

"Fine, chef. Thank you."

"You're such a liar," Benji jested. "I know this cool facade of yours is a farse, Wyatt. You're probably shitting yourself."

Marissa pointed a black polished finger at him. "If you can't act professional, I'm taking you home."

The corner of Benji's mouth twitched. "Tempting offer, little one."

Wyatt gave Bella a look like, *See?*

She smirked back at him, then kissed him on the cheek. "I think the chef needs a drink."

"Agreed," Marissa said, turning from them. "Let me get a waiter."

Wyatt placed a hand on Marissa's shoulder. "Hey, chill. We're not in my kitchen. We're here to celebrate."

Marissa conceded, her shoulders melting down into a more relaxed stance. "Fine. But I want a drink."

Benji winked at them. "That's my cue."

"No need," Matteo said, stepping up to them with a tray of champagne glasses. "I stole this from the bar."

Everyone cheered as they reached for one. Matteo raised his to the center, and everyone followed suit. "To Tri, the restaurant that has quickly become a New York staple, and the chef who made it happen."

More cheers ensued as they clinked glasses. Wyatt's smile in response was shy and humble, and it made her fall for him even more.

"So," Marissa started, the stem of her glass dangling between her fingers. "Should we talk about the fact that you're the internet's new favorite *short king*?"

Wyatt rolled his eyes. "Stop."

Benji slung an arm around him. "I think we should get him a crown."

"Ooh, if you're the king, does that make me your regent? Prepared to brood over the fact that I don't have the crown yet?" Marissa joked.

"I can teach you a thing or two about poison," Bella offered.

Wyatt dug his thumb into her side, making her yelp.

Marissa cackled in delight at Bella's quip. "I don't understand, but I absolutely love it."

The static tap from a microphone cut through the speakers. "Ladies and gentlemen, please take your seats. The ceremony is about to begin."

The group followed Matteo to their table. As they found their seats, Wyatt stopped her from reaching for her chair and grabbed the back of it himself, sliding it away from the table before taking her hand. He eased her into it, tucking her chair in, then took the one next to her.

"Such a gentleman," she teased.

He leaned over to whisper in her ear. She noticed his

hand was in his pocket, playing with the goodie he kept in there.

"You wouldn't be saying that if you knew what was running through my head right now," he rumbled in her ear.

"Want to find a closet and show me instead, chef?" she whispered back.

He huffed, then kissed her cheek. "You and that dress are killing me."

"Perfect. My plan is still working."

"*Tremendously.*"

She laughed. Benji cocked a brow in their direction, then gave Wyatt a cocky grin. He gave him the finger in response.

The ceremony started with a couple speeches from different committee members and judges. Hors d'oeuvres were placed in front of them as they waited, glasses of champagne swapped out with Sangiovese.

Bella crossed her legs, her knee making the slit drape open, revealing the bare skin at her thigh.

Wyatt smirked, reaching a hand under the table and slowly gliding it up. She placed her hand on his to stop him, which made him chuckle low under his breath. He traced small, torturous circles with his thumb.

The emcee listed off different awards, including Best Patisserie, Best Cocktail Bar, and Outstanding Pastry Chef. Then they moved on to the regional awards.

Wyatt's leg bounced under the table as they listed off the nominees for Best Restaurant in the Northeast. A Malaysian spot in Boston, a French bistro in Philadelphia, then Tri.

"And the winner is...Tri! With Matteo Lombardi and executive chef Wyatt Henderson."

Bella felt Wyatt's hand soften in her lap. His smile was

glorious, like a runner who made it to the finish line of his first marathon.

The rest of the table was too busy with their own celebrations to notice them. Marissa cheered and jumped from her seat, Benji catching her waist and lifting her in a fierce hug. Matteo shook hands with the other nominees as he made his way around the table.

Wyatt kissed her cheek as he stood up, shaking Matteo's hand and clapping his back as the two of them made their way to the stage. The emcee handed Matteo a glass awards plaque in the shape of a star. He said a brief thank you to the crowd, then they descended back to the table.

Bella leaned over as Wyatt took his seat, tucking a rogue wave behind his ear. "Congrats, chef."

To her surprise, he cupped her face and kissed her on the mouth in front of everyone. Benji's and Marissa's whistling didn't stop him from thoroughly finishing his job. When he pulled back, he placed one last soft kiss on her lips and whispered a breathless "Thank you" before leaning back in his seat, his thumb back to drawing circles on her thigh. The entire moment had her feeling delightfully dizzy.

After handing out a dozen more awards, the ceremony's emcee announced there would be a short break, and the lights brightened as nominees stood up and stretched their legs.

Matteo bolted up from his spot across the table, his eyes on whomever was approaching them from behind. "You made it!" he exclaimed.

Bella turned to see who it was. Her stomach dropped.

Matteo stepped aside and held out the chair next to him, his eyes sparkling with delight. "Everyone, I would like you to meet—"

"Nonna?"

Nonna stopped when she reached Matteo, her eyes wide. She wore a loose green sweater with a bow tied at her collar and loose black slacks. Her "fancy outfit," she always called it. The one she wore to holiday mass every year.

Matteo's lips tipped into a grin. "Surprise!"

Everyone at the table remained silent.

Wyatt's eyes darted back and forth between her grandmother and Matteo. "Is this your new client?"

"It is." Matteo beamed. "And I figured I would surprise Bella, given the circumstances."

Bella felt like she was going to throw up.

"What circumstances?" Wyatt demanded.

Matteo looked at Bella, waiting for her to say something.

"Oh *piccola*," Nonna said softly, the tone of her voice full of empathy. "I thought he knew by now."

She opened and closed her mouth once. Then twice. Her words were stuck. *She* was stuck. Her mouth felt dry, and she was convinced she was going to pass out.

Her lack of response had Matteo shifting his gaze to Wyatt, and to her horror, he told him the words she'd been unable to for months, ever since she met her chef.

"Sofia Russo asked me to meet with her a couple weeks ago to discuss management for Russo's," Matteo said to him. "Naturally, I was curious, given that my father said that he had a falling out with the owner of Russo's long ago. Which, it seems, he had a good reason for: Sofia Russo was his ex-wife."

Wyatt stopped sketching circles on her thigh.

"Wait, hold up," Marissa butted in, shaking her head. "So if this is your nonna," she started, pointing to Bella, "then that would make Matteo—"

"Her uncle," Matteo finished.

Bella's eyes remained on her nonna, who looked apologetic. She wanted to fume, wanted to be angry at her grandmother for not telling her that she was coming tonight, giving her any kind of warning. But then her attention dragged to Wyatt, who looked at his employer with a face that was stony.

Applause broke up the tension as the lights dimmed, not giving anyone a chance to respond. "Okay, folks, we'll now move on to the award for Outstanding Chef."

Wyatt's eyes were on the floating candles at the center of the table. "How long have you known this?" he asked her quietly.

Names and restaurants were listed off, including Wyatt Henderson from Tri. Benji whooped and hollered, the others at the table clapping politely. Nonna was now in the chair beside Matteo.

She closed her eyes, the words *finally* rushing out. "I found out through a DNA test. It was the reason I went to the restaurant in the first place."

When she blinked her eyes open, he still wasn't looking at her.

"And me?" he asked.

"You were close to him, and I..." She hiccupped, a tear trickling down her cheek. "I wanted to know more, but then I started hanging out with you and—"

"*Wyatt Henderson!*"

Their table exploded in cheers.

Wyatt blinked, realizing that he was being summoned to the stage at the front. He tossed his napkin to the table and stood up, buttoning his jacket as he made his way up to the stage without a backward glance.

Bella watched with tears in her eyes as her chef schooled his features, nodding as they handed him a similar glass plaque to the one now in front of Matteo. He thanked the judges and held up the award to the crowd.

Matteo, Benji, and Marissa shouted and whistled, but Bella sat there frozen. Wyatt's eyes locked on hers, his smile forced and cordial. It broke her heart. He'd *finally* won the award he rightly deserved, and she'd completely ruined it for him.

When he joined them again, he placed the plaque down. Benji got up to give him a hug, but he brushed him off.

"I'm going to need a minute," Wyatt requested.

Then he turned on his heels and left the banquet hall.

Chapter Twenty-Seven

Bella waited a beat, then two, then decided *to hell with it* and followed him out. She took the elevator down to the lobby, now quiet as everyone celebrated three floors above.

Wyatt stood outside in the snow, his head tilted up, flurries caught in his hair and tacked to the shoulders of his tuxedo jacket.

Bella swung the door open and walked out, not stopping to grab her jacket despite the fact that it was cold enough to snow in New York in November. She crossed her arms to fight the chill. "Wyatt."

He sighed, then gazed down at his leather Oxfords.

"Please say something," she croaked.

"Why did you keep so much from me?"

She rubbed her hands up and down her arms.

"You didn't tell me about your family, which I sort of understood at the time. But this, too?" He shook his head. "It's clear you don't trust me."

"I do trust you," she defended, but her words came out too soft, too weak. Like she didn't mean them.

"Do you though?" he asked, his voice getting louder.

His eyes finally met hers. "I get why you did it, why you said yes to hanging out with me. I would want to know more if I found out something like that, too. But what I don't get is after all this time, after..." He huffed, his shoulders dropping. "I opened myself up to you, Bella. But that didn't seem to be enough for you to do the same."

She shook her head. "It's not like that."

"Then what is it like? Spell it out for me."

"It's—" She started to cry. She looked away from him, feeling embarrassed.

"Is there something else you're not telling me?"

She didn't respond.

"*Bella.*"

She finally looked at him, and his expression was full of awful anger. And hurt. So much hurt.

He placed his hands on his hips, looking exasperated at her hesitation.

Bella wiped at the tears underneath her eyes, and after a long breath, she released the words she feared most.

"Lon didn't just leave me because he met someone else," she admitted. "I had three miscarriages when I was married to him, and...it *broke* me. I spent a year in hiding. I gave up on myself. I became a shell of a human. I slowly ruined our marriage. So he met someone, and he walked."

Wyatt ran a hand through his hair and pulled on it hard. He puffed out his cheeks, taking a step back, then let out a long exhale.

She shivered. "Besides diagnosing me with depression and putting me on meds, my doctors weren't very helpful. They couldn't give me a clear answer on whether having a baby would be possible for me, so I did the research. I went down a rabbit hole, wanting to know more about my health and what else was wrong with me. That's when I found out about Matteo. I felt hurt that my family never told me he existed, so I decided to find out what I could myself first. I found him and went to the restaurant...and then I met you.

"Wyatt, meeting you...it was the first time I felt *alive* in so long. Being with you has brought me back to life, has made me feel things I've honestly never felt. And I've been so scared to admit the truth because...because I'm damaged goods, and how could someone as good as you ever want to be with someone like me. You don't deserve that."

She let out a sob, tears spilling down her cheeks. "I'm not sure if I'll ever be able to carry children. You spoke of inadequacy? I'm a woman with all of the right parts to carry life, yet my body failed my babies three times."

They stood there in excruciating silence. Wyatt shoved his hands in his pockets. She watched as he fisted the thing she knew was in his left hand. He exhaled and looked at her. Then, without a word, he spun around and walked away, leaving her to shiver outside the Whitney alone.

BELLA WENT BACK INSIDE to retrieve her coat, then twenty minutes later, found herself on Percy and Yaz's stoop on the Upper East Side. As soon as her best friend threw open the door, Bella began to cry.

"You were right," she sobbed.

Percy responded by pulling her in for a fierce hug, then shutting the door. She went through the motions as Percy handed her a clean set of clothes to change into. After she washed her makeup off and emerged from the bathroom, Percy was standing there with a glass of wine in hand.

"Have anything stronger?" Bella grumbled.

Percy held up the bottle of tequila she had in her other hand. "Wasn't sure what kind of night it was."

Bella snatched the reposado and pulled off the cork, then took a swig.

"Got it," Percy said, handing the glass of wine to Yaz who appeared behind her, already in her pajamas. "Let's move this to the couch."

They settled down on the couch that took up the entire side wall of their small living room. Yaz undid Bella's hair and let it loose, guiding the back of her head down to her lap as she stroked the wavy strands. Percy sat on the opposite side, with Bella's legs draped over her lap, and demanded she spill everything.

So she did, explaining through the awards ceremony and how her nonna showed up, how the truth was revealed to Wyatt, but not from her own lips. Then she walked them through their conversation in the snow, and how he walked away.

"I'm such an idiot," she grumbled through tears. "I should have told him the truth like you said. I don't understand why it felt so impossible." She wiped snot on her upper lip with the back of her hand. "Or maybe I do. Maybe I was worried that he would walk away from me. And in the end, I was right."

"Maybe he needs time to think," Yaz said, her hands soothing her. "It's a lot to take in."

"He thinks I don't trust him."

"Do you trust him?" Percy inquired.

"Yes," Bella replied softly. "He told me he loved me tonight. And I...I said it back."

Percy squeezed her calves. "I'm so proud of you, Bells."

She frowned. "Why? It didn't make a difference. I still screwed up so bad."

"But you opened yourself up to him, and honestly? After the number of times I've peeled you off the floor from having too much to drink or talked you through your frustrations with your doctors and your health, I really thought this would never happen again."

Bella sniffled. "Really?"

"Really."

They remained silent for a few minutes, listening to the distant sirens and car horns on Lexington Avenue.

"What do I do?" Bella whispered.

"I think you should give him space, love. Let him work through it." Yaz rubbed her shoulders. "And I think it's time to speak honestly with your family."

"I'll deal with them on Sunday," she grumbled.

Percy patted her knee. "We'll be here for you if things fall apart. You will always have us."

Bella gazed up at Yaz. "I'm sorry for how I acted at the party, for ruining your night."

Yaz kissed her forehead. "You didn't ruin my night, Bells. We knew that night was going to be hard for you, and I'm sorry for that, too. I forgive you, and I love you."

"I don't deserve either of you," Bella grumbled.

"It's not about deserving," Yaz said. "Choosing to love someone has nothing to do with what you think you deserve or don't deserve. Love is deciding that despite it all, you still choose to love that person forever. And we will always choose to love you. No matter how messy it gets."

Bella sneaked a look at Percy, her best friend's eyes lined with silver and a watery smile tracing her lips. "No matter what, Bells."

The memory of a basket of toiletries popped into her head, and a soft smile from Wyatt as he sat on his bed, hair all over the place yet looking unfailingly happy. Then a half-eaten omelet on the table, mugs of coffee getting cold, and a warm chest as she sat in his lap.

I want to know every side of you too, Bella.

Even then, he'd chosen her, yearned to see every side of her, even the parts that were flawed and not perfect. Yet in her attempt to keep her heart protected, she might have lost the person who wanted to protect it. He wanted her to trust him with her scars, and still chose to take care of her and love her through it all.

She fell asleep like that, and only woke slightly to Yaz's and Percy's movements as they retreated for the night and tucked her under a blanket.

Her mind drifted into a familiar dream, in that same booth at Lombardi's. Her grandfather sat across from her, a slice of pepperoni on his plate.

"You made things so messy," Bella confessed. "And I did, too."

She watched as her grandfather took a bite of his slice, thinking it through. He chewed and swallowed, then returned his gaze to her. "Life is messy. I am not perfect, and neither are you. But we still choose to love one another."

"But choosing to love Nonna wasn't good enough for you? Choosing her deli, her family, her dream?"

"She deserved better than me."

Bella sat there in her dream version of Lombardi's, the streets abnormally quiet compared to the typical real-life version with bustling tourists and blaring music. She knew that what her grandfather said was her mind likely replaying her own thoughts and frustrations. But when it came from her grandfather's lips, she wanted to reach over the table, grab his shoulders, and shake sense into him. She wanted to scream at him about how much her nonna clearly loved him, how it was ridiculous for him to think that he wasn't good enough for her.

But...wasn't that exactly what she'd been doing, too?

The sound of her buzzing phone on the coffee table woke her up. She blinked her eyes open and reached for it, noticing it was a name that hadn't graced her screen in almost two years.

She snatched it and swiped it open, pressing her phone to her ear. "Lon?"

"You're going to want to get down to the first precinct."

She sat up. "Why? Is everything all right? Are you all right?"

"I was perfectly fine until *he* showed up."

Her stomach sank. She moved the crochet blanket off her lap and swung her legs around. "He?"

Lon let out a low, deep growl. "Your scary boyfriend is here. Covered in blood and behind bars."

Chapter Twenty-Eight

Bella threw open the doors at the NYPD, eyes wild as she stormed in looking for the front desk. Percy was close at her heels, the two of them quite the sight in the sweatpants and sweatshirts they'd thrown on before heading down to the station.

Lon's tall frame jumped in front of her, stopping her pursuit. "Bella."

She looked up at her ex. There was blood caked on his face, more dripping down from his nostrils to his chin. His nose was crooked. His eyes were bloodshot.

Bella glared at him. "What did you do, Lon?"

"What did *I* do?" He balked. "That psychopath you call a *boyfriend* came down to Gran Via and decided he was in the mood for a fight."

Percy cursed hoarsely under her breath.

Bella scanned his face and couldn't help the smirk that curved at her lips. "He broke your nose."

"You're *smiling* about that?" Lon spewed. "Bella, this asshole is clearly way too violent for you. He won't treat you right."

She puffed up her chest, her anger making her see red. "And what do you know about treating me right, huh? You didn't even have the decency to stick around and *try*."

"I *wanted* to, dammit! But you shut me out. What was I supposed to do?"

Life is messy. After everything she'd been through that night, or even in the past couple of months, the truth was abundantly clear.

She deserved better than him.

This whole time, she believed it was the opposite, that Lon was the one who deserved better after she gave up on him. Part of her knew she could have tried harder. But did she even have the tools to, when she felt like she was drowning in the depths of her darkness?

"You were supposed to love me unconditionally," she replied, head held high. "You were supposed to uphold your vow, in *sickness* and in health. You were supposed to take care of me."

"So is that what he does? Love you unconditionally? Take 'care' of you?" He lifted his hands into air quotes at that last part, his face livid with molten fury.

"Lon."

His back straightened at the sound of Katie's voice behind them.

Bella and Percy turned to their former friend, leggings tucked into soft boots, a thick puffer jacket wrapped around her frame, her nose pink from the cold.

"Stop talking to her that way," Katie added. Her voice was soft, yet somehow still firm. Quiet in her unwavering confidence.

"Agreed," Percy added. "Stop being a douchebag and let her through."

"I'm being a douchebag? He punched me in the face!"

"Something we've all been dying to do since the day you walked out on Bells," her best friend replied. "Except Katie, probably."

"Not anymore," Katie butted in. "You can add me to the queue."

Lon balked at his fiancée, but Bella wasn't paying attention to their responses. Instead, she was hyperfocused on the buzzing of a door at the other side of the station and the two figures that followed the police officer out into the main lobby.

Matteo said something to Wyatt, then followed the officer to his desk. Wyatt's jaw locked as he examined his now scuffed shoes then glanced up at the four people who were staring back at him.

He looked like absolute hell. His bottom lip had split open, his hair was in a haphazard heap, and his necktie was missing. She gazed down at his hands, knuckles split open and covered in blood. When he noticed what she was looking at, he slipped his hands into his pockets.

Bella rushed to him, stepping close enough so they could talk without eavesdropping ears. "What happened?"

"I'm sorry," he whispered, not meeting her gaze.

"What *happened*?"

"We're all set," Matteo said, walking up to them. He was still in his navy tux. "Need a ride home?"

Wyatt finally looked up at her, waiting for her response. Waiting for her to make the next move.

"No," she told Matteo, shaking her head as she faced him. "He can come to my place. His car is there anyway."

Matteo sighed. "We should probably talk at some point."

Bella swallowed. "We will."

He nodded as he held up a plastic bag of Wyatt's

belongings. Phone, wallet, keys...and a scrap of red fabric. Matteo's brow raised pointedly at the both of them, then with a squeeze to Wyatt's shoulder, he left the station.

She turned back to him. "You called Matteo?"

"I wasn't sure how you would react," he responded honestly, shoveling the items back into his pockets, including her underwear.

"But he's your *boss*."

"At this point you know it's far more than that between me and him." He paused, a muscle flexing in his jaw. "Something you should have picked up on during all of your prying."

She exhaled. "I deserve that."

"Yeah, you do." He peered around her at the others in the station. "Did he call you?"

She swallowed, then nodded.

Percy made her way toward them. "You guys good?"

"I think we're going to head back to my place," she replied. "Thank you for tonight."

"Of course. Call if you need me?"

"It's okay, I—"

Percy silenced her with a finger on her lips. "Remember what Yaz said."

Tears lined her eyes again, but she nodded, watching as her best friend herded Lon and Katie out of the station, the two now in some kind of heated argument that Bella couldn't quite make out.

She turned back at Wyatt, the picture of sheer exhaustion. She wanted to throw her arms around him and tell her how she felt, but under the harsh fluorescent lights of the NYPD's first precinct, she knew it wasn't the right time or place.

Instead, she took a step toward the door. "Come on, let's go."

HER APARTMENT WAS dark except for the orange glow from the city through her window. Bella flicked on her bathroom light and ordered him to sit.

He obeyed without a word. Bella ran a washcloth under the sink with warm water, then lifted one of his hands and began to clean off the blood. She could feel his eyes on her as she worked, but she didn't dare look into them, too afraid of what she might find.

She wrung the cloth under the sink, red water slowly swirling down the drain. Wyatt stood up and began to remove his wrinkled tux, stripping down to his white T-shirt and boxers. She brushed her teeth and tried her best to not pay too much attention as he folded his clothes and placed them on her couch, then climbed in her bed.

She slowly followed, slipping into the other side, keeping her distance from him. She wanted to close the space and hold him, to talk about the night and figure things out. But his breathing had gone heavy, his head sinking deep into the pillow as he fell asleep. She closed her eyes, forcing herself to do the same, despite how revved up she felt after the whirlwind night that they had.

As she started to drift off, she felt his hand reach up near her pillow. He laced his fingers through hers, and didn't let go as she fell asleep.

When she woke the next morning, Wyatt was already sitting up in her bed, his back leaning against her bed frame. He was examining his knuckles with a frown.

"You're awake," she said.

"Have been for hours." He pointed a finger to her living room. "I also removed the A/C for you. Put it in the empty spot on the floor of your pantry."

She sat up, brow raised. "Why?"

He shook his head. "Who the fuck knows. Despite everything, I can't seem to help myself when it comes to you."

She wrung her hands in her lap. Silence engulfed them as they sat next to one another, not touching or even looking. Simply staring at the dresser across from her bed.

She squeezed her hands together. "We should talk about it."

"Probably."

"Why'd you do it? Go after Lon like that?"

"I was an idiot."

"But *why?*"

His chest thundered with obvious frustration. "After you told me what happened, I couldn't believe he did that to you after everything you went through. And what makes me even angrier is that you felt like what happened was all your fault."

Bella tucked her knees closer and hugged them.

"On top of that, you also felt like all of it somehow made you unworthy of this." He pointed between the two of them. "So you kept it from me, thinking that the truth would drive me away."

She blinked back tears.

"That set me over the edge. This man made you think that you couldn't talk to me, and when it dawned on me, I found myself in front of Gran Via."

"I'm sorry. Wyatt, I'm so, so sorry."

He huffed and pressed the heels of his palms to his eyes.

"I do love you," she continued. "I meant it. I meant all of it."

He dropped his hands. "How can I trust you, though?"

Her heart dropped.

"I don't know where to go from here after you kept so much from me."

"Wh-what are you saying?" she asked, her lip quivering.

"I wasn't kidding, Bella. You make me crazy. I fell for you fast, faster than anyone in my entire life, and it still scares me. But how will I know if you're being truthful with me or not? Do I keep putting myself out there, hoping that you're actually doing the same? I don't think—"

"Don't," she pleaded. "Please don't do it."

He picked up one of her hands and kissed it, his eyes on her fingers instead of on her. "I need you to take some time and decide if you're ready. But until then—"

"*Wyatt*," she cried. "*Please.* Please don't leave me. Please stay. We'll work through this."

To her absolute horror, he shook his head. "I think this is something *you* need to work through, Bella. I can't do that for you."

He dropped her hand and stood from the bed. She remained in her spot and cried as she listened to him slip his clothes back on, lace up his shoes, then slide the deadbolt on her door to unlock it.

There was a pause before the door closed.

"I do love you too, *mia bella*."

Then the door clicked shut and he was gone.

Chapter Twenty-Nine

It was a Friday night when Lon walked out on her. Bella had spent the day on the couch in her sweats, hair tied up in a messy bun at the top of her head, computer on her lap as she scrolled through article after article about miscarriages and health precautions and treatments.

"I'm leaving," he said quietly.

She looked up from her screen to find Lon standing there, shoes on and a duffel bag at his feet.

"Like, for the weekend?"

Lon shook his head. "No. For good."

He told her everything, about falling for Katie, about wanting to be with her, about how their marriage wasn't working for him anymore. He told her to take her time packing up her things and finding a place, and he'd move back in once she was out. Then he picked up his bag and walked out of her life.

His leaving hollowed her out, even more than the grief she carried from the babies she'd lost. It felt like someone had scooped her insides and tossed them away, and she was left with this withering frame. And she existed like that—dormant, absent—for a long time.

Until she didn't. Until she met him.

Yet somehow, even though she'd only known Wyatt for a short while, this time felt different. She crumbled back into her bed after listening to the door shut, lost all sense of control, like she was being sucked into a dark hole that she'd never return from. Wyatt had filled her life with color, reminding her that life and love were worth fighting for. Yet in the end, he also left, and she wanted nothing more than to stay under the covers and let the world pass her by.

But it was Sunday, and she had no intention of missing supper with her family.

She mustered up all the energy in her reserves, threw on leggings and a sweater, and made the walk over to Little Italy. She ignored the tourists and the sounds that usually brought her joy and instead readied herself for battle. Bella had no idea what she would walk into, but she had a sneaking suspicion that it wasn't going to be good.

She unlocked the door of her nonna's apartment and was welcomed by the sound of two headstrong women fighting in fluent Italian.

"*Come hai potuto!*" Mom screamed.

"*Ti stavo proteggendo!*"

"Protecting me? From *what!*"

There was more screaming that Bella could hardly comprehend. The final step of the staircase creaked under her boot, and everyone fell silent as they gazed toward her in the open doorway.

Nonna was in her pink apron, her wooden spoon in her hand like a sword. Mom's face was splotchy and red, the sleeves of her worn Columbia University hoodie pulled up to her elbows, her brown-and-gray-peppered hair wild and loose at her shoulders. Dad sat at the table rubbing his chin, like he was contemplating how exactly he should proceed.

"Hi," Bella said to them.

Mom looked at Nonna, then back at Bella. "Hi, sweetie, sorry for the commotion."

Bella eyed her grandmother and was shocked by how serious her expression was. She tilted her head down and shook it slightly, then mouthed, *Don't*.

Anger flared in her belly. After everything her grandmother had done, the secrets she'd kept, the lies she'd told, and now the way she obliterated everything with the man who made her feel hopeful for the first time in years, she was done following in her grandmother's footsteps. Done making the same mistakes. She didn't want to hide like her, didn't want to keep things from the people she loved, all for the sake of protecting herself. It's exactly what she did to Wyatt, and she refused to do it ever again.

So she stood tall and faced her mother. "I know."

Mom frowned. "Know about what?"

"I know about Matteo. I know about Nonno's family in Queens, that he left Nonna, just like Lon left me."

Her nostrils flared as she turned back to Nonna. "You told her before you told *me*?"

"No," Bella corrected, her voice slicing right through her mother's bubbling anger. "I found out through a DNA test. I looked Matteo up, saw that he owned restaurants in New York, and Percy got us a reservation at one of them to see what we could find."

"So you met him?" Dad asked, his voice calm and curious.

Bella's shoulders slumped. "No. I met Wyatt that night instead."

"*Merda*," Mom swore.

Nonna placed her face in her hand.

"Wyatt and Matteo are close, so I befriended him to get more answers. And well…you know what happened there. Except it's probably over now."

Mom's back straightened. "What do you mean?"

"He broke things off this morning." Bella focused her attention on Nonna as she continued. "Said he couldn't trust me after all of the secrets I was keeping from him."

"Oh sweetie, I'm so sorry."

Bella shrugged. "I deserve it. I wanted to tell him the truth, but I never could seem to find the right words. Then Nonna showed up last night—"

Mom's head swiveled to her mother, eyes blazing.

"—and everything came tumbling out," Bella finished.

"Showed up *where?*" Mom demanded.

"The James Beard Awards," Bella answered for her nonna. "Apparently she's been meeting with Matteo about management."

"Oh dear god," Dad grumbled behind them, scrubbing a hand down his face.

Mom's nostrils flared. "*Management!* Are you kidding me?"

The two of them started screaming at each other in Italian again. Bella had never learned the full language, but she knew enough of it to catch on to phrases here or there. *Traditrice.* Traitor. *Non mi ami affatto.* You don't love me at all.

"After everything I've done for you and the shop, after fielding countless offers to expand or sell products or franchise…you go behind my back?" Mom asked.

"I haven't committed to anything. It was only a couple of conversations."

"But *without* me?"

"The situation would have been awkward," Nonna explained. "Especially when I was revealing the truth to him during our lunch."

"*Merda*," Mom swore again.

"Angela," Dad warned.

She held a finger up at him. "My outrage is valid right now. I've had a brother for almost fifty years that I did not know about."

"*Mi dispiace*," Nonna apologized.

Mom looked back and forth between her and Nonna, her eyes now rimmed with scarlet. "Why are we keeping so many secrets in this family? Do our Sunday gatherings mean nothing to you both?"

"I did what I had to, to protect you," Nonna replied, her voice soft and vulnerable.

"Protect me from what?" Mom spat.

Bella shook her head and looked at her grandmother, realizing the weight of what was really between them. She might have said she kept her secret in an attempt to protect her mother, maybe even her. But truthfully, it was a protection for her own heart. A feeling that Bella could completely understand.

"Protection from pain," Bella replied. "Protection from having to face what you feel is your biggest failure as a wife, and in some cases, as a woman. Protection for your own heart, because inviting someone else in simply opens the door for disappointing another person all over again."

Mom wept into her hands, her shoulders trembling.

"I love all of you, but I think I need some time," Bella confessed. Her mind was on Wyatt, how similar her words sounded to his.

He was right. She had baggage she needed to drag out into the light and sift through.

"I have things I need to figure out on my own," she said, then turned back toward the door and left before dinner was served.

SHE WANTED to fall into a pit of despair, but Bella knew that was no way of trying to actually figure out her life. Instead, she came back that Sunday night and thoroughly cleaned her apartment. She planned her week, cooked her lunches, and caught up on work emails. She refused to let herself drown this time around. She refused to let her life be controlled by the darkness.

Katie called in sick to work that Monday...followed by Tuesday, Wednesday, and Thursday. By Friday, Bella contemplated calling Katie from her personal phone, then thought better of it. Why should she waste her time worrying?

A soft knock on the door and a familiar head of red hair popping through her doorway saved her from making that call.

"You're back! How are you feeling?" she asked.

Katie shrugged, slinking into Bella's office. "Fine, I guess. I'm sorry I had to hand you all of my work this week. I know you already have a lot on your plate."

Bella flicked her hand. "No need. Let's just say it was a welcome distraction."

She wasn't lying; having to put together all of Katie's content and focus on her strategy plans kept Bella from cycling through thoughts of Wyatt. She edited images and videos, wrote captions, analyzed charts, and found keywords and hashtags to optimize posts. It was work she hadn't done in a long time, and she was thankful it'd fallen into her lap.

"That's good," Katie said. She swayed on the spot, her hands clasped behind her back, her gaze down at her ankle boots.

Bella frowned. "Everything all right?"

Katie let out a long exhale, then looked up at Bella. "I'm putting in my two weeks."

Her eyes widened. "Seriously?"

"I probably should have done it a long time ago, to be honest. But I really like this job, and despite the shit I put you through, you are actually a great manager and mentor. I learned so much working for you."

Bella nodded. "And I like having you as an employee. You've been a vital asset to the team."

Katie flushed. "I know. I'm going to miss it."

She folded her arms over her chest, confused. "Then why leave? Are you moving to a different company?"

"No. I'm moving to a different state."

Bella's stomach dropped. "You guys are...moving?"

"Just me. I'm moving. Back home to San Diego."

She blinked. "Just...you?"

"Can I sit?"

Bella nodded.

Katie took a seat in the chair across from her desk. She crossed her legs casually and threaded her fingers together on her knee. "Did you know that Lon was also arrested on Saturday?"

"No."

Katie sighed. "He was. I was out with a friend that night and had no idea. I found out when his mother called me all hysterical, saying that he'd called his father to ask him to wire money for his bail."

Bella rolled her eyes. "Lon is loaded."

"Something about not having his wallet on him or something, I don't know. But the moral of the story is, he called his father. Then once he had his phone again, he called you."

She sat up straight, understanding where Katie was leading her.

"He didn't call his fiancée, the person he is meant to love and trust. When I got down to the station and realized what had happened and heard the way he was speaking to you, it all came clearly to me. He may love me, but he's also still in love with you. I got swept up in him and was blind to what was in front of me. I want someone who speaks to me kindly and with respect, who wouldn't hesitate to make me his first phone call."

Bella rubbed her neck.

"I honestly don't feel like I deserve anyone now after what I did to you, but I've met with my therapist every day this week since breaking things off with him, and I can see that..." Her gaze moved to the window behind Bella, the plinking of raindrops the only sound between them. Tears trickled down her cheeks. "I see now that I can start over. Be around my family. Learn from my mistakes and do things differently.

"Bells, I'm so sorry for what I did. I'm so sorry for tearing the two of you apart when you were going through the hardest time of your life. I hate that I lost you as a friend, all for a man who didn't treat me right."

"He didn't treat me right either," Bella admitted. She pushed a tissue box toward her.

Katie plucked one from the top and blew her nose. "I feel awful. I know I shouldn't beg for your forgiveness, but I selfishly want to. I want to fix things between us."

Bella stood up and rounded the desk. She exhaled, then held out her hands. Katie reluctantly took them and stood.

"I think healing would take a lot of time and a lot of work," Bella said. "But I'd like to try. I miss you as a friend, too."

Katie sobbed and threw her arms around Bella. "I don't deserve you. I never did."

Bella slid her arms around Katie and squeezed. "A very wise woman once told me that choosing to love someone isn't about what you think you deserve or not, but about choosing to love that person despite everything."

Sobs racked Katie's body. Bella rubbed her back and waited for her crying to slow. When it did, Bella stepped back, hands on Katie's shoulders.

"Promise me you'll let me know if you need anything. Work reference, resumé update, whatever. And send me pictures of those gorgeous San Diego sunsets."

Katie gave her a watery smile. "Of course."

Bella pulled her in for one last hug. An idea struck her, like flicking on a light switch.

"Katie, how did you find your therapist?"

"Isabella Russo?"

Bella smiled and followed the receptionist through the narrow door at the other end of the office. The room was cozy, with green plants lining the windows and plush comfortable chairs. Blankets and pillows remained close by, along with a kettle and a basket full of teas and instant coffee packets.

A woman with voluminous black curls and dark brown

skin came through the door next, wrapped up in a comfortable cardigan and slacks. Her presence calmed Bella as she reached out to shake her hand.

"Gail," she said, "It's so great to meet you, Bella."

"Me too. Thanks for agreeing to see me at the last minute."

"Sundays tend to be my slowest days, so I'm glad you were available as well," she said. "Tea, coffee?"

Bella shook her head.

"Then let's begin."

They took their seats opposite one another.

"Why don't we start with why you're here," Gail began.

She took a long, deep breath. "In the past four years, I got married, had three miscarriages, got cheated on, divorced, and then found out that my grandfather had a secret family in Queens that my parents and I never knew about. He ended up having a son, my uncle, who owns a restaurant group in New York. I visited one of his restaurants, befriended his chef, and tried to find out more information. As I got to know this chef, I started to really like what I saw, and I fell in love with him. But I never told him the truth."

Gail clicked the pen in her hand. "All right. Let's start there."

Chapter Thirty

BELLA KNEW she wasn't ready for Sunday supper, so she asked Percy and Yaz to meet at Dante for dinner after her first therapy session. They sat at the counter, sipping on Negronis and discussing every minuscule detail they could about the wedding. Double bachelorette weekend that summer on Nantucket, ceremony and reception at the Central Park Zoo next fall, wedding party in lush dark greens with hints of silver and gold. They didn't mention Lon and his upended engagement, or even ask about Wyatt or her family, and Bella was thankful for them. So much so that she asked them if they would want to spend Thanksgiving together, just the three of them in the city. Percy bellowed out an enthusiastic "Fuck yes!" which Yaz tamped down with a hand over Percy's mouth.

It was the perfect way to spend a Sunday, even if it felt eerie not to be sitting at Nonna's table. She hadn't heard from her or her mother throughout the week, and decided it was probably good for all of them to take space. They would come together eventually. They always did.

Bella wanted more than anything to call Wyatt and see

how he was, but she owed it to him to leave him alone. The more she spoke with Gail and talked through her thoughts and worries, the clearer it became that she really *did* have her work cut out for her. Parsing through her emotional baggage about her body, her divorce, and her family wasn't Wyatt's job, or anyone else's for that matter. No, it was hers and hers alone. So, she would give it the attention it deserved.

A rainstorm swept through New York and knocked off the rest of the fall foliage. Crunchy leaves lined the sidewalks and sprinkled across Central Park. The city was bustling with tourists as they gathered for the Macy's Thanksgiving Parade, but Bella learned long ago to stay away from the crowds. She journeyed to the Upper East Side instead with three bottles of wine and a weekender, fully aware that she'd need to spend the night on the couch after what she expected would be a failed attempt at trying to roast their first turkey. In her bag were jars of Nonna's marinara, just in case.

Stoops lined with pumpkins were replaced with garlands and strings of twinkling lights. Splendent trees popped up in every office building, adorned with baubles and tinsel and topped with extravagant bright stars.

Katie had sent a selfie in front of a San Diego sunset her first night back home, her nose already pink from the sun. Bella sent her one back, frowning in the camera as she sat at Katie's empty desk. She'd responded with a series of laughing emojis. After Thanksgiving, Bella spent the subsequent weeks interviewing for Katie's position and getting ahead on work before the holidays. She filled her calendar with sessions with Gail and kept meeting Percy and Yaz on Sundays.

It was a week before Christmas, on a lazy Sunday afternoon, curled up on Percy and Yaz's couch, the three of them watching *Miracle on 34th Street* and eating Zabar's black-and-whites, when she finally felt like she got her courage to face it all. Percy yelped at whatever she was reading on her phone, then paused the movie.

"Bells...have you seen this?" she asked, holding up her phone.

Bella squinted and moved closer to get a better look.

It was a photo of Wyatt, carefully leaning over a white plate on a metal counter at Tri, a pair of tweezers in his hand as he placed pancetta curls atop charred cabbage. His hair was shorter now, but still long enough to tuck behind his ears while he worked, his concentration fixed on the dish before him. A chef in his element, intentional with every detail of his work.

It made her heart squeeze in her chest.

"*New York Times* did a whole feature on him," Percy continued. "Even bigger than mine. They're calling his restaurant 'New York's Newest Culinary Empire.'"

Bella scrolled through the article to find more images of Wyatt. One where he was talking to Marissa as they commandeered the kitchen during the dinner chaos. One of him without his chef's coat, cleaning a counter in the kitchen after everyone left. Another with him in his casual clothes, jeans cuffed at his ankles, a navy sweater pushed up his forearms, his hand casually holding the stem of a glass of orange wine on the table in front of him, his eyes on whoever was talking to him behind the camera.

She didn't realize she was crying until Yaz handed her napkins from the coffee table.

"Have you talked to him at all?" Percy hedged, like she wasn't sure if she should be asking.

"No." Bella sniffed, dabbing at her face with the napkin. "He told me I needed to figure things out first."

"And have you done that?"

In some ways, she had. But she still hadn't tackled things with her family—both new and old—and she didn't want to drag Wyatt through that. Part of her wondered if she should even bother dragging him through anything ever again.

"No, not yet," Bella said. She flung the blanket off her lap and stood up from the couch. "But there's something I need to do."

BELLA KNOCKED on the door of the red-brick house in Astoria. It was seven o'clock, meaning Wyatt was likely at the restaurant, so it was her best time to get him alone.

Matteo answered the door. He was in a pair of jeans and a faded Mets T-shirt, a dish towel slung over his shoulder.

She smiled and held up the bottle of wine in her hands. "Still up for gossiping?"

He smiled with his teeth and stepped aside, holding out his arm. "Come in, Bella."

She followed him into the kitchen. Claire sat at the table with Nicola and Haley Jo, the girls furiously coloring in the books in front of them, Claire assisting by handing them colors as she sipped on a glass of wine. When she saw Bella come in from the hallway, she lifted her brow.

"Did you eat?" Matteo asked. "We have some leftover carbonara if you need dinner."

"I had a cookie, like, an hour ago."

Matteo frowned, then pointed to the table. "Not acceptable. Sit."

Minutes later, a steaming bowl of pasta and a glass of red wine were placed in front of her.

"Let me finish the dishes, then we can talk."

Bella nodded, twirling her fork in the creamy pasta, trying to avoid Claire's gaze. But eventually their eyes met, and to her surprise, Claire smiled at her.

"I should have known you wouldn't listen," Claire started. "You are Nicholas Lombardi's granddaughter after all."

"Headstrong, stubborn, always getting my way?"

Claire chuckled. "Exactly."

Bella smirked. "Yeah, well, in the end, you were right. I should have walked away and stayed out of it."

"Pink!" Nicole cheered.

"No, *I* want pink!" Haley Jo yelled back.

"Girls, inside voices," Claire said, handing each of them a pink crayon, the shades slightly different. "I might have also come off a little strong. I was protecting my husband, and after everything Wyatt has been through..." She let out a long sigh. "I just want him to be happy."

Bella concentrated on swirling more pasta on her fork. "Yeah, me too."

"Then why don't you?" Matteo interrupted, taking a seat next to her. "He's miserable, by the way."

Her throat tightened. "He is?" she choked out.

Claire rolled his eyes. "You would never be able to tell, though. He hasn't stopped working. He's in his kitchen more than his apartment, and he hasn't bothered to pay a visit since everything went down."

Matteo shook his head. "That's how he gets. Tunnel vision. It's hard to pull him out of it sometimes. You're the only one who's ever successfully been able to," he said, lifting his chin to her across the table.

Bella set her fork down, no longer feeling hungry. She took a swig of her wine instead.

"All right, girls," Claire said. "Time for bed."

The desperate cries of *nooo* and *please* and *five more minutes* followed as Claire peeled them from their artwork. Matteo kissed the tops of their heads as Claire shuffled them around the table and up the stairs.

Matteo cocked his head to the back door. "It's kind of a nice night. Shall we?"

She nodded. "Sure, let's do it."

Wrapped up in their coats and refilled wineglasses in hand, the two of them took seats on the patio chairs overlooking the small gated backyard.

Bella waited a beat before she opened her mouth. "I'm sorry. For all of it."

His brow furrowed. "Why are you sorry?"

"I used Wyatt to pry into your life, to learn more about you and your family. I inserted myself into a situation where I didn't belong."

He shrugged. "I don't see it that way."

"Then how do you see it?"

Matteo sipped his wine. "Tell me, Bella. Are your feelings for Wyatt genuine?"

She squeezed her eyes shut. "Yes," she admitted softly.

"And if you'd come to the restaurant without everything you knew, and Wyatt still pursued you...would you have let him?"

"I don't know," she said. "I said yes to hanging out with him because—"

"Okay, let me rephrase." He mumbled something that sounded like *stubborn* before he continued. "Say if you *didn't* know everything, and he was simply a man trying to get a woman's attention, would you have said yes?"

She huffed. "Why are we not talking about our family?"

"I am talking about my family."

Bella blinked, unsure how to respond.

"Wyatt means a great deal to me. He was there for me when your grandfather died, took control of the restaurant group and managed everything while I was grieving...then did it *again* when my mom passed not long after. He's loyal to his staff and respectful to my wife and my girls. I know all about his past with Hyacinth, even some of the struggles he's had with women."

She felt her face flush.

"And I'm telling you right now, I have never seen him happier than when I saw him with you. The way he looked at you and held you that night we were celebrating the nomination..." He whistled and shook his head. "I knew he was an absolute goner. So, I ask you again, would you have said yes?"

"Yes." She didn't even hesitate.

"There you have it then. I don't think you pried yourself into my life when Wyatt was openly inviting you into it."

She frowned. "You make it sound like I didn't do anything wrong."

"Well, the lying bit isn't great, love," Matteo bantered. "But I'm glad to know your feelings for him are genuine."

She sipped on her wine and shifted in her seat, trying to get comfortable. "Now what about my family?"

Matteo sighed. "I'm having lunch with your mother this week."

Her brow shot up. "Seriously?"

"It was her idea. I'm also meeting with your grandmother again to discuss Russo's…and hopefully win her over."

"She's meeting with you, so you already won. She hasn't met with anyone before about the deli."

"Yeah, well, she's certainly making me work for it."

Bella couldn't help the smile that curled at her lips, but she quickly smothered it. She was supposed to be mad at her nonna, despite how impressed she always was by her grandmother's savvy business management.

She smoothed a hand down her ponytail. "So I'm guessing she told you everything?"

Matteo nodded. "I asked her why she wanted to work with me when she'd had endless other offers. Bigger offers. She told me the truth, that even though things didn't work out between her and her ex-husband, she would still trust him with her business and knew his son would be the same way."

Her breath caught in her throat. "And?"

"And naturally, I freaked. She didn't tell me why they separated to begin with, but I put together the pieces myself. Apparently they separated eight months before I was born."

Bella looked down into her wineglass.

"When Wyatt told me who you really were, I started putting more pieces together. I hadn't told him about my meetings with Sofia because the two of us were keeping them a secret, but I assumed he already knew everything from you."

She slammed her eyes shut. "Are you mad?"

"At you? No. At the fact that my father lied to all of us for decades? Yes. I know this business relationship won't fix everything between me and your grandmother, but I'm hoping that it will be the start of…*something*."

Bella nodded. "Me too."

They sat there in silence for a few beats, taking sips from their glasses, eyes on the lawn below the porch, blanketed in darkness.

"Could you ever see us hanging out as a family someday?" she asked softly. "Maybe for a Sunday supper?"

Matteo's mouth tilted into a smile, and it stole Bella's breath. It was that same look she knew well, the one she'd sat across from in a booth at Lombardi's for years.

"That's what I'm hoping for, love."

Hope took root in her chest.

"But only if I can have my whole family there."

"Whole family?"

Matteo leaned close to her. "My *whole* family."

Her cheeks heated again.

"Isn't it time you run after him?"

"I can't drag him through all of this again. How will he ever forgive me?"

"Bella. Forgiveness is one of the many ingredients it takes for being in love. Forgiveness from your partner...and forgiveness toward yourself."

She traced the rim of her glass with her finger, a faint hum ringing in the silence.

"Claire confessed things to me, you know. And I chose to forgive her."

Bella looked up at Matteo and caught his lopsided grin.

"Am I upset with her for not telling me? Yes. Do I understand why she did it? Also yes. Will we get through it? Absolutely. Because that's what you do for the people you love. You take them at their best...*and* at their worst. You don't pick and choose the parts to love and ignore the rest. You choose to love them wholly."

Images of Wyatt flashed before her eyes. Sleepy in bed

after a long shift, wet hair tickling the back of her neck. Blood caked on his knuckles, his face covered in shame. Sitting on a park bench, his fingers tugging on her jacket sleeve. His eyes on her lips, tormented by the push and pull of his desire.

She wasn't asking him to be perfect, she never would. Bella wanted Wyatt for who he was, every part of him. And he was simply asking for the same in return.

She looked up and smiled, and for the first time in months, she saw things clearly, like the cloudless sky and the glistening stars above her.

She sat forward. "Any chance you're up for a drive?"

Chapter Thirty-One

BELLA DIDN'T WAIT for Matteo to fully park outside of Tri before unbuckling and jumping out of the car. Customers huddled in clusters outside of the restaurant, shivering in the cold as they waited for tables to become available at New York's hottest award-winning restaurant.

She clutched the soft paper in her hand as she sailed through the front door and almost smacked right into Delilah. She grinned, then stepped aside. "He's in the kitchen."

Bella smiled as she rounded the hostess stand that proudly displayed two new star-shaped glass plaques and made her way through the restaurant, dancing around servers as they set plates of honeynut squash fries with rosemary pesto sauce and short rib ragu on tables. She saw Jayce pouring a bottle of wine across the room, and when his eyes met hers, he winked.

Feeling brave, she walked down the narrow hallway that led to the bathrooms, but instead turned and pushed through the double doors, heading right into the kitchen.

"Corner!"

"Behind!"

"Fire three crispy eggplant!"

Wyatt stood in the middle of it all. His back was to the door, facing the opening toward the center of the restaurant, approving each plate before sliding them across the counter for the waitstaff to grab. "Hands, please," he said, his authoritative voice bouncing off the gleaming tiled walls. "Eighty-six the mackerel for the night."

"Yes, chef!" they chimed.

Marissa turned from beside him to grab the new tickets that came through. She fired off more dishes, then added the tickets to the queue of other papers hanging across the counter. When she finished, her eyes met Bella's, and they widened like saucers.

She stepped up to Wyatt and said something to him softly. His back straightened as he looked at her, then around his shoulder to where Bella was standing.

Everything in the kitchen felt like it was moving in a blur as his green eyes met hers. His team moved swiftly around them, sliding plates on the metal counter to the waitstaff, line cooks working efficiently as Marissa called off different dishes and table numbers.

Eventually Wyatt moved, wiping his hands on the towel tucked at his belt. "Bella, what are you doing? You can't—"

She unfolded the receipt she'd snatched from her purse, the same one with his phone number on the front and his legal contract on the back, and flattened it on the counter. She reached for a pen in a plastic container beside them and clicked the top, then hunched over and began to write.

Wyatt wiped his palms down his slacks, looking uncomfortable, but he was patient. He waited.

She tossed the pen back into the container when she finished, then coughed to clear her throat. "I, Isabella Russo, hereby promise to always tell you the truth, even when it's borderline too much information. If it means sacrificing our former contract and revealing the meatball recipe, then so be it. Because I am in love with you, Wyatt Henderson, and I want to give you every part of who I am."

After taking a breath, she lowered her arms. She glanced around her, realizing the commotion of the kitchen had stilled, the eyes of his staff on the two of them. They'd picked up on every word.

Wyatt's expression was blank, his eyes scanning her face.

She sucked in a breath and waited.

"You barge into my kitchen without permission, disrupting my staff in the middle of a dinner rush, and decide this is the best time to win me back?"

Bella bit the inside of her cheek. "Is it working for you, chef?"

The corner of his mouth twitched. That earlier hope she'd felt bloomed at the sight of it.

He grabbed her waist and wrapped his arms around her, his eyes dancing with delight. Gasps from the staff surrounded them. Even the sounds of noisy conversation and clinking silverware against dishes dimmed.

"Tremendously," he told her with a grin, then closed the space between them, pressing his mouth to hers.

The restaurant exploded in cheers.

Bella draped her arms around his shoulders and kissed him back with a smile, the pressure of his lips on hers just as dizzying as she remembered. His arms tightened around her waist, a hand splayed on her back. He pulled away with three soft kisses, then pressed his forehead to hers.

"You still taste like strawberries," he whispered to her.

"You still smell like herbs," she teased back. She tilted

her chin up and looked at her chef, at the lines at the corners of his eyes from his smile. "Now that I'm here, want me to make the meatballs for the night? Show your guests what a true meatball is?"

He rolled his eyes. "All right, smart-ass, get out."

"No need," Marissa butted in, stepping up next to them. "Take five, I can handle it."

Wyatt nodded at Marissa, then looked back at Bella. "Make that ten, chef."

Her fingers tingled as he released his hold and grabbed for her hands, leading her out of the kitchen and to his office. He snapped the door shut, then leaned against his desk. The office was cramped, yet somehow tidy and homey and welcoming, and she wasn't surprised by it at all. It suited the man she'd come to know so well.

Wyatt pulled her close and cupped her face in his hands. "Are you sure?" he asked.

She grinned. "More than anything in my whole life."

He dropped a soft kiss on her lips. "You know things with me won't be easy."

"And you know things won't be easy with me either." She brushed a hand through his hair. He closed his eyes at her touch, the corners of his lips turning upward. "I'm still not sure if there's something wrong with my health, if I'll ever be able to—"

"*Mia bella.*"

The sound of those two words had her tearing up. They sounded warm. Nourishing. Healing.

His hands dropped to her hips as he pulled her flush against his chest. "No matter what comes next, you will never be alone in this ever again. You can count on me to be by your side." He tucked a strand of her hair behind her ear. "I'm sorry I created distance. I hope you didn't think—"

"I needed the distance," she admitted. "I had a lot to figure out."

He nodded once. "And what did you figure out?"

She placed her hand on the front of his chef's coat, directly on his heart. "Life is messy, but I can't keep hiding from it. I can't hide from the pain or the grief. I can't hide from the mess that comes with truly letting yourself be known by your family and friends. I can't hold back on telling the truth simply because I'm afraid of what will come next. I need to stop being so hard on myself for everything that happened and be kind to my body. Sure, there will be disappointments. But that shouldn't stop me from letting life in. From letting *you* in."

He brushed a hand through her hair and cradled the back of her head.

"I'm so sorry I put you through all of this mess," she murmured.

"I'm not."

"Really?"

He massaged her neck. "I've been doing some thinking as well."

"Oh? In between taking hot photos for the *Times* and running the new *culinary empire of New York*?"

"You saw that."

"The entire world saw that, short king."

"You are..." He chuckled, and the sound of it made her weak in the knees. She missed that raspy laugh.

"I figured out that while I was trying to do the honorable thing and give you distance, I was slowly going mad because I *despise* being apart." Wyatt kissed her slowly, tenderly, then pulled apart enough to brush a confession across her lips. "And I am so deeply in love with you."

She grinned. "You're so obsessed with me."

"*Bella.*" He dipped down and cradled her in his arms, his head burrowing into her neck. "You have no idea."

Bella woke to the sound of her phone buzzing on the nightstand. Being back at Wyatt's, in his bed and under his comfortable duvet, felt right. She'd missed him dreadfully, particularly their slower Saturday mornings. Lazy hands on skin. Coffee brewing in the kitchen. Breakfast in bed.

After a grueling week of training Katie's replacement and exchanging only a few words with Wyatt during late-night calls or check-ins before bed, she was very much looking forward to sleeping in beside the man she knew she could never live without again.

Her phone was a buzzkill.

She groaned and reached for it, and the name on the screen made her jolt upright.

It was her mother, and she was FaceTiming her.

Bella ripped off the duvet and shifted to stand, but a firm hand on her thigh stopped her.

"Don't," Wyatt pleaded, his voice groggy from sleep. His eyes were still closed, his head on the pillow. "Stay."

"It's a FaceTime call," Bella said. "From my *mom.*"

"Stay," he demanded. "I don't mind."

She sighed, throwing the duvet back over her legs and shifting closer to him. "So bossy."

Wyatt wrapped an arm around her waist and pulled her closer, his hand slipping underneath her big cotton tee. He rested his cheek on her stomach, so she used the top of his head as an armrest as she answered the call.

Her mother and father were both on the screen, sitting

at their kitchen table. The two of them had moved to Morningside Heights into faculty housing after Bella went to college, giving up their apartment in NoHo for something smaller and cheaper. You could see a clear view of the park out the window behind them, bare trees lightly dusted with snow.

She gave them a smile, which Dad returned. Mom did not.

"Morning," Bella said cheerily.

"Morning, sweetheart," Dad replied in kind.

Mom's frown deepened. "Are you still in bed?"

Bella coughed. "Still in bed. It's not a crime to sleep in on Saturdays."

"Ah, then we won't bug you." Mom moved to stand up. "We'll talk—"

"Angela," Dad said, gently grasping her wrist. "Sit."

Now Bella was the one frowning. "Is everything all right?"

"Oh yes, everything is fine." Dad beamed. "We wanted to catch up."

The tone of his voice was reassuring, so she relaxed. "How was the end of the semester?" she asked.

"Same as usual, students asking to push deadlines and for extra credit work to bump up their grades." He sighed. "Glad to have a break for a little while."

"How dare they want better grades," she quipped, which made her dad laugh. She turned her attention to Mom. "And the deli?"

Mom huffed.

"They haven't spoken to each other since our last Sunday supper," Dad admitted, filling the silence.

Bella nodded, knowing she needed to tread carefully.

She knew a lot of this was her nonna's fault...but it was hers as well. She'd also kept secrets.

"I'm sorry, Mom," Bella admitted. "I didn't mean to hurt you."

Mom's face relaxed. "Oh, sweetie, this isn't on you."

"It kind of is though. I'm the one who dug everything up."

She felt Wyatt's hand tighten around her waist, then rub circles into her skin with his thumb.

Mom opened her mouth to respond, but Bella cut her off.

"Mom. I know I screwed up. You don't have to explain it away."

Mom's mouth snapped shut and she nodded.

Bella continued, feeling anxious about everything that came next. "Did you meet with Matteo this week?"

Mom sighed. "Yes. He is energetic and full of life. Just like Nonno."

She smiled as she thought of Matteo and his boisterous laugh, the way he always made people feel loved and appreciated. "Yeah, he is."

"He has all of these great plans for the future of Russo's. I wanted to hate him for it, but it's kind of hard to do so. He's clearly good at his job, and he's about to make our lives easier." Mom rubbed her face. "Your grandmother has requested for all of us to meet for Sunday supper tomorrow to celebrate."

She watched a wrinkle form between her brows on the little square at the corner of her screen. "Tomorrow?"

"She wants to have a Feast of the Seven Fishes. With *everyone.*"

"Oh." Bella wasn't sure how else to respond. "No meatballs?"

She shook her head. "She wants each adult to bring a seafood dish to the meal."

"So she did speak to you?"

"No, she spoke to me," Dad said. "She also said someone will need to volunteer to make a second dish so it brings us to seven."

"No need."

Bella's eyes widened as Wyatt sat up, then shimmied closer to her, popping his face into view on the screen.

She watched her parents go bug-eyed at the sight of Wyatt and couldn't help the smile that stretched across her cheeks.

"I'll make the seventh dish," Wyatt continued.

Mom's mouth fell open.

"But the restaurant?" Bella squeaked. "Won't you have to be there?"

"I've already started working out a schedule with Marissa so I can be off on Sundays," he said matter-of-factly. Like the words didn't make her want to scream "THIS MAN!" into the sky right then and there.

"Y-you... Every Sunday?"

"Wait, I thought you guys broke up?" Dad sputtered, breaking their silence.

Bella flushed.

Wyatt smiled at her, then glanced at her parents on the screen. "Don't worry, sir. It won't happen again."

Yup, she thought. *I'm done for.*

He kissed her temple as Mom made a squealing sound paired with a shimmy and first pump on the screen.

Chapter Thirty-Two

"You ready for this?"

Bella looked up at the windows above Russo's. Snowflakes tickled her face as they fell gently from the sky, melting into her skin.

Wyatt gripped her waist and tucked her close. Bella looked back at her chef, snow lining the beanie on his head, a cozy sweater tucked inside his corduroy jacket.

"Yes and no," she replied. "But I'm really glad you're here."

He leaned in and kissed her gently, his lips warm against hers. "And every Sunday after."

She hummed. "I still think it's crazy that you're going to take off every Sunday..."

"To be with you and your family? Nonsense."

"You are such a sap."

He smirked. "If you're not ready, we can leave. I know something else we could do to pass the time..."

She rolled her eyes. "You got enough of that today."

"Not *nearly* enough."

Bella chuckled and grabbed the front of his jacket,

"

pulling him toward the door. He caught her arm and tugged her so she ricocheted into him instead, winding a hand around her neck as he kissed her again, lingering with each brush of his tongue and sweep of his lips.

She sighed, tucking her hands inside his jacket, then slipped them underneath his sweater.

He yelped. "Your hands are freezing."

"You're kissing me outside in the snow."

"Ah, right. Let's get back to that."

She laughed, hooking her *freezing fingers* in the collar of his sweater. "Come on."

They made their way up the stairs, listening to the tinkering of pots and pans, and to Bella's relief, raucous laughter.

She stepped into Nonna's apartment, propped open with a wooden chair as always, and stood in front of a number of familiar faces. Not just her grandmother and her parents, but Matteo, Claire, Nicola, and Haley Jo as well.

"Uncle Wyatt!" screamed the girls as they ran over, each of them claiming a leg like a barnacle.

"I wonder at what point they'll be embarrassed by you, Uncle Wyatt," Claire teased, pecking his cheek with a kiss.

He smiled, patting the girls on the head. "I hope never."

Bella's heart swelled with affection for him.

They shed their coats and tossed them to the pile of outerwear on Nonna's couch. Wyatt held up the tote bag he had in his hand. "Our contributions for the evening."

Mom groaned. "I don't even want to know what you brought, you're going to out-chef all of us. My calamari will certainly not live up to your standards."

Matteo crossed his arms. "Well, that depends, sis. I'm not so bad in the kitchen myself."

Bella watched the way her mom flinched at Matteo's

casual use of *sis*. But her mother rolled her shoulders and crossed her arms playfully in return. "Oh yeah, what do you have?"

"Cioppino, paired with a homemade Italian bread from a pastry chef I know."

Wyatt pointed at Matteo. "Getting Benji involved was technically cheating."

Matteo guffawed. "Says who?"

"Says me," Nonna said, placing a large pot of cod fish balls in tomato sauce on the table. "Only the family could contribute a dish to our first official Feast of the Seven Fishes."

Wyatt cocked his head, a mocking gleam in his eye as he stared up at Matteo.

"Bastard," Matteo grumbled. "What did you bring?"

He snatched a container out of the bag, then popped it open. "Tuna tartare, mixed with Italian fermented chili, with sourdough crostini."

The family groaned. Mom threw up her hands in defeat.

"Leave it to Nonna to make it a competition," Bella teased, slinging an arm around her grandmother and kissing her temple. "She loves proving she is the best."

"'Til the day I die, *piccola*."

"I also find it hilarious that you chose a dish that's essentially the fish version of a meatball," she teased.

"We can't have a Sunday supper without them, it's tradition. What did you bring, my sweet?"

Bella also reached into the bag and pulled out another container, much larger than Wyatt's. Matteo peered over her shoulder as she clicked the lid open.

He gasped in delight. "Are those—"

"Mini Neapolitan-style pizzas, topped with anchovies."

"*Pizza?!*" the girls squealed.

Claire laughed. "I'm sorry guys, but I think Bella might be the winner here."

"I thought the same thing," Wyatt added, tugging on the sleeve of her sweater.

"You're just saying that because you're *in love*," Claire cooed.

Wyatt shrugged. "Maybe. But I also already ate one and can confirm they are fantastic."

Bella squinted at him. "Fantastic, huh? Not *surprising?*"

He rolled his eyes. "You're impossible."

"Wait, did you say you're in love?" Dad asked from across the room. "Why am I always behind?"

"It's okay, sweetie," Mom reassured him. She looked at Bella and winked. "We have a lot of catching up to do."

Bella returned an easy smile. Based on the frigid interactions between Mom and Nonna, it was clear that much more needed to be said between the three Russo women. But tonight was about hanging out for the first time as a family, sharing a new holiday tradition as one. Putting the mistakes of their pasts behind them and moving forward together.

She linked her arm with Claire's. "What did you bring?"

"Crab dip with crackers. One of my momma's favorites."

Bella squeezed her arm. "Can't wait."

"And last but certainly not least," Mom said, turning toward Dad. "What did you bring, sweetie?"

Dad's eyes sparkled behind his glasses as he lifted up his arms, holding two colorful candy bags. "Swedish Fish."

Everyone lost it. The girls also squealed at this, already begging Dad to open the bags so they could have some.

Claire told them they needed to eat *real* food first, then asked Bella if she could remove the anchovies on one of the pizzas for them.

"Already a step ahead of you. I made them plain cheese pizzas instead."

"You're a darling," Claire said. "I knew I always liked you."

She squinted her eyes. "Always?"

Claire sipped on her wine and gave her a subtle wink. "Sure. Let's go with that."

Nonna demanded that everyone take their seats. A leaf was added to the center of the table to expand it, but it was still a tight fit. Apparently not tight enough for Wyatt though. As soon as Bella sat down, he wrapped his foot around the leg of her chair and dragged it close, then tapped her thigh and placed his hand on it, palm up.

She grinned and threaded her fingers through his.

Once everyone was seated, Nonna stood up at the head of the table. "Thank you all for coming tonight, it means a great deal to me to have all of your faces around my table."

To Bella's surprise, her grandmother lifted the corner of her pink apron and dabbed her eyes. "I have made many mistakes in my lifetime, of which I am not proud. But this particular mistake has been the worst regret of my entire life."

"*Mamma,*" Mom whispered, reaching for Nonna's hand.

She took her hand and squeezed. "No, my sweet. This needs to be said." She took a deep breath, then laid her eyes intently on the rest of them. "I am sorry for lying to all of you, for holding you back from knowing the family you had close by. For shutting Nicky out when we separated. I was heartbroken and foolish. I had no idea the pain I would cause. I hope this dinner is the start of many new traditions as a family. And the beginning of many more Sunday suppers to come."

Matteo lifted his glass. "Here, here."

Everyone clinked glasses as Nonna sat. She held out her hands—one to Matteo on her right, the other to Mom on her left. They took her hands, then everyone else followed as she led them in a prayer. They each signed the cross, Matteo and Claire included. Bella watched as Wyatt followed along, her chest bursting that he was beside her. Not because he felt like he had to be, but because he genuinely *wanted* to be.

He dipped his chin and looked at her, the two of them caught up in one another, not paying any attention to the passing plates around them.

"So," Dad coughed. "In love, huh?"

Bella grinned, not taking her eyes off her chef. "Yeah. In love."

"Bella!" Wyatt called out from his living room. "You forced me to get this damn tree and all of these decorations and you're not even *helping*."

She ruffled her hair as she stared at herself in the bathroom mirror, then pinched her cheeks to give them color. She flicked off the light and made her way to the living room, the cooing sounds of Michael Bublé playing over the speakers.

Wyatt was holding an ornament, his brow furrowed in concentration as he analyzed the perfect spot for it. Always intentional. Always taking his time to make everything just right. Like every dish from his new winter menu, which was already getting rave reviews. Or even the way he handled their relationship, intentional in the way he took care of her, the way he dug out every detail about her life, like he was insatiable. And she gave it all to him, without hesitation. She never wanted to hide from this man again.

Except now, of course. Wyatt didn't notice her approach, so she leaned against the wall and watched him work. His crewneck sweatshirt lifted as he raised an arm to place the ornament on the tree, his joggers low enough on his waist to reveal the dip of his hips. She smirked and leaned her head back, watching him work.

He lifted another ornament from the box and sighed. *"Bella!"*

"I'm right *here.*"

He whipped his head around, and she watched with smug satisfaction as pink crawled up his neck and up to his cheeks. The ornament slipped from his fingers and he yelped, bowing down to catch it. It fumbled a couple times before he firmly had it in his hands and placed it back in the box.

She stood there in what she thought was her favorite outfit yet.

His chef's coat.

Her lacy red thong.

And nothing else.

"Merry Christmas," she said wistfully.

He rubbed his mouth, then his neck, his eyes trailing up her bare legs and to his coat. "We're really not going to finish this tree now."

She pushed off the wall and pointed to the bedroom. "Would you like me to go change? I'm happy to—"

His approach was lightning fast as he grabbed for her,

his hands on her ass. "Don't you dare," he growled. He slid his hands around to her waist, realizing she wasn't wearing anything under his coat. "Are you trying to be the death of me?"

"The poison never worked. I had to think of another method."

"Then this is absolutely the way I want to die."

She laughed out loud as he grabbed her legs and lifted her up, then carried her to the bedroom and threw her onto his unmade bed. He crawled and pressed all of his body weight on her. He was hard—*everywhere*—and it made her squirm with anticipation.

He worked at the buttons of his coat at a painstaking pace.

"Faster, chef. I want your hands on me."

He shook his head. "Last time I had to rush. Tonight, I'm going to take my time and enjoy every damn second of this."

"God, you're so bossy."

Many...*many* moments later, they remained tangled up in one another, the Christmas tree long forgotten.

Wyatt pressed his chest against her back and traced his hand down her left arm, then lifted her hand and kissed it. He stared intently at it for a moment, then brushed his thumb up and down the indent on her ring finger.

"Way too soon, chef."

She could feel his grin as he cuddled her close, folding his hand over hers as he curled their arms around her waist. "Just tell me when you're ready, *mia bella*."

Bella twisted around to face Wyatt, welcomed by her favorite side of him. Tousled auburn hair. Pink cheeks. Sparkling green eyes. Soft. Warm. Kind. Loving.

She drew a heart on his bare chest. "I will. I promise."

Epilogue

Three Years Later

BELLA HEARD keys in the door, then soft footsteps climbing the stairs.

Wyatt entered the kitchen already shrugging off his coat and tossed the paper bags he had on the marble island. "I grabbed bagels for lunch."

"Those have to be the hottest words you have ever said to me," Bella cooed.

Rosemary slammed her fists on the plastic table connected to her high chair, spewing marinara sauce everywhere, including Bella's face.

"Ugh, Ro," Bella sighed. She looked down at the table and laughed, realizing that the meatball she'd cut up for her to eat was already polished off.

Wyatt appeared at her side and wiped the marinara sauce painted across her face. "Did you try giving her anything else?"

"She threw whatever sweet potato thing you made for her."

He frowned. "You sure you didn't just want to give her meatballs?"

She held her hand to her chest in mock exasperation. "Are you calling me a liar?"

Wyatt smiled and placed his hands on the arms of her chair, dipping down to kiss her nose. "Never."

She grinned as he pulled away. "Really, I'm not kidding. She picked it up and threw it across the room. We should consider her for the Olympics. I can see javelin throws in her future."

"Or maybe she's just as stubborn as her mother?"

"Eh, I don't blame her. She's a Russo, after all."

Wyatt returned to the table with pumpernickel bagels with veggie cream cheese on plates, then motioned for Bella to move so he could sit between his girls.

Rosemary squealed and reached for him with sauce-covered hands. Wyatt chuckled and wiped them clean, then let her play with his hair, which had come to be one of her favorite pastimes.

Like mother, like daughter.

Bella made Wyatt wait a year before placing a ring on her finger. She knew almost as soon as he did on that first Christmas together that she wanted to marry him. But this time she wanted to do things differently. She wanted to take her time, enjoy every second.

She found herself spending time at Wyatt's apartment more often than her own, and eventually packed up her stuff and moved in the summer after they met. Things felt solid between them, and by the time she watched Percy and Yaz exchange their vows, she confessed to Wyatt later that night that she was ready.

He put an emerald-cut diamond on her left hand a week later.

Seeing Lon at her best friend's wedding had no effect on her. Percy had told her about Lon's plans to move to the

UK after he accepted a promotion at their London offices. He left that winter, and she hadn't heard from him since. And she was more than okay with that.

Katie sent the occasional selfie, hiking or post-surf or cooking in the kitchen. Bella wasn't sure if she was seeing anyone, but their new friendship was cordial and frail, and she decided it wasn't worth the effort to pry. She hoped she was happy, and that maybe she could share that with someone new. Someone who treated her well.

Months after he proposed, on a warm spring day under a cherry blossom tree in the Brooklyn Botanical Gardens, they said their vows to one another, surrounded by their family and close friends. Percy stood by her side, Benji by his. She wore a cream silk dress with a strapless sweetheart neckline. He wore his black tux. They both cried the entire way through, and even during parts of the rowdy reception at Tri that lasted late into the night.

Bella and Wyatt weren't sure if children would ever work out for them, so they all but gave up on using protection. But she still dreamed. She took up Dr. Roscoe's advice and modified her diet and incorporated supplements, hoping it would somehow help her chances. She even broached the subject of attempting IVF, and Wyatt promised to be by her side if that was something she wanted.

Rosemary was an unexpected and very welcome honeymoon surprise. Wyatt took her to Sicily as a wedding present, and she gave him a positive pregnancy test for his. She would never forget the way he laughed and lifted her up when she walked out of the bathroom, then pressed her against the wall and kissed her senseless.

She was rightfully nervous during the first trimester, but true to his word, Wyatt was with her every step of the way.

He held her hand at every appointment. Rubbed her back when the nausea was overwhelming. Made sure she had whatever food she craved whenever she craved it.

It was what they did for one another. Bella stood by him as he made another attempt at seeking medical treatment and finally found solutions that worked. *Most* of the time. It was never perfect, but Bella didn't care. She loved Wyatt Henderson with all of her heart, and what he could or couldn't do in bed would never change that.

They celebrated her twenty-week appointment at a Sunday supper, surrounded by their whole family, digging into plates of meatballs and garlic bread, which seemed to be the only thing she could stomach during the tumultuous first trimester. Yet somehow, she never got sick of it. Rosemary's appreciation for her family's delicacy was a clear sign that love for meatballs ran deep in the Russo blood.

She didn't change her name, per Wyatt's insistence. And when their daughter was born, he signed the birth certificate for Rosemary Henderson Russo.

"Our girl has to carry on the legacy," he said, curled up on the hospital bed, their arms cradling the bundle of joy fast asleep in front of them.

Bella knew she would. When Rosemary's thirteenth birthday came, she would teach her everything, just like Nonna had taught her.

She hoped Nonna would be around for that moment, too. Her grandmother finally handed off business responsibilities to Matteo and everyday operations to Mom. Now she simply greeted customers at the counter and continued to do what she did best: love everyone who walked through Russo's doors with a plate of meatballs.

Wyatt kissed Rosemary's little hands. "Do you know what today is?"

Bella frowned. "September 26th?"

He smirked. "It's a special one."

Before she could reply, he reached into the pocket of his jeans and pulled out a faded receipt.

Bella laughed as he opened it up and placed it on the counter, pointing at the printed date at the top, barely visible after so many years. His number and their contracts in faded black ink on the back.

"It is a special one," she replied. "How should we celebrate?"

Wyatt pulled her into his lap and kissed her, slipping a hand underneath her shirt and running his fingers up and down her bare spine. "Want to teach me the meatball recipe?"

She squinted her eyes. He gave her a mischievous grin.

"Fine." Bella ruffled his hair. "But don't tell Nonna."

Wyatt's Menu

deconstructed italian meatball
sous vide veal, pork, and beef, green ricotta encased in a caramelized pearl onion shell, italian herb bernaise drizzle and dehydrated onion flakes

house made sorrel focaccia
quince jam, smoked salt, creamed butter

smoked oyster pate
preserved lemon and wild garlic, sourdough crackers

charred cabbage quarter
caramelized miso hollandaise, feathered pancetta curls

crispy tempura eggplant
basil aioli, house made italian red pepper flake chili crisp

baharat short rib ragu
charred okra, turmeric pappardelle

honey nut squash fries
parmesan crust, rosemary pesto dipping sauce

whole salted grilled mackerel

ground cherry sauce and melted leek parsnip puree

smoked salt cured wagyu beef cubes
cast iron charred mozzarella pancake, fennel shallot crispy mushroom salad, adobo finishing oil

polenta pistachio nectarine cake
cinnamon whipped coconut cream, candied ginger

lemon lavender panna cotta
cranberry compote

Also by K. Sinko

THE SCOOPS SERIES

Safe Harbor

Always Choosing You

The Offer

STANDALONES

Sunday Supper

Call Of The Loon

NOVELETTES

Please Be Mine

Notes & Acknowledgements

Sunday Supper is a work of fiction. While there are many aspects of this book that are real, some of them were changed in order to fit this particular story. This book includes a mix of fictional and real places that exist in New York City. However, the events that take place in these spots are purely fictional and not based on fact. The location and timing for the James Beard Awards will change around, but currently the awards are held in Chicago in June. For the sake of the plot, I took liberties to change around the when and where. Some of the awards mentioned in this book are also works of fiction, again to go with this particular plot.

Intimacy looks different for everyone. While erectile dysfunction is common—30 million men in the United States, and about 40% of men by the age of 40—the ways it manifests in one's body can be unique. Certain medications can work while others don't, and being comfortable enough to take medication is a personal choice. Wyatt's particular situation is how he chose to handle it, and may look different compared to how others decide to.

Similarly, miscarriages and fertility are also not a one-size-fits-all. Some people may experience multiple miscarriages and undergo years of IVF treatments to get pregnant, while others may become pregnant naturally and carry a child to term, even after experiencing miscarriages. The

National Library of Medicine states that up to 1 in 4 known pregnancies can end in miscarriage.

Again, for the sake of fiction, these characters handle their particular health in the ways they see fit. It may not be your experience, but there's never one right way to go about these things. Thank you to all of the brave souls who shared their stories for this book. For those who have gone through these, or have a partner who experiences it, I hope this book made you feel seen.

And with that, it's time to thank some people.

A special shout out to my friend Marissa Kennedy, my chef-in-chief for this book. Thank you for developing Wyatt's incredible menu, and for alpha reading this book as I worked through the story. For catching all of the restaurant inconsistencies, and for encouraging me to get even more detailed in certain scenes. (Wink, wink.) I'm so glad we got to share this book together. Thanks for your never ending support.

To my beta readers this time around: Meagan Williamson, Abby Hancock, and Alexis Wierenga. Thank you for all the encouragement and love for this story, and for freaking out just as much as I did over how hot Wyatt is.

My lovely cover artist, Hannah Hill. I love how one late night, drinks in hand, you told me you wanted to take a stab at designing a cover for my next book. Thank you for taking "sexy fall in New York" to a whole new level. This cover is *literally* a work of art. Ha. You're the best, I love you.

I would never be where I am without my amazing editor, Britt Tayler, and my proofreader Brooke Crites. Also, a special shout out to Shaily Yashar for double checking all of my Italian in this book. A true gem.

And of course, my family and friends who are always encouraging me to keep writing and keep following my dreams. To Cheyenne Buckingham who loved hearing little snippets as I was writing this book while we galavanted our way through Europe. To Amber Strickland, who has been a champion for this book even in the early stages of it in 2020. And to my husband, who never said no when I told him I had another restaurant on my list that we needed to visit, all for the sake of research. Thanks for always challenging me, and for caring about all of the little details that make my books even stronger. I couldn't do any of this without you.

About the Author

K.Sinko is an indie published author with a deep love for love stories. She is the author of *Sunday Supper, Call Of The Loon, Please Be Mine,* and the Scoops Series—a trilogy of stand-alone romances featuring the of a fictional ice cream shop. Her debut novel *Safe Harbor* became an Amazon best seller for young adult contemporary romance and is the winner of two Indieverse Awards. Follow her on Instagram and sign up for her newsletter to get the latest book updates.

tinyurl.com/ksinkonewsletter

instagram.com/authorksinko